THIS IS HOW IT ENDS

THIS IS HOW IT ENDS

JEN NADOL

Simon Pulse
New York | London | Toronto | Sydney | New Delhi

This book is a work of fiction. Any references to historical events, real people, or real places are used fictitiously. Other names, characters, places, and events are products of the author's imagination, and any resemblance to actual events or places or persons, living or dead, is entirely coincidental.

SIMON PULSE

An imprint of Simon & Schuster Children's Publishing Division

1230 Avenue of the Americas, New York, NY 10020

First Simon Pulse edition October 2014

Cover designed by Jessica Handelman

Designed by Mike Rosamilia

The text of this book was set in ArrusBT Std.

Manufactured in the United States of America

2 4 6 8 10 9 7 5 3 1

This book has been cataloged by the Library of Congress.

ISBN 978-1-4814-0210-1 (pbk)

ISBN 978-1-4814-0211-8 (hc)

ISBN 978-1-4814-0212-5 (eBook)

For Queenie

Acknowledgments

My agent, Melissa Sarver White, knows better than anyone how close this manuscript came to the circular file. Thank you, Melissa, for sticking with it and giving both gentle and pointed guidance that encouraged me to keep trying. Without you, this book would not be.

Thanks to Liesa Abrams, for believing in this story and helping me find the ending it was meant to have, and to Annette Pollert, who graciously shepherded it through title, launch, and probably a bunch of other stuff I don't even know about. And to the rest of the Simon Pulse team, especially Lauren Forte, Jessica Handelman, and Bara MacNeill, whose efforts and talent helped shape this novel—thank you.

I'm grateful to Bria Judkins for connecting me to my earliest readers of this manuscript: Basia Van Buren, Olivia Giacomo, Claudia Pou, and Amanda Patterson. Each gave thoughtful, candid feedback that I very much appreciate.

Last, but never least, many thanks to my family—Reardens; Bakanowskis; Nadols; newlywed Riches; my husband, Joe; and sons, Joey, Sam, and Jake—for their ongoing support and good times. Love you all.

CHAPTER 1

TRIP WAS LATE. AGAIN. I RAN MY FINGERS ACROSS THE ROUGH wood of the porch, counting seconds. Two hundred forty-seven, two hundred forty-eight. I'd been fidgety inside with my mom, but this was no better. The wind coming off the mountains made my nose drip and numbed my fingers. It was barely October, but that's Vermont for you. I dug through my backpack checking for gloves. I'd need them up at the cave.

Trip swung around the corner finally, the wagon's left headlight dimmer than the other, like it was winking. If anyone's car could wink and get away with it, it'd be Trip's.

He parked haphazardly, beeping before he noticed me on the step. I stood, catching the flutter of curtains next door. Mrs. McGinty watching me walk down the front path. Nosy old bat, Trip called her.

"You're late," I told him, sliding into the backseat.

"Sue me," Trip answered. "I had a hot date."

Sarah backhanded his arm lightly, then turned, smiling, her arm draped gracefully over the seat. "Hey, Ri."

"Hey," I said, trying to ignore the softness of her brown eyes, perfect lips. Hot date indeed.

We started up the trail toward the cave just past six, after picking up Tannis at her house a half mile from mine and Natalie at the ski shop. It was near dusk, but none of us needed much light to find our way. We'd been doing it all summer. Some of us for years before, too.

My dad first brought me when I was eleven, not to hang out with girls or go drinking like we were doing tonight. He and I were going hunting.

He'd stopped just outside the cave, his gun resting on his shoulder, breath coming hard after the steep climb. "My parents didn't know about this place," he'd said, peering into the dark opening. "Never woulda found me here, even if they'd come looking." He'd turned, scanning the clearing, a half smile on his scruffy face. "But *I* know about it, Riley." My dad had looked down at me sharply. "So don't think you'll be getting away with anything, Son."

I'd met his eyes, not sure if he was teasing, not sure what I'd try to "get away with" in this place that stank like our basement: stale beer and ash. "Okay, Dad."

He'd smiled and ruffled my hair, his hand still protection against the scary unknown. "C'mon. Let's head to the platform and see if you can bag us some dinner." He'd laughed loud, his heavy boots snapping branches as he'd started up the path to the hunting perch where he'd die two years later.

I thought of him a little bit every time I came here, wondered if he'd really have tracked me down if he'd still been alive. Or whether he'd have sat and had a beer with us.

"Move it, Riley!" Trip yelled down. He stood at the top of the trail, grinning back at me. "We're thirsty, dude."

Sarah stood beside him, her arm around his waist, dark hair blending into the dusk and woods behind.

"You could've carried this shit." I hitched my bag with the six-packs inside.

"I procured. You haul."

I flipped him the bird and continued walking—no faster—up the path. His laughter floated down, and I saw them turn away, Trip catching Sarah's hand, lacing her fingers through his as they walked toward the clearing.

Tannis was already working on the fire when I got up there. I let my backpack slide to the dirt by the pit.

"Hey, loverboy," she called. "How about a beer?"

"Don't mind if I do," I said, pulling one out of the bag.

Tannis snorted, poking at the logs with a stick that she tossed on top before walking over. She was easily an inch taller than me, and broad. I had to remind myself to stay put when she stopped solidly within my personal space, hands on her hips.

"Easy, motorhead." I handed her the beer, grabbing another from the backpack for myself.

"Shove it, Riley," she answered pleasantly, taking a long swig. Her blond hair fell heavily down her back, and I noticed a smudge of dirt under her chin.

I told her and she shrugged. "Adds character." But she wiped it away, her fingernails still rimmed with oil or lube or whatever they used to tune the cars in her front yard. It drove her OCD neighbor nuts, which I think was half the reason she and her brothers did it there instead of in their barn or at the track.

I took a drink, then bent for a fistful of twigs and listened to the sizzle and crack of the green ones as they landed on the fire.

"You guys need help?" Nat came up from behind. She waved off the beer I offered.

"Sure," Tannis said. "You and Riley want to collect some more wood?"

Natalie nodded, and I walked with her to the thickets on the opposite side of the clearing, both of us glancing toward Trip and Sarah, who were in soft conversation by the cave. Their foreheads touched and Trip's arm was around her waist.

"Gag," I said dryly.

"I think it's really sweet," Natalie said softly. "They're so happy together."

"I think you mean 'sappy together,'" I said, something hot and sour in my throat.

"Oh, Riley." She gave me a little shove. "Someday that'll be you."

I glanced past Natalie at Trip and Sarah, now walking hand in hand toward Tannis. If only she knew how much I wished that were true.

Twenty minutes later we had a pile of branches, seven empty beer cans, and the sky had turned purple through the tree line. The five of us sat on stones around our fire, me between Nat and Tannis, Sarah and Trip at the other end of the semicircle. I'd stacked the hollow cans in a pyramid by my feet, drifting in and out of the conversation—Trip complaining about the ski shop, Nat telling him not to, Sarah agreeing with one, then the other. Mostly I thought about how the air smelled crisp and smoky, like the bonfires my dad used to make at home after all the leaves fell. I remember him towering above the flames, even though in pictures I can see he wasn't much taller than my mom. Memories are funny like that.

Being here felt like those bonfires—warm, comfortable, ritualistic. I'd never have guessed it back when Trip first suggested bringing the girls. "C'mon, man," he'd said. "Think about it—drinks, dark, ladies . . ." He'd raised an eyebrow suggestively. "Anything could happen."

I'd agreed, because that's what you do when your best friend needs a wingman, but I'd known exactly what would happen with those ladies. Nothing. Not for me at least. I'd gone to school with Nat and Tannis since kindergarten. They weren't into me, and the feeling was unequivocally mutual. But over the weeks of summer, I'd gotten to like coming here with them. Gotten to like *them*. I was sorry to see it end and wondered if any of them sensed it too—the bite of ice in the air, the hard-packed feel of the ground now. This would probably be our last night.

"Why so quiet, Riley?" Sarah asked. "Whatcha thinking?" Light flickered on her pale skin, fragile and translucent beside Trip's, still tanned from summer. She reached up to tuck a stray piece of hair behind her ear, holding my eyes.

My heart hammered at her voice, deep and slightly raspy. "Nothing."

"As usual," Trip said.

I shot him a look. "Actually, I was thinking this is probably our last time up here for a while. Won't be long before it's snowing."

"And Nat's training all the time," Trip said.

"And Tannis is holed up in her garage," Nat added.

"And Sarah's studying all the big books in the library," Tannis said.

"And Riley's cleaning toilets for tourists," Trip said.

Nat snickered. "Sounds like a game show. Toilets for Tourists."

"I assure you, it's not," I told her.

"And Trip?" Tannis turned to him. "What are your plans for this winter?"

He took a long drink, belched softly, and said, "Finding us somewhere else to keep the party going."

"Hear, hear!" Tannis said. She raised her beer and stepped up on top of her stone. With her feet planted and her arms up, she looked about a hundred feet tall. She cleared her throat loudly. "I pronounce it time for a final game of truth or dare."

"Yes!" Trip agreed, standing too, his features strong and Nordic like hers. "Let it be so."

No, I thought. *Let it not*. "Do we have to?"

Tannis pouted. "Party pooper."

"Don't be a wuss, dude," Trip said.

"Fine." I threw back the rest of my beer. I'd known there was no escape.

"Just for that, you get to go first," Tannis said, grinning. "Truth? Or dare?"

Tannis could be a serious pain in the ass. I stacked my empty can on the pyramid. We'd need two more to finish it off.

She tapped her foot impatiently. "What'll it be . . . *loverboy*?"

That decided it. "Dare."

"Exxxxcellent." Tannis rubbed her hands together and jumped to the ground. "Go into the cave," she said. "Far enough that we can't see you."

"Okay." My skin crawled as I stood. Dark, spiders, mice, muck. In a closed-in space. I started walking.

"Hold it," Tannis said. "I'm not done."

Shit.

"Take Sarah with you." She smiled wickedly. "And tell her a secret."

I shook my head, my heart beating triple time as I looked across the circle at Sarah, beside Trip. "You can't drag someone else into my dare. That's not fair."

"Says who?"

"C'mon, Tannis. You—"

"It's okay, Riley," Sarah interrupted. "I'll go." She was already standing, looking at me. "If you want."

Her deep voice gave me shivers. "Thanks," I said. "But you shouldn't have to."

"What are you arguing about?" Tannis threw up her hands. "She agreed to go. Get on with it. Unless . . ." She raised an eyebrow. "You're too chicken."

I snorted, feeling like I was *definitely* too chicken to be going into the dark with Sarah. I looked at her, my pulse racing. "You ready?"

"Sure." That voice again.

I felt sweaty, hoped I didn't smell. *This isn't a big deal*, I told myself. *Don't make it one*.

"Be good!" I heard Trip call, laughing, as we walked toward the cave.

It was cool and dim inside. Musty, like our basement is now, the smell of late-night benders long gone. The cave's ceiling was less than a foot above my head, and my chest felt tight. Sarah's breathing was soft and quick behind me, and I could still hear Tannis outside. I slid forward, biting my lip so I wouldn't freak out as the dark surrounded us. "I think this is far enough," I said quickly.

Sarah bumped into me. "Sorry!" She laughed, nervous. Her breath was warm and minty like I remembered from sixth grade at Kelly Lipman's birthday party. "Yeah, I think it's fine." She stepped back, away from me. We were quiet for a second, and I could begin to pick out shapes in the darkness—the rough stone walls, the rise of Sarah's cheekbones, her full lips. We spoke at the same time.

"So I—"

"You know, you—"

Sarah laughed a little, and I told her, "Go ahead."

"I was just going to say, you don't have to tell me a secret," she said, her hushed voice echoing faintly. "I know this isn't your thing."

My pulse quickened with the idea of telling her my

real secret. Not that I would. I looked down, kicking at the dirt.

That's when I saw it.

A straight-line shape among the ragged leaves and rocks. I nudged it with a boot.

"What?" Sarah asked.

"There's some kind of box down here." I squatted and ran my hand over the cool leather surface.

Sarah knelt too, her hand brushing mine as she touched the box. I felt the whisper of her breath as she leaned closer, and I thought about how it might feel to kiss her. Not like we had in sixth grade but like we might now. Like she and Trip kissed.

"What's inside?" she asked. It was rhetorical, of course, but I had a weird sense of déjà vu, like I'd been here, heard these same words before. Like I almost knew the answer. "Let's take it out to the fire," she said.

"Yeah," I agreed, not moving. A dark, unsettling worry crept through me.

I felt Sarah watching. "Riley?" Her voice saying my name in the quiet of the cave sent chills up my spine. "Are you afraid?"

There was gooseflesh on my arms, under layers of clothes, and I realized I was. "No," I told her. "Of course not." To prove it I lifted the box, and something inside shifted as I tucked the case under my arm. "Let's go."

* * *

We stepped back into the clearing, the bright fire raging against the shadowy woods. "Did he tell you a secret?" Tannis asked suggestively.

"Lots," Sarah said.

"We found something," I said. Everyone crowded around, peering at the box.

"Cool," Trip said. "Open it up."

No. It was an immediate and primal response. But I pressed the button anyway, and the latch on the front sprung open with a sharp click. I remember thinking maybe it'd be worth something, whatever was inside. The box was old, hidden for who knows how long. Childhood stories of pirates and treasure jumped to mind, and I felt a sharp disappointment as I lifted the object out. Not gold coins or jewels or important documents.

Tannis wrinkled her nose. "Are those . . . binoculars?"

"Yep," I said, though they weren't like any I'd ever seen before. Clunky, with strange knobs and gears and lenses longer than they should have been. They looked like a cross between a small telescope with two barrels and a brass View-Master, dirty with bits of green where the metal had oxidized.

Forgotten by some old bird-watcher or hunter, I thought, turning them over. *Someone sheltering in the cave or camping up here*. I rubbed the lenses, which were clear and unbroken. I'd have

Morris Headley at the antiques shop check them out. He always had junk like this in the window. If I were lucky, maybe they'd turn out to be worth a few bucks.

I put them to my eyes and turned toward Trip, expecting to see his face magnified when I looked. I even had a joke ready—*I knew you had a big head, man, but . . .*

Only, I didn't see Trip through the glasses at all.

There was a show of colors and light instead. Patterns swirled slowly in and around one another, like when my mom made squash soup, her wooden spoon cutting white lines of cream as she stirred in figure eights. In the binoculars the lines twisted, folding in and out, new colors emerging. A kaleidoscope, I realized vaguely. An expensive one. Not like they sold at Miller's General in town. *Some rich kid's toy,* I thought thickly. I was mesmerized by the changing view, fluid purple merging into yellow, then green, a burst of red. A tourist must have brought it up here.

I could hear Trip and Natalie talking. Someone saying my name. I tried to drag my eyes away and listen, but it dawned on me just then that there was something else.

A picture was taking shape slowly, coming out of the colors, but also, not. Something was happening somewhere between the gyrations in the kaleidoscope and the dead center of my brain. Like the ghost images you see when you stare at brightness for too long, shadows burned into the back of your vision.

It was a room, I realized. That shape, a bed. A dresser behind. There were clothes on the floor and hung over chairs. A table, books, computer. The image was sharpening, and I saw a window. Outside, a blue sky broken by a building, long and uneven, with row after row of tiny squares. The whole picture was there but not, vivid but translucent, like something remembered from a dream.

Then suddenly there was movement. A rustling in the bed.

The image shifted as a figure rolled over and sat up.

I stared, focused, and sucked in my breath.

Holy shit.

It was me.

CHAPTER 2

"RILEY?" TRIP'S VOICE WAS FAR AWAY.

In the glasses, patterns were still swirling, moving in and out of each other. I watched the scene unfold, projected in front of or behind the changing colors.

The guy looked like he—*I*—hadn't shaved for days. My hair was long enough to curl around my ears in a way it hadn't since I was ten. I looked exhausted, rubbing my scruffy face like I'd just woken up from a two-month nap.

Then something moved and I realized the Riley in the picture wasn't alone.

There was someone beside me in that bed.

I watched my other self turn toward the rustling sheets that were twisting slowly as a girl pushed up on one arm, a glint of metal by her throat. Her skin was soft and silky down to her shoulder, where her body disappeared, bare, beneath the covers.

Sarah.

I dropped the binoculars. A dull clang sounded as they hit a rock. A weird noise escaped my throat, every nerve in my body jangling.

"Hey!" Trip said, surprised.

I'd recognized her faster than I'd recognized myself, had known almost before I saw her face—the sense of it deep inside me. She was thinner, beautiful, but too pale. Her hair was heavy and dark and messy in a way I'd never seen it. *Bed-head*, my brain whispered. *Because she was in bed. With you.* My heart was jackhammering, and I felt like my face was on fire.

What the hell?

"Riley?" It was her voice drifting across the fire. "You okay?"

I nodded, trying to swallow, not daring to look up.

"Hey." Trip gripped my shoulders. My chest was still pounding so hard, I wouldn't have ruled out a heart attack. Could you have one at seventeen? "What's wrong, man?" I had a flashback to third grade, when I'd blacked out after Paul Peterson punched me because he thought I'd stolen his Lugia EX Pokémon. Trip had sat beside me with that same watchful look, and my brain had felt like it did now, like nothing made sense.

"I'm okay," I squeaked, coughing to find my voice. "Sorry."

Trip looked at the woods, then scooped up the binoculars. "What's out there?"

Oh no. No, no, no, I thought as he raised them to his eyes. He was going to completely *freak—*

Get a grip, Riley.

I breathed, slowing my heart so my brain could work. *Trip isn't going to see you in bed with his girlfriend.* You *didn't just see that. Not in those binoculars. It's in your mind. Imagination or fantasy or whatever. Beer, and fumes from the fire.*

Yes, I thought, muscles unclenching. *Of course*.

After a minute, Trip laid the binoculars aside. "You scared the crap out of me," he said. "I thought the cops were here."

"You didn't see anything?"

"It's a kaleidoscope." He shrugged. "I saw shapes and stuff."

I nodded, relieved even though Trip was looking at me like I was nuts. Which I might have been.

"What'd you see?" he asked.

"Same thing," I said weakly.

Trip frowned. "Did you drop acid on the way up here, Ri?"

"You know I don't do that stuff."

"Colors and shapes are only scary if you're whacked-out."

"Yeah. I just . . ." I shook my head. "It must have been,

like, a panic attack or something." I looked down at my hands, could feel them trembling. Thankfully Trip didn't ask more. I'd had exactly three panic attacks in my life. All around the time my dad died. It was a sure out with Trip, though. Talking about stuff like that made him even more uncomfortable than it made me.

I ventured a quick glance at Sarah, who was still watching me.

She smells like spices and coffee and sleep.

The thought sent my heart racing again. Something was messed up. Was the beer spiked? I'd just been in the cave with her. She'd smelled like mints, maybe a flowery perfume, but I knew she smelled like that other stuff too. It had been so vivid in the binoculars, like it was real.

I could still feel the tangles of her hair, the coolness of the room we'd been in, the warmth and silkiness of her skin when I—

"Ohmygod," Natalie gasped.

Hallucinations. The thought flashed in my brain just as the binoculars fell out of Natalie's hand. Her face was pale, eyes wide and glistening with tears. My stomach fluttered with a hundred dread-filled butterflies.

"Jesus," Trip said, looking from her to me. "What's going on here?"

Natalie was rocking gently back and forth, hands covering her mouth like she was stifling a scream. I went over, squatted in front of her. "What, Nat?" I said, hearing a quaver in my own voice. "What was it?"

Her eyes found mine, and I saw she was scared. "God, Riley . . ." She took a deep, shuddering breath. "I saw my dad," she said shakily. "In our house. There was blood *everywhere.*" Natalie breathed quickly, like she could barely suck in the air. "I think he was dead."

My body felt cold, every hair on end. *Go,* my brain whispered. *Walk away. Pretend this never happened.* But I was frozen.

And in that moment, Tannis leaned forward and picked up the binoculars. I'm not sure if I thought she wouldn't look or if I hoped she wouldn't see anything. Maybe I was just too stunned to act. It wouldn't have mattered; Tannis would have looked anyway. That was how she was. Or at least I tell myself that now.

The dark lenses reflected the fire, with Tannis's thick blond hair spilling loose around them. When we were kids, she wore it in ponytails, dirty and messy by the end of the day from climbing trees and riding BMX bikes with the boys. Tannis was tough. I knew no matter what, she wasn't going to freak out or cry. I wasn't even sure she knew how to do those things.

I held my breath, staticky nonsense in my brain, until finally she lowered them.

"Well, that was really fucking weird," she said softly. She looked at Nat, who was rubbing her temples. "It was me, on the mountain," Tannis said. "I was walking Wraparound in summer. You know, like, hiking?" I nodded. "There were a couple kids with me. The way I felt about them . . . I think"—she hesitated—"they might have been mine." She laughed nervously, looked at me. Waited.

She wanted me to tell what I'd seen.

Not a chance.

Natalie stood suddenly and lurched away from the circle.

Trip jumped up. "Nat?" He followed her to the edge of the woods. She stumbled, and he grabbed her arm. Then she threw up.

"We should go," I said, the voice—*Get out!*—now screaming in my head. I started to gather our things, robotically stuffing my backpack with beer cans, matches, sweatshirt. This wasn't okay. Something was wrong here. Very wrong.

Tannis nodded, dumping her beer onto the fire, scraping up handfuls of dirt to put out the flames. She gestured toward the woods. "I'm going to help Trip. You guys pick up the rest?"

"'Kay," said Sarah, already folding the blankets.

I collected the last of the trash and scanned the circle. The fire was out. There was nothing left.

Except the binoculars.

Sarah saw them too. "You want these?"

I shook my head. It seemed stupid not to take them, but no, I didn't want them. No way.

"You think we should just leave them?" she asked doubtfully. "Here?" Sarah looked around the clearing. "They might get wrecked."

"We could put them back in the cave."

"Okay." She nodded. "I'll take them."

"Are you sure?" I forced myself to say, "I can do it."

"I won't go far." She was already reaching for the box, flipping it open.

"Riley?" Tannis called.

"Yeah?" I could barely make out her silhouette against the trees.

"We're going to start down. You guys okay to follow?"

I checked the flashlight. "Uh-huh," I told her. "We'll meet you at the car."

I heard the crunch and snap of their receding footsteps as I zipped up my bag. I looked over, expecting Sarah to have tossed the binoculars into the cave and be heading back my way, but she'd stopped just inside the dim opening.

She was frozen, and for a second I thought she'd seen an animal or something. Then I noticed a glint of metal in her hands, near her face.

She was looking into the binoculars.

CHAPTER 3

TRIP PICKED ME UP FOR SCHOOL JUST BEFORE EIGHT ON MONDAY like he did most mornings. I slid into his passenger seat and wrinkled my nose. "Dude. It reeks in here."

"Says the guy who spent yesterday cleaning toilets," Trip answered.

"Actually, it was rotting mice." It had been my week to clean and reset the traps at Oknepa Hotel and Restaurant, the only place to stay in town, and my employer for the last three years. "And toilets," I added.

"How'd you score such a sweet job?"

"Must be my good looks." I swiveled around, looking for rancid food. Trip's gym bag was on the floor, surrounded by McDonald's wrappers. Bingo. I hadn't seen him since he'd dropped me off Saturday night after the cave. I'd spent half of Sunday at work and an even longer half at the hospital

ER with my mom. I guess I knew how Trip had spent his. "You ever clean this thing?"

"My car or my bod?"

"Either."

"Rarely," Trip admitted.

"I bet that impresses the ladies."

"Seems to be working out okay," he said pointedly.

I let that go. I didn't want to talk about Sarah, or worse—*him* and Sarah.

"Don't you think it defeats the purpose of a workout to have fast food afterward?" I asked instead.

"You're in a shitty mood," Trip observed, glancing over.

I took a deep breath, then exhaled hard. "Sorry."

He studied me for an extra second, then zeroed in on it. "Your mom all right?" Trip had a way of reading people like that, especially me.

I shrugged, my chest tight, thinking of her in the hospital wheelchair last night. I wanted to blow it off, tell him it was nothing, she was fine, but I was having a hard time unclenching my throat.

Trip noticed and pulled over, turned on the bench seat to face me. "What happened?"

And just like that, it felt like the end of eighth grade, Trip and me standing by our lockers—side by side that year—after the first time she'd been sick. I'd tried to hold it together back then, telling him the stuff the doctor had said.

Normally you wouldn't take your fourteen-year-old son to your medical appointment, but I'd found my mom in bed that morning, barely able to sit up. I'd been so worried, I'd insisted, and I guess she hadn't had the energy to fight it. But when we'd sat together in the doctor's office after she'd come out of the exam, I wished I hadn't gone with her. The things he'd said scared the crap out of me.

". . . cardiomyopathy, inflammation, muscular dystrophy—"

"Or it could be just strained muscles," my mom had added, seeing my reaction. "I probably overworked them yesterday."

I'd wanted that to be it. My mom's job was physical, moving things, lifting people who couldn't walk, helping them into and out of bed. It wasn't the first time she'd come home sore, but Dr. Williams had given her a look. "There are the other symptoms to take into account," he'd said.

I'd thought back to every incriminating thing, my heart sinking as I realized there were plenty: headaches, dizziness, days when she'd dropped dishes and blamed tiredness, days when she'd had trouble driving because her eyes were bothering her. Stretching back months, at least.

"We've done some tests," he'd said. "The results should tell us what we're dealing with."

Only, the tests had been inconclusive, and we were taking the "wait and see" approach. It was years later, and none of us liked what we were seeing.

"She went to the hospital last night," I told Trip now as we sat in his car. "They did more tests. She's home today. I don't want to talk about it." Which was the God's honest truth, because just thinking about it was like suffocating under a thick wet blanket of worry.

I pinched the underside of my forearm, focusing on the pain instead of all the other crap. Finally Trip nodded and faced forward. "Sorry, man." He pulled back onto the road. "Let me know if I can help."

We split in the parking lot, Trip stopping to talk to his football teammates while I jogged toward homeroom. I had a sudden weird certainty that Natalie wouldn't be there. She'd called off work Sunday at the ski shop, Trip had told me on the drive to school, and hadn't answered his texts or calls either.

"Because of Saturday night?" I'd asked. I'd managed to put aside most of my anxiety about those binoculars. We must have been hallucinating, I'd decided. It had been weird, but I was okay.

Trip had shrugged. "I guess so."

With anyone else, you'd swing by their house or maybe call their parents to check in. But, of course, we couldn't do that with Nat.

I held my breath crossing the threshold to homeroom, expecting an empty chair, but there she was: second seat by the window, as usual. I tried to catch her eye, but she stared outside through announcements, not talking to friends or looking my way.

I waited by the door when the bell rang.

"How're you feeling, Nat?" I asked, trailing her toward the music room.

"Fine." Natalie kept her head down, but I didn't need to see her face to know something was wrong. She walked in long, stiff strides like she couldn't wait to get away from me. I didn't take it personally, but it cranked my nerves up a notch.

"We were worried about you," I told her. "After Saturday. Trip said you missed work yesterday."

She still didn't look at me, her long hair swinging as she walked. Nat usually wore a braid so her hair wouldn't tangle—lots of the skiers did—but today it was loose, hiding her face.

"I'm okay, Riley," she said. "Thanks."

"It was really weird, wasn't it?" I asked quietly when we'd gotten to the stairs without another word. "What happened up there?"

She gave me a quick, hard look. "I saw my dad dead. It was beyond weird."

I felt a lump in my throat, but not because of what she'd said. "Nat." I reached out, held her arm gently, the hallucinations forgotten.

Natalie stopped, staring at her shoes, but her whole posture sagged.

I looked around quickly, letting a few nearby kids pass before I lifted Nat's chin, forcing her to look at me.

"Jeez, Nat," I said softly. There was a Band-Aid under her left eye. A soft yellow bruise spreading out from it. "What happened?"

"I tripped," she said, forcing a smile.

"You tripped? How?"

"There was a box on the floor in the living room, and I had my arms full. Just didn't see it. And *whap*! Smacked my face pretty good, huh?" She chuckled, the sound brittle. I could picture her standing in front of a bathroom mirror, rehearsing. My stomach clenched as I thought of all the ways it might have actually gone down.

"Listen, I've gotta run," she said, pulling her arm away. "I'll see you later." Nat spun on her heel and trotted down the steps toward the music room, leaving me to consider the things I knew about how she lived.

We picked her up almost every weekend, but never went inside her house. Natalie would slip out like she'd been waiting, the door cracked just enough for her to squeeze through.

I knew what was in there, though. Moose, from work, had taken me up to her place one night when he'd offered me a ride. It would have been a long, cold walk home, so I'd gladly accepted.

"Just gotta run a quick errand on the way," he'd said as I'd followed him to his car. Moose had waved me to the rear door, and I'd noticed an arm hanging out the passenger window. I recognized the ripped-up surplus jacket. Wynn Bishe. Another Buford High deadbeat who'd graduated—or at least left—a couple years before.

"What the fuck's he doing here?" Wynn asked, tossing a butt on the gravel lot as I slid into the backseat. He shot me a dirty look, the dark wisps on his upper lip twitching—the world's most pathetic mustache.

"He needs a ride home," Moose said.

Wynn snorted. "What're you, his babysitter?"

"Jeez, Wynn—" Moose said.

"I can walk," I said, reaching for the handle. But Moose had already started the car and now threw it into reverse.

"Forget it." He glared at Wynn.

Wynn just shook his head. "Not smart, Moose."

I sat stiffly in back, ignoring the cold air whistling in from the open windows. I felt like somebody's kid brother no one wants around, even though Moose was in my grade. Not that I'd said a word to him since elementary school before he'd started at the restaurant. Moose went to vo-tech most days, and when I did see him, he was usually smoking with the other 'heads two steps off the Buford High curb—not school property. But despite his crappy choice of friends, habits, and death metal T-shirts, Moose was mostly okay.

We sped down back roads, then up a winding, unlit lane, Wynn smoking and Moose nodding randomly to Zeppelin, tapping his lucky skull-and-crossbones lighter against the wheel. Finally we pulled off the road and parked by a run-down trailer.

I'd never seen the place—wasn't friends with Natalie then, and certainly didn't know she lived there. Wynn got out without a backward glance, but Moose gave me a quick "Wait here; be right back" before jogging across the weedy yard.

It wasn't until the last bit of daylight had gone and I'd had way too much time to examine every dented strip of aluminum hanging from the mobile home that I started to worry. The place was pretty remote. I'd seen maybe one other house on the way up, and it didn't look like somewhere that'd welcome visitors. It was pretty obvious what kind of errand Moose was running, and I kicked myself for being lured along. I was late, my phone was out of juice, and my mom was waiting for me, probably calling work, expecting that I'd have been home for dinner thirty minutes before.

Moose had said "Wait here," but he'd also said it would be a quick errand, which had been a total lie. Either that or he and Wynn were lying dead inside, something that seemed possible as I walked toward the trailer. I stood on the front stoop and knocked softly. For a long minute nothing happened. Then I saw dark messy hair and eyes peering through the small window beside the door. The handle rattled and the door opened a crack.

"Who're you?" The guy squinted at me, his face haggard and unshaven.

"I'm looking for Moose," I said. "I've been waiting for him."

The guy grinned, but it looked more like a snarl. One of his front teeth was missing. He turned his head, yelling back into the room, "Moose! You bring this Boy Scout up here with you?"

Moose was at the door a second later. "I told you to stay in the car," he hissed.

The guy opened the door wider, and I saw all of it—the dank living room, crumpled beer cans by a beat-up recliner, a low table littered with ash and papers, lighters and baggies, mismatched curtains dangling from metal rods.

Wynn was sitting on the couch beside a little woman with matted hair. She looked half-asleep, slumped sideways like she'd fallen over and no one had bothered to pick her up. "C'mon in then, Boy Scout," the guy offered. "Join the party."

I took a step back. "I've gotta go, Moose," I said, looking at him. "Sorry, but my mom's waiting—"

"Don't wanna keep Mamma waiting," the dirty guy agreed. "Ain't that right, Crystal?"

He looked back at the woman, but she didn't stir.

"S'all right, Moose," the guy said. "S'all good. Take your boyfriend home to his mamma." He winked in a way that made me hope he never crossed paths with my mamma.

"You want me to drive?" I asked Moose as I trailed him down the walkway. Wynn, thankfully, had decided to stay. I had no idea if Moose would go back for him or if Wynn would just sleep there beside Crystal. And I didn't care.

"Why would I want you to drive?" Moose barked without looking back. He was pissed. "I thought I told you to stay in the car."

"Yeah," I shot back. "You also said it was a quick pit stop."

"It was."

"You were in there for almost an hour."

"No way." Moose squinted at his watch, then grunted. "Huh. Time flies when you're having fun."

I never told any of my friends about that night, even after the first time Trip and I picked Natalie up, my heart freezing at the memory of the inside of that sad, dented trailer.

Now I trotted down the hall away from where I'd left Nat, back past homeroom, and then slipped through the door to physics just before the bell.

"Welcome, Mr. Larkin. To what do we owe this distinct pleasure?"

"Rocks for Jocks was filled?"

"Of course." Mr. Ruskovich shook his head ruefully.

"Sloppy seconds. Story of my life." He smiled as my classmates laughed. My eyes skated across them, and paused briefly on Sarah. She smiled, making my ears redden, and I looked away. I wondered if she'd seen Nat yet. "Okay, everyone," Mr. Ruskovich was saying as I slid into my seat. "Today we discuss"—he paused, leaning forward—"particle theory."

"Again?" Matty Gretowniak moaned.

"Unless you can tell me what it means, Mr. Gretowniak."

"That I'll have a splitting headache in exactly forty-three minutes," Matty grumbled.

"That's what happens when you only use your brain once a day," Chuck Lee told him. "It gets rusty. Creeeeeak!"

"Okay, suck-up," Matty said mildly.

"Gentlemen, gentlemen," Mr. Ruskovich interrupted, holding up his hands. "Please. Save your verbal sparring for debate club. In here we do intellectual sparring only."

"Then why's Gretowniak here?" I asked, grinning at Matty. He flipped me the bird where Mr. Ruskovich couldn't see. The truth was, Matty was probably smarter than all of us, which was what made it fun to rag on him. Plus you had to lighten up physics somehow. Mr. Ruskovich gave his AP groups, especially our tiny class of four, pretty free range like that.

"Actually," Mr. Ruskovich said, smiling, "I'm joking, Mr. Gretowniak. In reality we're going to begin a crime scene investigation."

Matty sat up straighter. "Cool!"

"What's the crime?" Sarah asked.

"Murder, of course."

"Awesome," Chuck said.

We listened closely as Mr. Ruskovich continued, his voice low and spooky. "It happened in the supply closet." He pointed at the door behind his desk, all of us eyeing it as he spoke. "In there right now you will find a gruesome scene of splattered blood. Your job? Describe the killer." He beckoned us to his desk, where an array of supplies was laid out: protractors, rulers, notebooks, tape, pencils, and string. "With these few simple tools and an understanding of physics, you will determine where the perpetrator was standing, how tall he or she might have been, and what sort of weapon was used—"

"Like Clue," Matty said.

"Exactly like Clue, actually," Mr. Ruskovich agreed. He spread the character cards from the game on the table. Beneath each he'd written their height in pen.

"It was definitely Professor Plum," Matty said. "He's a creeper."

"I've been told I resemble him," Mr. Ruskovich said.

"Exactly." Matty laughed.

"I bet it was Miss Scarlet," Chuck said.

"Oh, sure," Sarah teased. "Blame it on a woman."

"Isn't that what they're for?" Chuck asked.

"Well, actually, Chuck . . . ," Matty started, eyebrows raised.

"Hold it, Matt," Sarah said. "You should quit while you're ahead."

"I'm going to have to agree with Miss McKenzie on this one, gentlemen," Mr. Ruskovich said firmly. "Now if we could get back to the lesson . . ." He went on to explain circular versus elliptical splatters, angle of spray, and impact. "Once you've identified the point of contact, you'll be able to test the various weapons"—Mr. Ruskovich flashed a second set of Clue cards showing a lead pipe, candlestick, revolver, and the rest—"reenacting the crime to see how close our new splatters come to the old ones."

He told us to take turns with the measurements so we wouldn't disturb the crime scene. Then he pivoted and opened the door behind him.

"Nice," Chuck said appreciatively. The walls and shelving in the closet had been covered with long sheets of white paper, splattered with drops of dark red. Right away I could see the ellipses and spray Mr. Ruskovich had talked about. Of course, I could also think of at least ten things wrong with this experiment—how the force of impact or part of the weapon used might change the pattern, that Mr. Ruskovich wouldn't have been able to precisely record locations. But we all—Mr. Ruskovich especially—knew those variables weren't properly accounted for. That he turned boring lectures about cosines, angles, and projection into a murder mystery was at least half of why physics—and all of his science classes—were always my favorites.

The forty-three minutes flew by, and no one really wanted to move on to our next class when the bell rang. Reluctantly we stood, closing our notebooks as Mr. Ruskovich shut and locked the "crime scene," the inside now taped and marked where we'd begun work.

"Guess you were wrong about that headache, Matty," I said as we started down the hall.

"I'm telling you, man, particle theory burns my brain. I might have run screaming from the room."

"Or committed hara-kiri," Sarah suggested.

"At least we'd be able to figure out what he used and where he was standing when he did it," I said.

Sarah rolled her eyes. "It's always with a sword, Riley. That's the definition of 'hara-kiri.'"

"I knew that," I lied, feeling my ears redden.

"Hey, did you guys get your SATs back?" Chuck called, jogging to catch up to us.

"No." Matty whirled to face him. "Yours came?"

Chuck nodded. "On Saturday."

"And?"

"Twenty-one forty."

Matty whistled. "Nice."

Chuck smiled, embarrassed. "I'm sure yours'll be better."

"You didn't leave me a lot of room," Matty said, turning back to me and Sarah. "Did you guys get 'em?"

She nodded. "Twenty-two hundred."

"Well, well . . ." Matty grinned, raising an eyebrow at Chuck. "Whaddaya think about that, Chuckster?"

"I think your margin for claiming the Brainiest Brainiac title is shrinking."

"Indeed." Matty looked at me. "Ri?"

"Nope." I shook my head. "I got nuthin'." I hoped Matty would leave it at that, but I could tell the way his eyes narrowed that he wouldn't.

"You still didn't take them, did you?"

I could feel all of them watching me, Sarah's stare especially penetrating. Matty had gone down this path with me before, but never with her there. And definitely not with the memory of her naked in bed floating around in my brain. I'd thought my Sunday night at the hospital had made me forget the feel of her in the binoculars, but the way she was looking at me brought it rushing back. My throat felt hot and tight. I shook my head. "No."

Matty stopped, turning to face me. "What are you waiting for, Riley?"

"I'll get around to it."

"When?" he demanded. "Next year? The year after?"

There was a lump in my chest. I knew this was how it started, the kind of future he was talking about—being stuck here majoring in grunt labor, Drinking 101, and hating life instead of chem or physics. The kind of future Moose and any number of our classmates were headed for. It shouldn't be mine, but I didn't know any way around it. Not right then. I hoped if I worked full-time for a year, maybe I could save enough to go to school. Maybe things with my mom would get better and she wouldn't be out of work so much. Maybe she'd even find a better job.

Maybe pigs would fly, too.

"You're too smart to get stuck here," Matty said.

"That's high praise, coming from the Brainiest Brainiac."

"Joke about it if you want," he said shortly, "but I don't think you'll be laughing next year." He turned and started down the hall with Chuck toward their next class.

I wasn't laughing *now*. But I also wasn't about to spell it out for him. If Matty was so damn smart, he should have been able to figure it out. I was hardly the only kid in Buford with money problems.

Sarah was still there, watching me. I glanced over, but she didn't ask.

"Have you seen Nat today?" I said.

She shook her head. "No. Why?"

CHAPTER 4

AT LUNCH I WALKED TO THE QUAD WITH SARAH, TRIP, AND Tannis. Nat had a student council meeting but had told Trip she'd find us later. A bunch of kids were already outside, sitting on steps or benches with their food. It was cold, but there was no snow on the ground. We all knew that wouldn't last much longer.

We passed Moose with a few of his buddies, headed in the opposite direction. He barely acknowledged my brief nod. I'd have done the same if he'd nodded first. That was how we rolled at school.

"What do you think really happened?" I asked once we found a free spot on one of the stone walls around the quad.

Trip unwrapped a sandwich, shaking his head. "Man, I don't know," he said. He'd been the first to bring up Nat and her bruise. They'd had earth sciences together, and she'd given him the same story she'd given me. Verbatim.

"Do you think her dad—"

"Hit her?" Trip finished. "The million-dollar question. I've never seen him violent, but it's been a long time since I've really been around him." Trip used to ski with Natalie when they were kids, before her mom left and her dad holed up in that trailer. "Nat's so crazy-protective of him. It's hard to imagine it."

"Classic sign of abuse," Sarah piped in.

"Yeah, I know," he said. "Believe me, I've been wondering for years."

We all nodded. If you didn't spend a lot of time with Natalie, maybe you wouldn't notice—a scrape here, bruise there. Competitive skiing is rough, and when you fall, you fall hard. But not in summer. The five of us really started hanging out last year, when Trip and Sarah got together, and after a few months I realized that for an athlete at Nat's level, she was awfully clumsy.

God forbid you mentioned it to her, though.

"Did she say what went on at her house this weekend?" Tannis asked.

Sarah snorted. "What? And make us all accessories?"

"I just meant, you know, whether her dad was around. Or if anyone else came over . . ." Tannis trailed off at Sarah's pointed look. "Yeah, okay. I guess that *would* make us accessories."

"She's not about to rat out the town's junkies," Sarah said. "It'd put Daddy out of business."

"What a fucking mess," Trip said.

Tannis wolfed down the last of her sandwich and stood. "No wonder she's thinking of him dead."

"You mean the thing at the cave?" Trip asked.

Tannis nodded, walking to the grass a few feet away and motioning for Trip to toss her the Nerf football he'd brought out. "If he was my dad, I'm pretty sure I'd daydream about that."

"I don't think those were daydreams," I said.

"You don't?" Sarah asked.

I shrugged, suddenly uncomfortable. As if she knew how I'd pictured her, in my bed.

"What do you think they were?" Sarah pressed.

"I don't know."

"C'mon, Ri," Tannis butted in. "Sounds like you have some ideas. Let's hear 'em."

I knew these girls, and they weren't going to back down. "Hallucinations?" I offered.

"What do you mean?" Trip said. "Like from acid?"

I nodded.

Trip tossed the ball thoughtfully, but Tannis said, "I don't know, Ri. I'm no expert, but it wasn't like any trip I've ever had. You?"

I'd tried drugs exactly once, the summer before junior year, when Trip had dragged me to a football party. "I don't know, Trip," I'd hedged. "Some of those guys seem kind of . . ."

"Kind of what?" he'd said impatiently. "Older? Fun? Cool?"

I'd shrugged, thinking of the way they'd jammed Chuck Lee's locker shut one day. "Like trouble," I'd finished.

Trip had snorted. "Don't be a loser, Ri. It'll be fine."

It hadn't been, of course. The acid had come out around midnight, and like fools, we'd put the tabs on our tongues when the other guys did. I made some crack about how it was like second grade, when Trip ate the corners off all his worksheets. It was the last thing I said all night, because my head got really cold and divided into three compartments, the tongue not connected to the brain. Definitely not my thing.

"No," I told Tannis now. "It wasn't like that at all. But lots of things can make you hallucinate," I said. "Maybe different stuff gives you different reactions?"

"But we didn't take anything," Sarah said.

"Not that we know of," I said. "But 'shrooms and peyote both occur naturally."

"And you think there's some up at the cave?" Trip asked.

Sarah shot him a look. "Don't get any ideas, Trip."

"Buzz kill," he said, mostly joking. LSD hadn't been Trip's thing either.

"Maybe we touched something in the cave or on those binoculars," I said.

"So how come I didn't see anything?" Trip asked.

"Maybe you're immune to it," I said.

"Just my luck."

"It *is* your luck," Tannis said. "Trust me. It was freaky."

"So you don't think it was a daydream either, do you?" I asked her.

"Guess not," she said. "I *don't* daydream about kids. What'd you see, anyway, Ri?" Tannis asked. "You never told."

No, of course I hadn't. "Nothing much." Blood rushed to my face, and I felt all of them watching me. I didn't dare look at Sarah. "Just me in a room with some books . . ." *And Trip's girlfriend. In my bed.* My heart was pounding. "And some, you know, papers and a little fridge and a bed," I finished quickly.

"Like a dorm room?" Sarah asked.

My eyes locked with hers, and it was like a jolt of electricity. "Huh?"

"A dorm room," Sarah repeated. "It sounds like a college dorm."

I nodded slowly, the words finally sinking in. "Might have been."

"What were you doing?" Tannis asked.

"Sleeping."

Trip laughed. "Always the party animal, dude."

If only he knew.

"Why do you think you guys saw *that* stuff?" Sarah asked.

Tannis shrugged, but I was struck by how Sarah had asked the question. "You guys." Not "we." I was pretty sure she'd seen something that night. She'd stared into the binoculars for too long and had come away from the cave unusually somber, but hadn't said a word about it. Even when I'd asked if everything was okay before we started down. She didn't want to tell, and what's more, I realized now, she didn't know anyone had seen her look.

I could have called her on it, but for some reason I didn't.

"Maybe it was, like, our hidden thoughts," I said, watching her reaction. "Our deepest wishes or worst fears or something."

Sarah held my eyes, her expression unreadable.

"It's definitely *not* our wishes," Tannis said vehemently. "I saw *kids* in mine."

"So?" I said.

"Dude. I do *not* want kids." She chucked me the ball, and missed by a mile.

I jogged to where it'd landed. "Not *now*, Tannis—"

"Or later," she interrupted.

I threw the ball to Trip. "Don't all girls want kids?" I asked Tannis, only half-teasing. "Isn't it like a biological imperative?"

"No, dumbass, not all girls want kids. And if it's a biological whatever, it would be for guys, too, wouldn't it? Last time I checked, it takes two. Do all *guys* want kids?"

"Don't know," I said. "I've never really thought about it."

"Well, I have," Tannis said. "Because I've watched how it is for my mom, stuck in the house—every minute she's not working, that is—washing and cleaning and cooking and then washing and cleaning and cooking again. She's been doing it for twenty years, and my mom's awesome, but she's never done any of the stuff she wanted. Live in a city, fly on an airplane, do a job where she gets to wear a suit. Kids are a straight-up dead-end boring job, and it is *definitely* not for me."

I had to agree with that. It was impossible to imagine Tannis as a mom.

"I want to get the hell out of Buford and race on the circuit," Tannis said, swatting away the ball Trip had thrown, too upset or angry to play along anymore. "You thought that was my secret desire, huh?" Tannis demanded. "To be a slave to a bunch of rug rats? And Nat's was for her dad to die?" She didn't even wait for me to answer. "Jeez, Riley. You really think a lot of us, don't you?"

"Hey, relax," I soothed. "I'm just guessing, you know? Maybe it was our fears or stuff we worry about—"

"She's coming," Sarah said quietly.

The four of us turned simultaneously, looking toward school. I could almost see Natalie stiffen. Then she squared her shoulders and joined us with a smile.

"Well, that was a total waste of time," she said breezily.

The four of us exchanged a look.

"Nat," Sarah said gently. "What happened to your eye?" Nat's smile faltered, and Sarah added, "For real."

Natalie went totally still, then clenched her jaw. "I tripped."

No one said anything. It was the longest, most uncomfortable silence I think I'd ever sat through. I wanted it to be the truth. We all did. Maybe it was.

Nat seized her chance to change the subject. "Everyone's running the Dash on Saturday, right?" she asked brightly. "Lu really wants a good turnout. We need it after last winter."

"The football team's running together," Trip said. They did every year, just like Nat's ski team.

The Warrior Dash was a two-and-a-half-mile race through rocky paths and mud with no reward other than some trophies and a stocked bar at the end for anyone legal. The resort owners cooked it up years ago to lure people to Buford before ski season and sell winter passes, condos, and rentals. And the tourists love it—it's Buford's busiest weekend and the unofficial kickoff of the season for the town and the mountain, which are pretty much interchangeable. We all pitch in, one way or another, all of Buford holding its breath and on its best behavior, hoping this winter will be better than the last, in a series of tougher and tougher years since newer resorts opened a few exits north.

And after, we all celebrate. The ski team's annual post-Dash party is not to be missed.

"I'm doing it with Jed and Tyler," Tannis said, raising an eyebrow at Trip. "And we're going to kick your ass."

They probably would. Tannis and her brothers, one of them a marine, were built like Vikings. But Trip snorted. "Uh, yeah. Good luck with that, Janssen."

"What about you guys?" Nat asked me and Sarah.

"I'm not sure—" I started, but Sarah interrupted.

"Riley and I are racing as Team Independent. And we'll kick all of your butts!"

"Team Independent?" I asked.

"Lame, right?" Sarah admitted. "Best I could come up with on the fly. Got anything better?"

"How about Team Invisible . . . like, we don't show up?"

But Trip was already on it. "I bet Ri doesn't even cross the finish line." He turned to me. "Have you even done it before?"

He knew I hadn't. "I'm not sure."

"What are the stakes?" Tannis asked. "Make it worth my while."

"What do you want?" he asked.

Tannis thought for a minute, then grinned. "How about you come to the track and wax my car?"

"Oh, I'll wax your car, baby."

She laughed. "You're a pig, Trip."

"Yeah," he agreed. "If I win, you guys wax mine?"

"Fine," she said. "But what about Nat and Team Indigestion over here?"

"Independent," Sarah corrected.

"Whatever."

"You guys can take turns carrying my gear for a month," Nat suggested.

"A month?" Trip said dubiously. "What time do you start training?"

"Six thirty."

Trip winced. "How about a week?" he asked, looking to the rest of us for approval.

Nat shrugged. "Fine by me."

"And what about us?" Sarah asked Trip.

"What do you want?"

"Ri?" She turned to me.

I thought for a minute. "Come to the restaurant and do toilet duty for a week."

"Will they let us?" Nat asked.

"I'll sneak you in," I told her.

"If I thought you had a chance in hell of winning, I'd say no way," Trip said. "But, sure." He grinned. "Why not? What about you, Sarah?"

"Shovel our driveway and walk for the first snowfall," she said immediately. "My dad's back has been killing him, and I hate doing it."

"You could just do like us and not bother," Nat suggested wryly.

Tannis snorted. "So we're on. . . . Best time wins?"

We all nodded, and with that, we let it go, Nat's mysterious injuries swept under the rug again.

Until the weekend that changed everything.

CHAPTER 5

I RAN INTO THE LIVING ROOM AFTER MY SHIFT, HOPING I COULD make it to the mountain on time. It had been a brutal morning. "Georgie's got his panties on extra tight because of the Dash," Moose had told me as soon as I'd walked into the restaurant. He'd been right. Our manager usually saved his cursing for Moose, but today we'd both been fair game. He'd had us scrub every surface, roll extra tubs of silverware, mix vats of coleslaw. I was over an hour late getting out of there and would have just enough time to shower and change before I was supposed to meet Sarah near the starting line. It was probably stupid to get cleaned up, but there was no way I was going to show up smelling like bacon and eggs.

But I stopped short in the living room, seeing my mom on the sofa. It had been almost a week since our night at the hospital, and she'd gone back to work a few days ago, but she wasn't one to sit still, much less lie down in the middle of the day.

"What?" she asked, looking up from her book.

"How are you feeling?"

She smiled. "Fine, Riley. Really." She swung her legs over the edge of the sofa, stood, and turned around in a circle. "See?"

She looked solid and steady, the way I'd always pictured her. She'd been a runner in high school, had always hiked the trails behind our house and gone camping with me and my dad when I was little. I'd thought of her as strong like that long after it was true.

"Do I pass?" she asked, returning to the sofa.

"Yeah," I said, thinking that if she were just honest with me about stuff, we wouldn't have to go through this.

"Are you going to the Dash?"

I nodded, starting up the stairs. "You running this year?" I teased.

"Ha-ha."

Twenty minutes later I hopped onto my bike after telling her, "I'll be late. Don't wait up."

"I'm working till five in the morning," she said. "Try to beat me home, 'kay?"

Sarah was watching for me, and waved when I swung off the bike. "Hurry," she called. "The juniors are almost done."

I nodded, locked up, and jogged to the base lodge patio, where the Stones were blaring across a crowd of at least a hundred people. As much as we complained about Buford, there was something pretty special about Dash weekend. People were smiling and laughing. Bill Winston, one of the mountain partners, moved through the crowd, glad-handing the seasonal people and chatting up the weekenders. A good winter was important to all of us—no one ever forgot that—and at this time of year there was always the sense it could happen. This could be the year people rediscovered Buford, the season we got record snowfall. It was probably like spring is in most places—the sense of a fresh start, new blood, a chance to re-create our town and ourselves.

I saw it in Sarah's face, her eyes shining with excitement as we wove through people toward the red banner at the starting line.

Trip and Tannis were already there.

"You're late," Tannis told me. "The ski team's about to take off."

I craned my neck and saw Nat clustered with her teammates, all of them wearing red-and-white T-shirts emblazoned with the mountain logo.

"Sorry," I said. "Had to work."

"We're going with the two forty-five group," Sarah said, handing me our number.

I taped it onto my shirt, glancing at the huge clock on

the peak of the base lodge. Thirty-five minutes. That should be enough time to get my heart rate down from the five-mile ride over.

"When are you guys running?" I asked Trip and Tannis.

"Trip's in the third group, just after all the ski teams," Tannis said. "My brothers and I are with you. We can say good-bye at the starting line," she added, "since you'll be looking at our butts the rest of the way."

"Puh-leeze," Sarah said, flipping her palm at Tannis.

People ran the Dash individually or in whatever haphazard teams they cared to put together, a semi-organized free-for-all. The starts were every fifteen minutes up until the last runner, which, by the looks of this year's crowd, might be near dark. Times were posted on the lodge windows as teams came in, with trophies for each age category as well as a Worst Time, Dirtiest Finish, Youngest Runner, Oldest Runner, and a bunch of other nonsense. The course wasn't long but it was tough, a combination of hiking; running; rope climbing; and sloshing through streams that, depending on how rainy it'd been, could be three feet deep. Pretty much everyone in town ran it at least once at some point or another, and lots of people did it every year. While we'd been rolling silverware that morning, I'd asked Moose if he was going.

"Are you crazy?" he'd said. "I get my recommended daily allowance of tourists right here."

"You'll miss the after-party."

Moose had given me a funny look, like he was going to say something, then thought better of it. "Thanks, but I get my daily allowance of assholes at school," he'd finally said, adding, "No offense," as an afterthought.

"Gee, why would I be offended by something like that?"

"I didn't mean you," he'd said. "But that guy you're friends with . . ."

"Trip?"

He'd nodded. "Yeah. That dude's a jerk."

I'd shrugged. "Sometimes."

"Anyway," Moose had said, "I've got my own after-party planned."

I knew better than to ask him about that.

The loudspeaker announced the next group, and a few minutes later we heard the starting gun pop, and Natalie's team took off. Within a minute they were around the first turn and disappearing into the woods.

"How are we going to beat that?" I asked Sarah.

"Where's your positive attitude, Riley?"

"I knew I forgot something."

Sarah smiled. "Remember, their whole team has to cross before their time counts. So having more people isn't necessarily better."

"Even if they're all strong, well-conditioned athletes who know this mountain like the inside of their own house?"

She nodded. "Even if."

Trip checked his watch. "I'd better get with the team. Good luck," he said, adding suggestively to Sarah, "I can't wait to watch you wash my car, baby."

"That's too bad," she answered. "Because it's going to be a loooong wait."

"I like confident women." He winked.

"Oh my God." Tannis rolled her eyes. "How can you stand him?" she asked Sarah.

"I don't know." Sarah considered Trip with a grin. "He has a certain je ne sais quoi, don't you think?"

"That's French for 'ridiculous arrogance,' right?" I asked.

Even Trip laughed. "Nice smack talk, Ri, but let's see how you race. Later, losers." He jogged toward the starting line and a few minutes later took off.

They called us soon after. Tannis lined up with her two huge, muscular brothers. Sarah and I were at the other end of the starting line with a motley assortment of townies and tourists.

"Nervous?" she asked as we waited for the gun.

"Why do you ask?"

"The foot-to-foot dance is sort of a tip-off."

"Maybe I just have to use the bathroom."

She frowned. "Do you?"

"No. I'm nervous."

She reached out, squeezed my shoulder. "Don't be. It'll be

fun." Her cheeks were flushed pink with the cold, her eyes still sparkling. She looked beautiful, and I felt scared and excited being there as her partner. I hoped I didn't screw it up.

Then the gun went off and we were running hard, a pack of twenty or so headed up the long, slow slope of the bunny hill. I could feel the burn in my lungs as we neared the turn where I'd watched Natalie's team disappear. Already Tannis and her brothers had fallen back, not as light or nimble as me and Sarah. I wondered how they liked the view of our butts. I let Sarah set the pace, and I trailed a few steps behind. Trip had told me she ran regularly, and even though I didn't, I was pretty sure I could keep up, thanks to having to bike whenever our car broke down or my mom needed it.

Sarah veered onto the first of the hiking paths that wove through the woods. I kept my eyes down like I did whenever we went to the cave, watching for loose stones. Behind us I heard someone call out as they stumbled. I knew from the course map that this trail kept going up about a quarter mile before we got to the first obstacle—a rope wall twenty feet high. Beyond that was the stream and the mud pit and a rock wall that was part of one of the terrain parks when the snow fell. And in between each, lots and lots of running.

I glanced behind, saw no one. We were clearly in the lead, though I had no idea by how much or how our time would stack up against anyone else's. I didn't expect to win, but it sure would feel good to beat Trip and his football friends. Not that they were bad guys—not all of them, at least—but I couldn't help holding a small grudge at the way they'd become his go-to buddies at exactly the wrong time.

It had started the summer before eighth grade. Trip had been playing Pop Warner for a few years by then but had somehow gotten it into his head he was destined for more. He'd gone down to the rec field almost every day that summer, and I'd gone with him. Eventually I'd drift to the bleachers with a book, bored with the repetitive drills he was willing to run endlessly with whoever was there that day. Maybe I'd have joined in if I'd had any idea how *not* joining would come back to bite me. In August, he tried out for the team. I did too, but when they posted the final roster, his name was on it. Mine wasn't. I remember standing outside the coach's office, looking at that list, not surprised but feeling a bitterness in my throat as Trip high-fived the other guys. "Bummer, Ri," he told me, not bothering to suggest I try again next year. He walked away chattering with all of them without a backward glance. I tried to shrug it off. Told myself it was just one small part of his life. But I already knew it wasn't. If I'd made the team, I realized belatedly, I'd have been along on their bus trips and practices, I'd have been going to the Hull after. But since I hadn't, from then on a huge part of our days and weeks had no overlap.

"How you doin'?" Sarah called back breathlessly. We were nearing the top, but she kept a steady pace up the steep hill.

"Good," I panted. "You?"

"Fine. We're almost to the ropes."

Sure enough, a big net stretched across the trail around the next bend.

"Hello, warriors," the attendant called as we ran toward her. "Up the rope—one at a time, together, however you like. Continue onto the trail to the right."

I could see a yellow sign with an arrow pointing the way she'd said.

Sarah ran to the net and started to climb without hesitation. I waited a beat for her to scale about two feet of it, then started up myself, feeling the tug and pull of the ropes, our weight causing them to swing at odds and together.

And then another tug, harder, as someone else started up. I looked down to see Jed, Tannis's marine brother.

"Thought you'd lost us?" He grinned up at me.

I didn't answer. But I did climb harder. Sarah had already swung her leg over and was descending the other side as I reached the top.

"We're doing great," she said through the net, her voice low. We were close, as close as we'd been in the cave, and I could see sweat on her brow, her messy hair, not unlike how it had looked in my vision. "Keep it up," she said, continuing down. Then she jumped to the dirt, and I clambered down the ropes and followed her onto the next trail.

We kept a steady, quick jog along the path to the stream,

which was thankfully only about a foot deep. Our sneakers squished and squashed as we started up the hill on the other side, one of the ski trails near the top of the mountain. Steep, but with easier footing.

At the summit Sarah paused, and I pulled up beside her. "Beautiful, huh?" she said.

"It is," I agreed, surveying the valley spread out below us. No one in Buford ever got tired of this view.

Sarah checked her watch. "We're at eleven minutes," she said, her voice breathy. "Not bad, but we've gotta pick up some time."

"Tannis is behind us," I reminded her.

"Forget her. We had her beat at the starting line. Ready?" She took off without waiting for an answer.

I followed her onto the second half of the course just as Jed emerged from the woods.

We did great on the first part of the descent and the rock wall, but the mud pit was a disaster. I think we were both feeling the exhaustion by the time we got there, but Sarah plowed right in, immediately losing her footing and falling face first into the muck.

"Yuck," she spat.

"Yer not the first to do that today, honey," called the attendant.

"I feel so much better," Sarah muttered, wiping mud off her face and taking the hand I offered. But instead of pulling her up, I lost my footing too and slid down beside her.

"Sorry," I said, scrambling to get back up. We slipped and slid, falling three more times and losing at least that many minutes trying to get across.

"What are we doing wrong?" Sarah stormed in frustration after her third fall.

"I'm not allowed to tell you, sweetheart," said the attendant. "But here comes yer competition."

I turned back and saw all three Janssens starting into the pit.

"Lookin' good, guys," Tannis called, laughing.

Sarah climbed out, with me just behind her. "I'd love to watch you have a swim," Sarah called back, "but we've gotta run."

We half-jogged, half-stumbled onto the last trail, still trying to clear our eyes. I'd watched a mud wrestling movie with Trip once, and the girls in that had looked pretty good, but Sarah looked like some kind of wild mud zombie, her face smeared and streaked with dirt, clumps of it sticking to her shoes. I'm sure I was no better.

I followed her down the path strewn with rocks, trickier under our slippery sneakers, and around a bend, and then suddenly she stepped off the trail.

"Come on!" she said when I didn't follow.

"That's not the path." I pointed to the yellow arrow. "It's over here."

"This way's faster."

"But you can't do that, can you?"

Sarah snorted. "This is the Warrior Dash, Riley, not the Mary Sue Mud Run. You can do whatever gets you to the finish line." Sarah grabbed my hand and tugged me toward her. "Come *on*!"

I followed her onto the tiny path, barely cleared, and could see right away she was right. It cut straight down the mountain, more treacherous but shorter than the route outlined on the Warrior Dash board at the base. A minute later we emerged onto the main Dash trail, still out of view of the patio, but I could hear the pumping beat of the base lodge music. Then the trail joined the bunny slope, and we could see people cheering and yelling where another group of runners was just taking off.

"Mud monsters!" an attendant yelled at us through a bullhorn. "Clear your numbers! I can't log your time."

I swiped at my shirt, hoping it was good enough, because I was pretty much completely out of energy. Sarah and I crossed the line side by side, and she grinned at me, white teeth against her filthy face.

We bent over, breathing hard for a minute, then straightened up.

"Nice job," she panted, holding up her hand.

I smacked it in a high five that sent mud flying everywhere. We burst out laughing, and were still trying to stop and catch our breath when Trip came over.

"Nice run," he said, genuinely impressed. "But you guys are *disgusting.*"

Sarah snorted more laughter.

"What was our time?" I asked Trip.

"You beat me," he said, answering my real question. "But Nat's team was *fast*. Looks like we've got some early mornings ahead of us." He looked up, then pointed to the course. "Here come Tannis and her brothers."

I glanced at Sarah and found her watching me, eyes sparkling. She winked. "Way to go, teammate," she said, her voice low.

"You too." We stared at each other for a beat too long, neither breaking eye contact, and I felt a different excitement, beyond the thrill of the race. I got why people ran the Dash now. You came out feeling different from when you went in, like you'd passed a test. Trial by fire. There was something special about doing it with someone else, which I guess is why they always had the ski teams and the football teams run together. Bonding.

Tannis had just crossed the finish line and was doubled over and panting when the commotion on the patio started. I didn't really notice it at first, loud voices among lots of other loud voices, but then a few became clearer. Not just loud but wrong somehow. Angry.

I walked closer.

". . . going to have to leave. Now!"

"What? I can't join the rest of you fancy people? You too good for me? I see lots of other townies here."

I recognized that voice, even though I'd only heard it once. I could tell Trip did too by the way he stiffened, then moved quickly toward the patio. We followed him and stopped by the edge of the crowd, where a circle had cleared around the man in the center.

Natalie's dad stood, hands on his hips, facing off against Bill Winston, who was neat and tidy and absolutely furious. Mr. Cleary's shirt was stained and misbuttoned, and he looked like he'd aged about fifteen years since I'd seen him last. "Randall," Mr. Winston said quietly, "this isn't the place—"

"I can't come here and watch my own daughter?" His voice was louder. "Can't even cheer on my—"

Natalie stepped out of the crowd then, and I felt myself cringing for her. Everyone watched as she approached him. "Come on, Daddy," she said. "Let's go."

"Natty!" He gave her a big grin. "There you are!" He took an unsteady step toward her, stumbled, and almost fell. He frowned as she took his arm and pulled gently. "Why you doin' that?"

"We have to go," she said, desperation creeping into her voice.

His frown changed to a hard disappointed look. "You, too?" he said. "You're too good for your own daddy now?

I seen that coming, Nat. And I told you what happens, you let these fancy ski people get in your head." His voice had gotten louder and louder, and he swept his arm toward the crowd. "Fucking tourists," he spat more quietly. But not quietly enough.

Nat looked ready to burst into tears.

And then Trip stepped in. "Mr. Cleary," he boomed, striding across the empty space surrounding Nat and her dad. "I haven't seen you in forever!" He gave Mr. Cleary a huge grin, shook his hand, and clapped him on the back like they were old friends.

Nat's dad squinted at him, then grinned. "Holy shit. Is that little Trip Jones? How'd you get so damned big?"

Trip leaned in close and, though Mr. Cleary looked like he reeked, kept up a smile. "Broccoli," he stage-whispered, and gave a huge, hearty laugh. Trip sounded half-crazy, but he didn't stop until Mr. Cleary started laughing along with him.

"Hey! Did Natalie show you the new lockers and lounge? Holy crap, they're awesome. Totally first class. You gotta come see . . ." Trip kept talking, pulling Mr. Cleary like a kid dragging his dad to a candy store. Nat tagged along, Bill Winston close behind. The rest of us stared after them as they went down the steps, away from the patio.

Music continued to pound, like it probably had the whole time, but to me it felt like everything had stopped, like everyone had been watching when Nat's dad showed up. In reality most people probably hadn't noticed anything amiss. But it wouldn't feel like that to Natalie.

Or Bill Winston.

Or Mr. Cleary when he sobered up or came down or whatever.

"Wow," Tannis said.

"Yeah," I agreed. "Wow."

CHAPTER 6

I FIGURED NATALIE WOULD SKIP THE DASH PARTY AFTER THE scene at the mountain. She and Trip didn't come back to the patio, but Sarah, Tannis, and I hung around, watching the rest of the race and letting the last of the mud dry on the parts we hadn't cleaned yet.

Trip called about an hour later. Tannis and I didn't bother trying to hide that we were listening, so Sarah just put him on speaker.

". . . with me. We're going to shower up here and head to the party a little later."

Tannis raised her eyebrows.

"Does Nat need clothes?" Sarah asked. "I could bring her some."

"No. She grabbed some when we dropped off her dad."

"How is she?" Tannis asked.

Trip hesitated for a second. "Fine." Which of course meant not fine at all but that she was sitting right there.

"You think there's anything we can do?" Sarah said. "Is she okay to go tonight?"

"Yeah," he said. "I think that's the best thing. We'll just all stick together, right?"

"Definitely," we agreed.

Sarah hung up, and she, Tannis, and I looked at one another, Tannis saying what was on all of our minds. "I wish she didn't have to go home. Like, ever."

"What a shitty way to live," Sarah said tightly. "I can't imagine why she puts up with it."

"He's her dad," I said. "People are willing to forgive their parents a lot sometimes. At least as much as they blame them for."

Sarah cocked her head, looking at me with a little smile. "That's very philosophical, Ri," she said. "And very true."

After that, I took off for home and my second shower of the day.

The five of us walked into the party at John Peters's house just after eight. Music was blaring on the deck that overlooked the town down in the valley. It seemed like half the crowd from the base lodge was already there. Inside, a bunch of Nat's ski team friends were clustered around a table, playing a game with dice and poker chips. A couple of guys stood near the TV, watching football, while other people were playing darts and foosball.

Natalie was sandwiched between Trip and Tannis, looking like she half-hoped the floor might swallow her up. John Peters broke away from the other skiers and came over as soon as he saw her.

"Hey, Nat. Glad you made it. Nice Dash today."

"Thanks, John." She smiled wanly, waiting for the obvious questions about her dad. But John completely sidestepped it.

"My parents put in a hot tub this year, out on the deck. You guys want to come see?"

She looked up at him gratefully. "Sure."

Tannis, Trip, and I watched them go out, John walking carefully beside Natalie, Sarah tagging along behind.

"Hey, Trip!" Galen Riddock came over and exchanged a fist bump with Trip, ignoring me and Tannis. "You bring any beverages?"

Trip shook his head. "No time. I had that thing with Nat's dad—"

"Yeah, that was something, huh?" Galen shook his head. "That dude's a fucking mess. Man, was Winston pissed. My dad said he ripped mountain security a new one. Couldn't believe no one stopped Cleary before he got out there. I heard he fired the shift manager on the spot."

"Jesus," Trip said. "How could they have known?"

"I don't think Winston really gave a shit," Galen said. "Listen . . ." He leaned in closer to Trip. "You score anything when you were up there? You know, with Nat's dad?"

Trip frowned. "You know I'm not into that stuff."

"You're no fun, Jones."

"I'm lots of fun."

Galen snorted. "Gonna be a different kind of party this year, I guess. Good, clean small-town fun, eh, Tripper?"

"Nothin' wrong with that," Trip said evenly.

Galen rolled his eyes. "Later."

We all knew the Dash after-party would be tamer, after last year's had gotten out of hand. It had been at Marshall Blume's farm a few miles outside town. His parents had been away, and pretty much everyone knew it. Lots of people showed up who weren't friends with him or anyone else on the ski team. Lots of alcohol and drugs. Two weeks later some freshman had been found dead in her bedroom. An overdose. It hadn't happened at the after-party, but word travels, and adults aren't stupid. Between Marshall's party and the girl's death, they'd figured out there was a problem. Someone even went up and questioned Nat's dad, but word had traveled to him too, and whatever usually went on up there was tucked away by the time the police showed up. There probably wouldn't have been a party this year at all if John Peters's dad hadn't offered to host it. He was a town cop, and I'd already seen him talking with kids out on the deck, making sure everything stayed well under control.

"I'm going to see if I can get in on the game," Tannis said, nodding toward the dice table. "You guys want to come?"

Trip shook his head. "Nah. I'm gonna go find Sarah and Nat. You coming, Ri?"

"Sure."

We grabbed sodas and made our way through the crowd and out onto the deck. The Peterses lived one ridge over from the ski trails. Not prime real estate, since you couldn't get to the slopes from there, but the view was pretty sweet. John's dad had grown up in this house. It wasn't big or done up like the trailside homes, but he was pretty handy and had built an addition and I guess saved enough for a hot tub. They had it running, underwater lights changing from blue to purple to green. It looked really cool. If it had been at Marshall Blume's house last year, there would have been about twenty people in it by the end of the night, naked or fully clothed. I was pretty sure the Peterses' hot tub would stay empty, just there for decoration.

"Hey, loser." Someone tapped me on the shoulder, and I turned to find Matty Gretowniak leaning against the railing.

"What are you doing here?" I said, still feeling the sting of his comments about the SATs but otherwise glad to see him.

Most of the kids there were skiers or partiers or jocks. I was none of the above, and neither was he, as far as I knew.

"Having a Coke. Enjoying the view. You?"

"Trolling for chicks."

Matty laughed. "Good luck with that. I came with my sister," he admitted. "She's on the ski team this year."

"Awesome," I said. "Point her out, and I'll troll in that direction."

"Don't you dare."

Trip had continued on without me, and I saw him on the far side of the deck with the girls and John. "You run today?" I asked Matty.

"Are you kidding?" he said. "That course is brutal. You ever done it?"

"About five hours ago."

Matty whistled. "Impressive. Brains and brawn."

"You know, Matty," I said, "you keep talking like that, and I'm gonna start thinking you have a thing for me."

"Well, now that you mention it . . . ," he joked. "Actually, I was checking out your friend."

"Trip? He's got a girlfriend."

"No, you idiot." Matty cleared his throat, suddenly uncomfortable. "The girl. Tannis."

"Tannis?" My eyebrows shot up. "She's not—" I stopped, realizing that what I'd been about to say—*She's not a girl*—was mean. I might rag on Tannis to her face, but I didn't want to do it behind her back. "Not seeing anyone," I finished.

Matty nodded, glancing out at the view. "Maybe you'll, you know, make the introductions later or something?"

"Yeah," I said, a little shell-shocked at the thought of it. "I'm gonna go catch up to Nat and those guys." I nodded toward where they stood.

"Yup," Matty said, and then added, "I heard there was a bit of a scene at the base lodge today with her dad."

"A little. No biggie," I told him, hoping it was true. If there was one cardinal rule in Buford, it was that you didn't mess with tourism. I guess Nat's dad hadn't gotten the memo. I walked toward Nat, feeling bad that even Matty knew about it. His sister had probably told him, but still. It was one of the things I hated about Buford. Everyone knew too much about everyone else.

By the time I made it across the deck, Nat and John Peters had ducked back inside, where the rest of the ski team was, and Mr. Peters had taken their place with Trip and Sarah.

"It was nothing," Trip was saying.

"You're too modest," Mr. Peters said. "That was damn ugly. Bill Winston was steaming mad. Wants to press charges. I don't think anyone at the mountain knew what to do, but word is, you diffused it perfectly."

Trip waved his hand in an *Aw, shucks* sort of way.

"What are your plans after graduation?" Mr. Peters asked him.

"I'm not sure," Trip said. "College, I guess."

Mr. Peters nodded. "Well, whatever it is, I'm sure you'll do great. Thanks for helping us all out today." He stuck out his hand to shake. "I'm off to make sure there's no other trouble. After that Milosevich girl's OD, a snowless winter, and now today, it's the last thing we need."

"Bad things happen in threes," Sarah said.

"Hope you're right." Mr. Peters waved and walked away.

Trip, Sarah, and I stayed there for a while, talking to the kids around us, some of them from our classes, some having run the Dash today too. At one point I spotted Matty talking to Tannis, both of them half a head taller than anyone else around. Unbelievable.

The football guys started an arm wrestling tournament inside and summoned Trip. "You mind?" he asked Sarah, already being dragged off by Galen.

"Go." She smiled, waving him away, leaving just her and me.

"You want to get a drink or anything?" I asked after a few seconds of quiet.

"I'm okay," she said. "You want something?"

"No. I'm fine too."

We stood, awkwardly looking at the people around us, until Sarah suggested we move closer to the hot tub. "I like the colors," she said.

The Peterses had put it in the far corner, with the most sweeping views of the valley.

"Not quite as good as when we were at the summit today," I said, looking out over the smattering of lights. "But not bad."

"We had a good run," she said, smiling. "Didn't we?"

"We beat Trip," I said.

"And that's all that matters." Sarah laughed and held up her palm for another high five.

I clapped her hand gently, and she tilted her head, grinning. "You can give me a real high five, Ri. I won't break."

"Sorry," I said. "I didn't want to be too rough."

"You're not the rough type," she said, holding up her hand again. I hit it harder, the smack loud enough that the person behind her looked over.

"Ow!" Sarah frowned, shaking her hand.

"Oh!" I said. "I'm sorry—"

"I'm *kidding*, Riley." She grinned, rolling her eyes. "You worry too much about other people."

"I do?"

Sarah nodded, looking out across the dark hills. "It's not a bad thing," she said. "But sometimes you have to worry about yourself, too."

"I worry about myself plenty."

She smiled. "Maybe 'take care of yourself' would have been a better way to phrase it."

"Hmmn," I said noncommittally, not sure what to think of what Sarah thought of me or that she'd been thinking about me at all or whether I was overthinking this. Which I'm sure I was, because I worried about myself plenty. Like I'd told her.

"Do you like it here, Riley?" she asked.

"It's better than standing in the middle of the crowd."

"Not here, next to the hot tub," she said. "I meant in Buford."

My "no" was automatic—on the tip of my tongue—but I stopped to really consider it, and finally told her, "Yes. But I don't want to stay." I picked at the railing, adding, "Mostly because the people who make me like it will be leaving."

She was quiet, and I could feel her watching me, the party noise all around us but feeling far away. "Will you leave too?" she asked.

"Someday."

She nodded. "That's why you're dreaming about dorm rooms, huh?" I knew right away she was talking about the binoculars. Deepest wishes. She continued before I could ask her what she'd seen, "You know what I like about you, Riley?"

I looked at her, my heart beating harder at the way it sounded. Her dark eyes reflected the underwater lights—green then pink then blue. *I should say something funny*, I thought. But it was hard to think with her so close, and the sweet warm smell of her intoxicating. "What?" I asked thickly.

"You're a thinker," she said. "You're deep but not morose. You're funny, and there's just . . ." She paused, gesturing for the words that were missing. "There's so much there."

I held her gaze, aware—like she must have been—that we were looking at each other for way too long, but unable to tear away. I think if we'd been anywhere else, I might have tried to kiss her then. But we were on John Peters's deck and she was my oldest friend's girlfriend.

"It's all bullshit," I said hoarsely.

She smiled wryly. "It sure is." Her comment seemed to mean more than just the way I acted or what she thought of me.

Natalie came back to us then, smiling and more relaxed than I'd seen her all day. Eventually Trip drifted over too, and I stepped aside, letting him take the spot beside Sarah, where he was supposed to be. We only saw Tannis briefly when she and Matty Gretowniak came over, bizarrely hand in hand. I smelled alcohol on her breath as she said, "Matty's driving me home."

I'd seen the flask and had known it was circulating, even under Mr. Peters's watchful eye. I wasn't surprised Tannis was drinking, but Matty? I gave him a hard look, and he grinned sheepishly. I had no idea if he was drunk or just feeling foolish or something else entirely.

"You okay?" I asked Matty. "You shouldn't drive if—"

"I'm fine," he said. "Ninety-eight percent sober." He held up a hand. "Scout's honor."

"Well, then . . ." I shrugged. "Mazel tov."

"Dude," Tannis said fuzzily. "You know I suck at Spanish."

Trip dropped me off sometime after midnight, Sarah asleep on his lap in the front seat and Nat already deposited at home. My mom was at work, and I crashed hard, feeling the full exhaustion of the Dash and the high of being with Sarah and everything else.

I woke up to the shrill ring of my phone, the red numbers of my clock blurry but definitely not double digits.

I checked the caller ID, then picked up hesitantly. I couldn't imagine why Tannis would call me at all, much less before six on a Sunday.

"Riley," she said breathlessly. "Natalie's dad is dead."

CHAPTER 7

I STOOD IN MY ROOM STUPIDLY, TRYING TO FIGURE OUT WHAT to do. Trip was on his way.

"Shot." Tannis's words echoed in my head. "And, Ri?" she'd said. "Nat found him."

"Oh my God." But she'd already hung up.

I couldn't remember the last time there'd been a murder in Buford. The girl who'd died last year had been a big deal because before that it had been just the usual stuff—heart attacks, old age. My dad's shooting four years ago had made all the papers, and a TV station had even showed up. Maybe they'd thought that was a murder, instead of what it had turned out to be—a hunter shot by a stray bullet, bleeding out in the woods. I'd been thirteen, and now I remembered only fragments: my mom crying; people bringing food; dishes and dishes of it piling up, uneaten. Staying in the McGintys' old-people-smelling house, wondering when my mom would be back, worrying that she wouldn't be. And after, the absence of my dad, a gaping and permanent hole of never. He'd never take me hunting again or teach me to drive, see me graduate, get married, have kids. There was an icy feeling in my gut, thinking of him and of Nat and her dad. And what she'd seen that night at the cave.

Trip's honking out front startled me. I zipped up my backpack and went out to meet him, careful—for once—to lock the house door.

They were all there—Trip, Tannis, and Sarah—their faces pale and serious. Sarah had been crying.

"What happened?" I asked.

"He was shot in the head and chest," Trip said bluntly.

"Who . . ." I couldn't even finish the sentence.

"I don't think they have any idea yet, Riley," Sarah said. Her voice was shaky. "And Nat—"

She stopped, trying to catch her breath. My brain called up the inside of Nat's trailer, painted it in the splattered blood from the physics closet. "Jesus," I whispered.

We rode silently, Trip's headlights swinging across the bramble as he turned onto Ohoyo Road. Everything looked gray in the early morning light, a sheen of silver dew coating the bushes and grass. I kept hoping we'd round the final bend to find the trailer quiet, all of it a case of mistaken address or identity.

It wasn't, of course. Every police car in Buford was there—all six of them—lights flashing, colors and shadows bouncing off the woods. I got out of the car slowly, eyeing the yellow tape already strung around the yard. A handful of gawkers had gathered—a fat lady in a housedress, an old guy, three men I recognized from the restaurant.

Trip was already talking to the old guy when I reached them. William Johnson. He lived up the road a mile past Nat's house.

". . . heard the sirens an hour or so ago. After 'bout the third one, figured I better come see what was goin' on." William Johnson shook his head. "They already had the girl out by the time I got here. Saw her sitting in the back of a cruiser. She was still there when they brought out the body. I'da thought they'd take her away before that, but I guess seein' the black bag prolly wasn't any worse than seein' what she did inside."

"Do they know what happened?" Trip asked.

"If they do, they didn't tell William Johnson."

"Where's Natalie?" Sarah asked.

Mr. Johnson looked her over. "I reckon they didn't tell that to me neither, sweetheart," he said. "Maybe you'll have better luck with them police types."

We turned toward the house, watching silently as shadows moved inside. John Peters's dad had to be in there somewhere. Maybe he could tell us more. But it was Bob Willets and Lincoln Andrews who came out first and stopped to talk by the door. Then Lincoln went back inside and Bob headed down the yard, toward the police van parked just outside the tape. I moved to that part of the cordoned-off area.

"Hey, Bob," I called. He was a regular at the restaurant, friendly with everyone there.

He glanced up, his face grim. "Riley Larkin," he said tiredly. Some guys probably were excited by the idea of "real" police work, but Bob wouldn't be one of them. He had a little girl and a pretty wife and seemed content to shoot the shit with the townies and write the occasional parking ticket. "What are you doing here?"

"Natalie Cleary's a friend of mine," I said. "Is she okay?"

He pursed his lips. "She's not hurt, if that's what you mean."

"What happened?"

He shook his head. "I can't tell you anything, Riley," he said. "You've seen enough cop shows to know that."

I nodded. "Can you at least tell me where Nat is? Or how to get ahold of her?" To our left, the tight knot of Trip, Sarah, and Tannis were all staring numbly at the house.

Officer Willets followed my gaze. "They took her down to the station," he said finally. "She's going to be there for a while, I'd guess. And frankly, she's not really in a state to chat, even with her friends. I'd go home and get some sleep." He gave me a once-over. "You look like you could use it."

He started to walk away, but I called after him. "Where was she? When it happened?"

He paused, and I saw his jaw tighten. He shook his head, and I thought he wasn't going to answer, but he did. A single word. "Inside." He sighed heavily. "Go home, Riley. Hug your mom. Say some prayers for that poor girl."

The four of us stood out in the cold for more than an hour. The sun rose gradually, light bouncing off the white trailer, but there wasn't much else to see or learn. Nat was gone. The police came in and out. Mr. Peters waved to us, his face tight and unsmiling, but aside from what Bob had told me, no one was talking.

I told the others what he'd said. That was why we stayed, hoping to get even the smallest clue what it meant. "If she was inside, she must know who did it," Tannis said. "Right?"

"You'd think so," Trip answered simply. We stood, watched, waited.

Eventually we gave up, piling back into Trip's car. It wasn't until we were driving slowly down the hill that Tannis brought it up. "You don't think . . ." She paused. I knew what she was getting at but wasn't about to be the one to say it.

"What?" Trip glanced at her in the rearview.

Tannis shifted uncomfortably. "Well, you know how the other day when she had the bruise . . . and, I mean, this is what she saw, right? In those binoculars."

"Oh! Shit," Trip said. It hadn't occurred to him before.

"What are you saying, Tannis?" Sarah asked. Her voice was low and controlled. I could tell she'd already considered it, just like I had.

"I don't know," Tannis backpedaled. "Just that . . . you know, what Riley said at lunch that day—about, like, our hidden desires . . ."

"You think *she* did it?" Trip's eyes in the rearview were wide in disbelief.

"Nat would never, in a million years—" Sarah started, but Trip didn't even let her finish.

"No way, Tannis," he interrupted. "Nat's been putting up with his shit for years, and she was fine when we dropped her off last night—"

"But who knows what happened after?" Tannis argued. "You saw the way he was acting at the mountain, Trip. How was he later? When you guys got him home?"

"I don't know," he said. "Wasted? Unstable? Fine one minute and pissed off the next."

"And if he was in the same mood when Natalie got home from the party . . . ," Sarah said slowly.

"Or was whacked-out on some drug . . . ," I added.

None of us said anything else, letting it hang there. The idea that Natalie might have shot her own dad was suddenly fairly easy to imagine. Trip turned down Main Street. The town was just starting to wake up. A few tourists walked quickly from the coffee shop, steaming cups in hand. We let the radio play, watched sun light the metal ski lifts strung across the mountain face. We'd run there yesterday. The start of the season, almost anything seeming possible. Except this.

I turned to Tannis, thinking about the after-party. "What happened to you last night?" I asked.

"What do you mean?"

"Matty?" I said, raising my eyebrows.

"God," she muttered, rubbing her forehead. "Don't remind me."

It was just after eight when Trip dropped me at work. I'd texted George that I'd be late, explaining why. He'd already heard, of course, and I knew by the end of the day, it'd be all over town.

CHAPTER 8

THE FIRST REPORTER WAS ALREADY AT THE RESTAURANT WHEN I arrived. A skinny guy in jeans and a button-down. He'd come from Burlington the day before to cover the Dash—I guess it was a slow news week—but suddenly found himself with the scoop on a much juicier story.

Not that any of us were answering his questions.

"You're not gonna tell him anything, right?" Moose asked, his eyes darting to the restaurant floor, the entrance, then me.

"What would I tell that half the town doesn't already know?" I asked.

"Yeah, yeah, exactly," he said, bobbing his head. "Just . . . you know . . . nothing about that one time we went up there with Wynn, right? I mean, I didn't even know Mr. Cleary. I was just doing a favor. It—"

"Moose. Calm down," I interrupted, taking a step back. "You're freaking out. Talk like that, and they'll think you did it." I raised an eyebrow. "You didn't, did you?"

I was joking, but Moose didn't think it was funny. "Jesus Christ," he exploded, "that's exactly what I don't need!"

He stalked away, and I stared after him. I'd never heard him yell before. Maybe I shouldn't have said anything. Nat had found her dad dead, and there'd been a murder in our little town. People were *going* to be freaking—it wasn't something to joke about. I kept my head down the rest of the morning, busing and cleaning and trying to ignore pretty much everyone and everything.

"You must go to school with Natalie Cleary."

The guy behind me at table ten was sipping a Coke and wearing a flannel shirt that looked fresh from a package, still creased down the front. There was a pen and notebook open on the table, the page clean and white. Reporter number two. I wondered how many others would follow.

"No comment," I told him, loading the last of table nine's plates into the bus pan and heading for the back.

Bob Willets and Lincoln Andrews walked in just after one p.m. "Too busy to make it this mornin', I reckon," Patti said. They looked less rumpled but more exhausted than when I'd seen them behind the yellow crime scene tape six hours earlier. "There's some outta towners at yer table." She gestured to a pair of city people. "But I can seatcha by the fountain."

I was busing table three and watching them from the corner of my eye. Patti was pulling menus from the rack when Bob said, "Actually, Patti, we're here to ask some questions. About the Clearys."

She froze. I did too.

"We'll need to have a few minutes with a couple of people here," Bob continued.

"I best get George out here, then," she told them.

Lincoln nodded. "Yep, we were figuring to talk to him first. Where's his office?"

They followed Patti back to see the manager. Moose was fidgeting beside me as soon as they disappeared.

"You think they're gonna talk to all of us?"

"I don't know." I surveyed Moose, who looked ready to jitterbug right out of his uniform, tap-tap-tapping his fingers on the seat back. "Dude," I said. "Calm down."

"Yeah." He nodded, a little manic. "Sure, sure."

"Just be straight with them, Moose."

He hesitated. "You know I can't," he said softly.

"Look," I said. "So you did things up there that"—I looked around at the empty booths nearby before continuing—"weren't exactly legal. So what? When was the last time you went up?"

"I dunno. A couple months ago." He flicked his eyes

toward the ceiling. It was a classic tell. Trip had taught me that back in third grade, after his mom had caught us taking quarters from her purse.

"Look them in the eyes," he'd said sternly when his mom had finished scolding us. "And don't fidget. That's how they know." I'd never gotten good at it.

"Moose," I cautioned now. "Don't lie to them. You'll just get in bigger trouble."

"I'm not lying."

"Even I can tell you are," I told him. "You think the police aren't going to figure it out? This is what they *do*."

He looked down, then nodded. "Yeah, you're right. I saw him yesterday, though. Last night." He looked at me hopelessly. "What if they think . . ."

"Moose," I looked at him carefully, not even sure I wanted to ask the next question. "Did you do it?" I whispered.

"God, no!"

"Do you have anything . . . any drugs on you?"

He shook his head.

"Then be honest," I said. "What do you have to lose?"

"You don't get it, Riley," he said, shaking his head angrily. "I'm already on probation. For last year?"

I frowned, but then it came back to me. The girl who'd OD'd. Moose had been involved in that somehow. He'd been out of work a bunch of days after it had happened. It'd been right after first snow, and I'd gotten stuck picking up dead mice almost every time I'd come to work, since he hadn't been around to take turns.

"I could go to jail if they nail me for anything," he said. "Basically, I'm fucked."

I thought it sounded like he kind of was. "Well, Jesus, Moose, why'd you go up there?"

He looked at me hard, then shook his head. "Forget it," he said. "You wouldn't understand."

George pushed through the swinging doors, and stopped when he saw us. "Riley," he said. "The police want to talk to you."

I felt a flutter of nerves at how that sounded. And I hadn't done anything wrong. I couldn't imagine what Moose was feeling.

"I know this must be hard for you, Riley," Bob started gently once he'd closed the office door behind us. "You bein' friends with Natalie Cleary and all."

"I didn't really know her dad," I said.

"No?"

"No."

"You never met him?"

"Not really."

Lincoln, who'd been writing notes, looked up. "Either you did or you didn't. Which is it?"

"Well, I saw him at the mountain yesterday," I hedged. "Just like everyone else."

Bob nodded, like he'd expected that. "How did Natalie seem to you before that?"

"I didn't see her before," I said. "She was already with the ski team when I got there."

"What about in the days before?" Bob asked.

"She seemed fine."

"Really?" he pressed. "Not worried about anything? Acting strange? Upset?"

I thought about the bruise on her face. "She was upset on Monday morning at school, but she was fine later on that day. Fine all week."

But Lincoln leaned in. "Upset about what?"

"I—" I paused. "I don't know, actually."

Lincoln frowned. "Well, how do you know she was upset? Tell me exactly what happened."

He was watching me closely, and my brain was churning through how she'd looked, hair hiding her face. Her reaction when I mentioned the night at the cave. "She was just really quiet in homeroom," I said. "When I tried to talk to her, she wouldn't look at me, and then I saw she had a cut on her face. And a bruise."

Lincoln's eyebrows lifted. "Did she say where she got it?"

"She said she tripped and banged into a wall."

He studied me for a minute. "You didn't believe her."

I shrugged uncomfortably.

He exchanged a look with Bob. "Did she often get hurt like that?"

"Sometimes," I said.

"More than you might expect?" he pressed. "More than other people?"

I shrugged again, unsure of the right answer.

Lincoln exhaled, hard. "Could you help us out a little, Riley?" he said, clearly frustrated. "We're trying to get a sense of the Clearys' home life, and I feel like you're not being very cooperative." He ran a hand through thinning hair. "Is there more?"

"I'm sure there is," I said, frustrated myself. "I'd imagine her home life was pretty shitty. Yeah, Nat had cuts or bruises or scrapes more than you'd expect. She said it was from skiing or just her being clumsy." I took a breath. "If you're asking if her dad hit her, I have no idea. I don't know if she was upset at him last week or if something else was going on or if she had, you know, girl problems or what. She's private. I try to respect that."

"Even though it meant she might have been abused right under your nose?"

I glared at Lincoln, feeling my ears burn. "If she was abused," I said evenly, "it was under all of our noses. Don't tell me you didn't know her dad was a user and a dealer."

His face darkened, and I knew I'd crossed a line I probably shouldn't have. "You saw drugs at her house?"

"No," I said flatly. I knew they were there that night Moose dragged me up to the trailer, but I didn't actually *see* any. "I've never been inside Nat's house."

"Never?"

I shook my head. "We'd go up to get her sometimes—me and my friends—but we always waited in the car for her to come out."

"So you'd never met her dad? Never talked to him?"

I hesitated, knowing I should lie. "Just at the door of her house."

"When you were there to pick her up?"

"No," I said. "A year or so ago."

"What were you doing there?"

My hands felt damp. This wasn't going the way I wanted. "I was with a friend."

"And you went there because . . ." Lincoln drew it out, waiting like a cat who's spotted a mouse. He knew exactly where this was heading.

"My ride needed to stop by."

"For what?"

"What does it matter?" I said. "It has nothing to do with what happened last night."

"How do you know?" Lincoln said, leaning close enough that I could smell the sourness of his morning coffee. "*I* don't know what happened, and I'm investigating the case. So how could you?" He took a deep breath and, his voice calm but dead serious, asked, "What were you there for, Riley?"

"Look," I said, "I don't really know. I never went in, didn't hear what they talked about or see what they did. All I know is we drove up there, I waited, we left."

Lincoln looked ready to tear into me, but Bob interjected, "You said you met her dad."

I nodded. "Yeah. It was late. I had to get home, so I knocked on the door. Nat's dad answered."

"And?" Bob asked. "What was your impression?"

"I don't know. Same as it was yesterday, I guess. That he was . . ." I paused. "Kind of a mess."

Lincoln snorted.

Bob ignored him, asking, "Did you see Natalie there?"

"No. We weren't really friends back then," I said.

"Did you ever tell her about that night? Stopping up there with your 'friend'? Meeting her dad?"

I shook my head.

"Why?"

"She'd be embarrassed," I said. "Natalie doesn't talk about her dad or anything. I didn't want to make her feel bad."

No one said anything for a few beats, but I could feel the air in the room soften. Until Lincoln jumped in with the next question, "Did she know he kept a gun in the house?"

"I don't know."

"Does she know how to shoot?"

I saw where this was leading. "You think she did it?"

Bob shot a look at Lincoln, who asked, "Do *you*, Riley?"

"No!" I said. "No way." I felt guilty. Like they'd somehow overheard our conversation in the car and gotten the idea our friend could shoot her father point-blank in the head.

"Why?"

"Why?" I echoed, thinking of Nat who always remembered birthdays and never let kids sit alone in the cafeteria. "It . . . it's just . . . not something Natalie would do."

"Why?" Lincoln pursued.

"She's not like that. Not violent," I said. "I've never even seen her argue with someone, much less, you know, try to hurt them."

"Sometimes people just snap," Lincoln said.

"Maybe. But Nat's so protective of her dad. She's never said a bad word about him. And won't let anyone else, either," I said. "She doesn't have other family that I know of."

"What happened to her mom?" Lincoln asked.

"She never talks about that, either."

"But you have some idea."

"No. I really don't. I mean, I guess she just left. A bunch of years ago." The rumor that she'd up and split was pretty common knowledge. "But I don't really know."

Bob was nodding, but Lincoln was looking back at his notebook. "Does she have a boyfriend?"

"Nat's mom? I have no idea."

Lincoln frowned, like I should have been able to read into his poorly phrased question. "No. Natalie."

"Oh," I said. "No." Though John Peters seemed to be auditioning for the role last night. I wonder what he was thinking this morning. Would he believe Nat could kill her dad?

"Anyone on the ski team she's especially close with?"

"Not that I know of."

"How about at school?"

"Nat's friends with lots of people. Pretty much everyone likes her."

Lincoln scribbled some things down while Bob took over the questions, switching angles.

"Who do you think might have done something like this, Riley?"

"Me? Who do I think?"

He nodded.

"I have no idea."

"Can you think of anyone who hated Nat's dad?"

"Well, sure." I frowned at them. "Bill Winston, for one. Not that I think he did it or anything," I hurried to add as Lincoln kept scribbling.

"Do you think he's a more likely suspect, or Natalie?" Lincoln asked, glancing up.

"So this is a multiple-choice test?"

Lincoln scowled. "We're just trying to get some clarity here."

"I think I'd have to go with 'neither.'"

"Uh-huh," Bob said. "Who else?"

"Who else what?"

"Who else might want Randall Cleary dead?"

I was not comfortable with this. At all. "I don't really know," I said, deciding to plead the Fifth on the rest of this conversation before I got my ass kicked by someone.

Lincoln took a few more notes and flipped another page or two. Bob smiled at me, and I felt everything inside me unclench. We were done.

Then Lincoln asked, "Who took you there that night, Riley?"

"What night?"

"The night you met Randall Cleary. Natalie's father."

I didn't answer, my face burning, sweat starting on my brow.

"I know you don't want to tell on anyone," Bob said gently. "But it's important. This is a murder investigation, Riley."

"Listen, kid." Lincoln stepped forward, forcing me to look at him. "You don't want an obstruction of justice charge or anything else that'd mess up your record. You're a senior, right?"

I nodded.

"Smart, too, from what I hear. Colleges don't look too favorably on a criminal record." Clearly he was the bad cop.

"It was Moose," I said softly. God, I hoped he'd understand. And that he had nothing to hide.

"Moose?" Lincoln said impatiently.

"Eugene Martin," Bob told him. "That other kid out there."

I looked up in time to see them exchange a meaningful glance. My stomach rolled. "Are we done?" I asked, starting to stand. I'd just thrown Moose under the bus.

"One more thing," Bob said, holding up a finger. "Where were you last night?"

"Me? I was at the Dash party. At the Peterses'."

Bob nodded. "Until when?"

"Uh . . ." Holy shit, were they checking my alibi? It was amazing how even the idea of it short-circuited my brain. I couldn't remember at all what time we left. "Till maybe twelve? One?" I shook my head. "I'm not sure."

Lincoln wrote something down. "And what happened after you left?"

"Trip drove me home."

"Just you?"

"No, all of us. Me and Sarah, Natalie . . ." I trailed off, staring at Lincoln, who was scribbling furiously in his notebook.

"So you were at the Clearys' house last night." Bob met

my eyes, and I could feel that my ears were bright red.

"For a minute. To drop off Nat."

"But you don't remember what time?"

"I . . . I'm not sure."

"And then you were back there. First thing this morning," Bob said. "When we spoke."

I nodded.

"How did you know her dad had been killed?"

"Tannis called me."

"Tannis Janssen?"

I nodded.

"How'd she know?"

"Trip heard it. On the police scanner."

Bob nodded. Lincoln looked up from his notes to ask, "So where were you between midnight and two a.m.?"

"At home," I said. "I mean, I think I got there before midnight. And then I went to bed."

"Can anyone verify that? Your mom?"

I shook my head. "No. She was at work."

Lincoln wrote something down, then looked up at me, his eyes sharp. "Is there anything else you think we should know?"

Immediately that night at the cave jumped to mind. How could it not, after Nat had predicted this very thing? I could feel my neck hot, cheeks flushed. There was no way I was going to tell them. I shook my head. "No."

Lincoln raised his eyebrows, slowly. “Nothing?” he asked.

It occurred to me in that instant that they’d be talking to the rest of them—Trip, Sarah, Tannis. Maybe already had. And maybe one of them had talked about the binoculars. But I couldn’t backtrack now. “No,” I said. “Not that I can think of.”

Lincoln eyed me for an extra second, then slowly closed his notebook. “If you change your mind, Riley, you give us a call, ’kay?” He stood, eyes on me the whole time.

“Thanks for cooperating, Riley,” Bob said. “We’ll be in touch.”

I nodded, stifling the urge to wipe my forehead or throw up, and left the office.

CHAPTER 9

WALKING INTO SCHOOL MONDAY, YOU COULD SEE IT IN EVERY-one's eyes, even before you heard the whispers.

"The gun belonged to her father," the principal's secretary was saying when I went in for my late pass. "It was still at the scene, and—" She saw me listening and dropped her voice.

". . . questioning her *all night*," Caitlin Trahn told a friend at her locker, flipping her dark hair before adding, "I mean, my dad said she was *in* the house . . ."

The best information came from Matty Gretowniak. His mom worked for Children's Services. "Yeah, she was inside," he answered when I caught up with him in the hall before physics. "Said she was in her room sleeping. Didn't hear or see a thing."

"Really?"

"Seems pretty far-fetched," he observed. "I know you're

friends with her, but c'mon, a gun goes off in your house—your *trailer*—and you don't notice?"

I could see it on other people's faces too. I wasn't the only one wondering if Nat might have done it. But I didn't want to hash that out with Matty. "Soooo," I said, looking at him pointedly. "You and Tannis?"

His response was immediate. "What'd she tell you?"

"Plenty."

"Really?" He had such a weird, nervous look that I was pretty sure I didn't want to hear any more about whatever had happened. I was already getting some awful mental pictures of the two of them. "No, man. I'm just messing with you."

"Oh," he said, relieved. "Okay."

Matt and I headed for our seats in physics, and I peeked over at Sarah, who was already watching me, her eyes serious. Trip had told me the police had been to see her on Sunday too. And him. And Tannis.

Mr. Ruskovich shut the door, facing us somberly. "I'm sure you've all heard about Natalie Cleary's father?" Everyone nodded. "Tragic," he said, shaking his head. "In light of it I think it appropriate to suspend our study of forensics." He scanned the room and, maybe seeing some disappointment, added, "At least for today. These things take time to sink in, and I don't want to move ahead with this project if it hits too close to home for anyone." He paused, and then added, "We'll decide sometime next week, but in the interim, please feel free to talk to me about it—in class or privately—if you like. Okay?"

We nodded.

"What I'd like to cover today instead is—"

"Please, not particle theory," Matty muttered.

"I'll spare you," Mr. Ruskovich said. "But only because I think we're all processing enough right now. Let's discuss kinematics."

The four of us huddled up at lunch: me, Trip, Sarah, and Tannis. The eyes of all of Buford High followed us, blazing into our backs as we sat at a table near the center aisle. I was afraid to talk or look around. We lasted less than five minutes before Sarah suggested, "Want to go to the quad?"

Even though it was forty degrees outside, we all did. The eyes followed us to the doorway, eager for scraps about our conspicuously absent friend. I still felt them as the four of us split down the halls toward our respective lockers for coats and hats and gloves.

Tannis was already at the picnic table when I went out. She was bundled into a blue down jacket and scarf, picking at her fingernails, her head bowed.

I climbed onto the bench across from her.

"She's still down there, you know." She didn't have to tell me who she was talking about.

"With the police?"

Tannis nodded, flicking her eyes to me. "Does that mean they think she did it?"

"It could mean lots of stuff," I said, trying to picture Nat with the cops, being questioned like I'd been, her dad dead. Natalie was tough, but not like that. Not hard. "Maybe she doesn't have anywhere else to go. Maybe they just have her with, like, a foster family or something. Who else does Nat have?"

"I don't know. No one?" She rubbed her forehead, admitting shakily, "I'm freaking out, Riley."

"We all are."

Trip and Sarah joined us then, Sarah's cheeks red from the cold. They matched her coat, one she'd complained mildly was worn at the edges, last year's style. She looked beautiful, and I thought of how it had felt to stand beside her at John Peters's. Two nights ago that felt like two million.

"What do you think happened?" I asked when we were all at the table. No one else was outside today; the air was sharp with the brittle cold. Sarah shook her head, still looking spooked.

"Damned if I know, Ri," Trip said. "Sounds like the police don't either."

"People think it might have been her," I said.

He nodded. "I got that from the stuff the cops asked. I don't believe it."

"Really?"

"It's just not Natalie." Trip was adamant.

"Yeah, I know, Trip. But her dad—"

"Has been out of hand for as long as any of us can remember," he said, cutting me off. "But we don't know that he's ever done anything to hurt anyone. Except himself. It's all speculation and suspicion and rumor." He shook his head. "If he was really abusive, don't you think Natalie would have done something about it? In all these years, with all the people who've offered to step in? Why would she suddenly decide to shoot him?"

"Maybe she just snapped," I said. "Maybe he came after her."

"Then she'd have done whatever she's been doing the last ten or fifteen years to deal with it," Trip said angrily.

"So if it wasn't her," Tannis said, "who was it? And how could she have been there and not heard anything?"

"We don't know that she didn't," Trip pointed out. I was about to tell him what Matty's mom had said, but realized it was just more hearsay. "Maybe it was a disgruntled client," Trip continued. "Or a girlfriend?"

"Ewww." Tannis wrinkled her nose. "He had girlfriends?"

I thought of the woman passed out on the couch, and Sarah said, "Nat mentioned his 'lady friends' a couple times."

"Ugh," Tannis said. "Parents and dating? Awkward."

"I'm not sure you'd call what they did dating," Trip said.

"Ewww," Tannis said again.

"The cops were asking about drugs and stuff," I said, realizing that I'd actually been the one to bring it up.

"And?" Trip asked.

"Maybe they have a suspect." One I gave them. Moose had looked like he wanted to strangle me when he'd walked out of his chat with them.

"If looks could kill, Randall Cleary would've been dead at the mountain," Sarah said.

"Yeah," I agreed. "But I don't think Bill Winston hauled up to the trailer in the middle of the night and shot him."

Sarah nodded.

"The cops were asking me who I thought might have done it," I said. "'Who would have wanted him dead?' were their actual words."

Trip snorted. "Everyone?" He said. "Except Nat."

"Trip," Sarah said, "you're not supposed to speak ill of the dead."

He rolled his eyes. "Sorry, grandma," he said. "The fact is, there probably isn't anyone in town you could come up with a longer list of suspects for."

I nodded. "It sounds like the cops are keeping it wide open right now."

"So they think Nat did it or don't?" Trip asked.

"I don't think they have a clue."

"That's not likely to change," Sarah said. She was joking, but there was more than a kernel of truth there. Buford's finest hadn't had much to investigate since someone had stolen Larry Bushman's lawn mower six months ago. And they'd only dug into that because Larry had called them about it every day. People up here tended to live and let live. It was the way we were all brought up. Why stick your nose into other people's business unless it affected you? People gossiped plenty but rarely got involved, and the cops tended to look the other way unless their hand was forced. I don't think it had ever been forced like it was being forced now.

"But, guys," Tannis said, "what about those binoculars?"

We stared at her. "What about them?" Trip said.

"I mean, I know I'm freaking out, but what if . . ." Tannis took a ragged breath. "What if we saw the future?"

There it was. None of us said anything right away, but I'd be lying if I didn't admit I'd wondered the same thing sometime between watching the red-and-blue police lights outside Natalie's trailer and now.

I ignored the shiver down my spine. "That's impossible."

"I don't know," she said. "The stuff I saw was so *real*. Not like it'd be if I made it up. The strangest things came to me about walking with those kids. I mean, I felt like I loved them or something." Tannis looked embarrassed. "I don't even *like* kids. And my shoes hurt and it was blazing hot. And I was crampy—"

"TMI," I said, trying to calm the anxiety racing through me. I'd smelled French fries in mine and had felt a weird nervousness that definitely wouldn't have been part of a fantasy or hallucination.

"But it was like it was really happening," Tannis insisted. "Or would. And now this."

"It's impossible," I said again.

"How do you know?" she demanded.

"It's against the laws of physics. We studied it in class last year." Another of Mr. Ruskovich's lessons. But even as I said it, I wondered if it was true. You couldn't *go* to the future, but did that mean you couldn't *see* it? I wasn't about to share any doubts with Tannis. "All that stuff in books and movies . . . it's all just fantasy."

"Really?" she asked hopefully.

"There's one way to find out for sure," Trip chimed in.

I knew immediately what he meant. "I'm not going back there," I said. "That's crazy, Trip. After what happened?"

"You're not curious?" he countered.

Oh, I was definitely curious. Could it really be my future? Me with Sarah? I glanced at her and saw the weirdest expression on her face. Nervous, almost guilty. What had she seen that she was afraid to tell?

"What are you guys talking about?" Tannis asked.

"Going back to the binoculars," Sarah said. "Right?" She looked at Trip.

He nodded. "You just said it couldn't be the future, so what can looking hurt?" he asked me.

"It was definitely *something*, though," I said. "Hallucinations or whatever."

"So?" Trip said.

I looked around but could see that none of them got it. "What if it's what we first talked about—subconscious desires or something? What if whatever happened that night called up things we'd been thinking deep down." I saw Tannis about to interrupt. "Maybe *so* deep we're not even aware of it."

"And . . . ," Trip prompted.

"And changed how we think or act. Maybe it didn't predict what happened to Nat's dad but caused it."

No one said anything for a minute.

"You really think she did it?" Trip said quietly.

"Not the Nat we've always known," I said. "But what if it *was* a hallucinogen? Something chemical that got on our skin? Into our brains? That night last year when we were on acid? We were acting pretty weird."

"You think?" Trip said sarcastically.

"And to tell you the truth, I didn't feel right for a few days after."

He nodded slowly.

"What if this is like that and somehow it changed Natalie?" I said, then added, "We have no idea what we're dealing with."

Trip pursed his lips, thinking. Finally he said, "Don't you think we should figure it out, Ri? I mean, the police are investigating a murder and holding our friend—maybe as a suspect. She saw it coming. Don't you think we should check out the thing that showed it to her?"

I was silent because I didn't want to go back. "You didn't even see anything," I said to him.

"All the more reason to look again," Trip countered. "So I can see if you're all just nuts. We're the only ones who know about the binoculars," he continued quietly. "If they have anything to do with what happened to Nat's dad—by changing things or predicting them or whatever—the police will have no idea to even consider them.

"Which could be good or bad," he added after a few seconds.

"Depending on . . . ," I said.

"On whether or not Nat had anything to do with it."

I realized that for all his certainty, Trip actually wasn't that certain at all. Typical.

"So let's just tell the cops about them and be done," Tannis said. A confused look passed over her face. "Actually, that wouldn't be a very good idea, would it?"

"They'd think we're crazy," Sarah said.

“Or worse,” I said. “Find out that we’re not.”

“We have to go back,” Trip said. “I don’t think there’s really a choice.”

“There’s always a choice,” I said, but it was halfhearted. I didn’t want to admit it and definitely didn’t want to *do* it, but Trip was right. We had to look again.

CHAPTER 10

"TELL ME AGAIN WHY WE'RE WE DOING THIS?" TANNIS ASKED as she climbed into my car.

"Because you live close to me and I've got the car tonight and I'm gentleman enough not to make you walk."

"No, you moron. I meant, why are we going back to those binoculars?"

I knew that's what she'd meant, but I was trying to avoid thinking about it, my stomach a tight ball of knots.

Tannis poked my shoulder. "Hey. Loverboy."

I rubbed the spot where she'd jabbed me. "Could you please stop calling me that?"

She snorted. "Truth hurts?"

"What's that supposed to mean?" I snapped, wishing immediately I hadn't. I suspected Tannis knew I had a thing for Sarah, but I sure didn't want to hear it out loud.

She smirked. "I think you know."

"Whatever." I waved it off. "You heard Trip," I said, returning to her original question. "We're going back because we need to know what the binoculars are. And whether they had anything to do with what happened to Nat's dad."

"And if they did?"

"I don't know. I guess it depends on how they're connected." I didn't want to think about turning Nat in. Or turning the binoculars in. Though I wouldn't mind seeing the look on Lincoln Andrews's face if he saw the crazy shit we had.

She was quiet for about ten seconds. Which might have been a world record for Tannis. "What if it really is the future?"

"It's not," I said automatically.

"But what if it is?"

"Okay, fine," I said. "Let's just say—for the sake of argument—that it is. So what?"

"So what?"

"Yeah," I said. "Does it matter? Does it change anything?"

"It changes everything." Tannis's voice broke on the last word.

I looked over, surprised.

"It's all wrong," Tannis said.

"What? That you have kids?"

"Everything," she said miserably. "It means all of the stuff—my races, the trials, the time I've been fixing cars instead of studying or whatever—it's all been a huge waste. None of what I want happens. I never leave. I'm stuck right here, raising kids, living in a falling-down house, just like my mom, and her mom before her, and—"

"Whoa, Tannis. Hold it," I said. "How can you know that?"

She stared at me, her face tight for a second, then crumpling. "Because I have three kids. And I'm not old." She wiped at her eyes, and I felt my head swimming a little. I'd never seen Tannis cry. Or go off like this. "I'm in, like, my twenties. And I'm walking on a trail on that same damn mountain." She took a short breath. "I'm not racing; I'm not training. It means I never make it on the circuit. So, what do I do? I'm not smart like you or Sarah. It's too late for me to go to college or figure out something else. This is the only thing I'm good at. The only thing I've ever wanted. And it *doesn't happen*."

Tannis wiped at her eyes, sniffling.

"Tannis," I said softly, "you're getting *way* ahead of yourself."

"Am I?" she demanded, whipping her head up to look at me. "Was yours like mine? So real you could smell and feel stuff in it like it was really happening?"

I thought about Sarah's weight next to me in that bed.

The way my chest flooded with warmth when she smiled. I didn't answer, and I think that was answer enough. Tannis had been so quiet about the things she'd seen, not bringing it up at all in the week between the cave and the Dash. I'd assumed she'd blown it off as nothing, had forgotten it. I couldn't have been more wrong. It was itching at her, just like it had been at me.

"You're not really going to look, are you?" she finally asked.

"No, I'm not going to look." It was Trip's idea to go back, and even though I knew he was right, I wasn't willing to be the guinea pig. Trip seemed more than happy to do the honors, which could only be attributed to the fact that he'd seen nothing last time and he hated to be left out.

I turned up the volume on the radio then, which was kind of rude, but it kept Tannis from asking me any more questions. Eventually she sang along instead. Loudly, the way Tannis does most everything.

Lights were blazing in the living room when we pulled up to Trip's house. I saw his dad pass by the oversize window as we went up the walk, and my teeth clenched. The last person I wanted to see. Great.

Tannis rapped on the door three times, then pushed through without waiting for an answer. "Domino's!" she yelled.

I took a deep breath, assaulted at the threshold by the

smell of Pine-Sol and the candles Trip's mom always lit to cover her cleaning obsession.

"Hey, guys," Trip's dad greeted us, giving me a hard clap on the back. I mumbled hi and ducked into the living room, hoping to catch the score before going downstairs. I could hear him chatting up Tannis: ". . . looking lovely as ever. . . . Got a hot date?" "Not tonight, Mr. Jones. . . . Are you free?" Hardy-har-har.

Then his footsteps. "They're losing again."

"I see that," I said without turning around. Trip's mom passed by on her way to the kitchen, calling a quick hi.

"Terrible about Natalie Cleary's father," he said, stepping closer and shaking his head with exaggerated sympathy. It was what people had been saying for days, but like everything else Mr. Jones did, it was too much—too loud, too hearty, and now, too sad. A big, fake, lying façade.

When I was a kid, I'd liked how his big smiles had been different from my dad's moodiness. I remember roasting marshmallows beside him. He ate his charred, and I'd liked watching them burn.

"Ready, Riles?" he'd ask, puffing on his cigar and holding the stick just outside the campfire's flames.

I'd nod, barely hearing my dad across the fire. "You're making my son a pyromaniac, Pete."

Trip's dad had grinned. "I'll drop off some fire extinguishers. Consider it a housewarming gift."

We'd just moved into our place, and my parents had been scraping wallpaper and painting most weekends, their home improvements nearly steamrolling right over our annual camping trip with the Joneses. That year Trip and I had our own tent, which I'd been psyched about until he'd sprung his plan to set up his SpyToolz Lazer Wire to trap bears. I hoped I wouldn't have to crawl into my parents' tent overnight. I'd never hear the end of it.

"Better blow that out, Pete," my dad warned, nodding toward the marshmallow as he stood. "You're gonna catch the stick soon." He tossed the remains of his cigar into the fire, then hooked a thumb toward the woods. "Gotta drain the main vein."

Trip snorted. His dad didn't say stuff like that, and Trip thought it was hilarious.

Mr. Jones had me hold his cigar while he steadied the stick and blew hard on the marshmallow until the fire went out, leaving a drippy black glob that he sandwiched between graham crackers and chocolate, then offered to me.

I wrinkled my nose. "No, thanks."

His eyebrows shot up. "Have you boys been sneaking chocolate?"

I shook my head, but in fact we had.

"Reeeally," he drawled. "Not sure I remember a time in your ten years when you've turned down a s'more, Riley Larkin."

He winked so I'd know he wasn't really mad. I liked that Trip's dad never left you wondering about that.

He offered it to Trip, who also shook his head. "Don't want it."

"Hnmmmm." Mr. Jones rubbed his chin. "Curiouser and curiouser."

Mrs. Jones had ducked into their tent for some drinks, so Mr. Jones turned to my mom.

"Melissa?"

I was surprised when she said, "Sure."

He smiled, crossing to her side of the fire. Trip scooted next to me, bringing the bag of marshmallows and chattering about whether we should set the wire up by the entrance to the cave or the trail and where a bear'd be more likely to come from, but I was busy watching Mr. Jones feed my mom, both of them laughing as strands of marshmallow dripped down her chin.

I'd felt only surprise then, seeing my mom giggle like that. Maybe a hint of apprehension. Not the hot, seething anger I felt standing beside Mr. Jones now. "Yeah," I answered shortly as the Sox struck out again. "Terrible about Mr. Cleary. Is Trip in the basement?"

"Him and his girl." He winked, somberness vanishing instantly. "Proceed with caution."

Bastard, I thought. Which is pretty much what I always thought when I saw him these days.

I flicked the basement light on and off before clomping downstairs. Mr. Jones was a creep, but he was right. I definitely did not want to see Trip and Sarah doing whatever they did when we weren't there.

Which today was only playing checkers.

I lugged a beanbag closer while Tannis, who'd followed me down, messed with the music. Trip took Sarah's piece, and she responded with a triple jump, clearing the board of red checkers.

"I let you win," he said, standing.

"Yeah, okay." Sarah rolled her eyes and smiled at me. Typical Trip.

"You hear from Nat today?" I asked her. We'd all left messages and texts, but Sarah was the most likely to hear back.

Sarah shook her head. "The police probably have her phone."

"I wonder when they'll let her go," Tannis said. "I mean, they can't keep her forever."

"Unless she did it," I said.

Trip scowled at me and pulled on his fleece. "You ready?"

No. But I trailed him back upstairs anyway. All of us waved to his parents on the way out.

Twenty minutes later we pulled into the deserted dirt lot. I stepped out, the wind rushing past with more than a hint of frost. The four of us huddled by the car, zipping jackets and rewrapping scarves before following Trip up the half-frozen path like a parade of mummies. It was hard to believe it had been less than two weeks ago that we'd come up here with beers, made the fire, played Tannis's stupid game of truth or dare.

Now one of us was in police custody, her dad dead.

The clearing seemed much more exposed, with the leaves gone and the cave yawning black behind the half circle of stones. No one mentioned gathering wood. There was no beer to stow.

"Where are they?"

It took me a minute to realize Trip was talking to me. "The binoculars?" I asked.

"No, dude, your balls." Trip snorted. "Of course, the binoculars."

"In the cave."

"I'll go with you," Sarah told him. "I put them in there."

Trip slipped his hand into hers and they walked toward the cave, the beam of the flashlight bobbing ahead of them and twigs crunching under their boots. The moonlight made Sarah's skin even paler than usual, and I could see her biting at her lip, the way she did when she was nervous. The first time I'd noticed it had been in sixth grade at Kelly Lipman's party. The day we kissed.

Rich Fowler had shoved the Coke bottle toward me. "Your turn, brainiac."

I'd stared at it, wishing I could melt into the floor. Galen Riddock whispered something to Trip, the three of them nudging each other and laughing across the circle. That was the year Trip discovered football, and Rich and Galen were the captains of the Pop Warner team he hoped to play on. He'd been buddying up to them, so I was an outcast, sandwiched between the new girl who'd come with Natalie Cleary and Kelly, whose mom worked at Woodside Manor with mine and had probably made her invite me to this stupid party just like my mom had made me come. Angrily I sent the bottle skittering, trying not to think about Rich yammering by the pretzel and soda table earlier. I had no idea how to "slip them some tongue," since I'd never even kissed a girl on the lips.

The bottle slowed, clicking softly and finally stopping with its neck pointing squarely to the girl on my right.

She looked at me silently, her dark eyes solemn. My heart was thudding. *Does she expect me to slip her some tongue? Does she* want *me to?*

"Uh, Riley? You want to get on with it?"

Trip. Fucking loudmouth.

"I don't think she bites," he said, adding suggestively, "Or maybe she does."

Everyone laughed. Except me and the girl.

Her brown eyes seemed nice. But also sad. Like my mom looked the time we found a puppy with broken ribs at the park.

For God's sake, stop thinking about your mom. Just do it. I leaned forward. *Don't slobber.* She smelled sweet, like gum or candy, her eyes on mine until I was too close to see them anymore. Then my lips touched hers, soft and hot, and I felt weird and nervous and tingly. *Okay, that's long enough*. I sat back, my face burning, hoping I hadn't messed it up somehow.

"Didja get some tongue?" Galen yelled. Trip and Rich cackled.

The new girl looked at him. "No," she said blandly. "And please keep yours to yourself next time too."

"Ooooooh!" Natalie said.

Galen shot Nat a dirty look, and I stared at Sarah McKenzie, wondering at this new girl brazen enough to take my side over one of the most popular guys in school. That was when I saw her hand clenched by her side, the knuckles white and the corner of her lip puckered where she was biting at it. *She's nervous*, I realized, filled with admiration. *Much more than she's letting on*.

"Yo!" Tannis yelled toward the cave now. "Trip! Should we send in a search party?"

They came out seconds later, before I even had time to hope maybe the binoculars were gone. Trip waved the box toward me. "Want to go first?" he asked.

"No."

"What are you . . . chicken?"

"What are you . . . ten?"

Trip stuck out his tongue.

"I guess that's a yes," I said. "And, sure, I'm chicken."

"Anyone else?" he offered. The girls shook their heads, Tannis even taking a step back. "All right." Trip sighed, setting the box on the ground. "I guess it's all me."

He reached for the lid.

"Wait," I said. "Are you sure you want to do this?"

Trip looked up, blue eyes shining silver in the moonlight. After a second he nodded. "Yeah, Ri. I am."

"What if you see something bad, like what Nat saw?"

"I've thought about that," Trip answered. "But we need to know. It's gotta be killing Natalie if she really saw it, somehow knew ahead of time—"

"Unless she's the one who did it."

"You keep saying that," Trip said. "But, fine. If she is the one, don't you think we should know if these had anything to do with it? Plus," he added, "the curiosity's killing me."

"It's like Pandora's box," Sarah observed.

Trip winked at her. "Is that the porn we watched last night?"

Tannis laughed, and Sarah smiled. It was the first time the mood broke, maybe since we'd heard about Nat's dad. "Were you napping during lit class again, T.?" Sarah asked.

"Wait . . . they show porn in lit class?" he said. "Shit, *now* when am I going to sleep?"

"It's a myth," I told him.

"I knew it was too good to be true."

"Not porn in lit," I said. "Pandora's box. She opened it out of curiosity, releasing evil into the world."

"Well, that's a brick," Trip said.

"But there was something left in the box," Sarah reminded me. "Hope."

I'd forgotten that part.

"See? It's not so bad, Mr. Doom and Gloom," Trip said. He unlatched the lock, flipped open the lid, and took out the binoculars. They looked heavy and cold. Sinister and promising. There was a tangy taste in my mouth as Trip rubbed the lenses quickly, then looked.

I held my breath, feeling the thud, thud of my heart. After a minute Trip pulled them away, frowning. He messed with the knobs and looked again.

"What do you see?" Tannis leaned forward.

He didn't answer, but I knew, and was surprised by the wave of deep disappointment that washed over me. He'd seen nothing. My chest felt tight, and there was a single, unexpected thought: *No*.

"There's nothing there," Trip said, his voice slightly muffled.

"Really?" Tannis sounded hopeful. "Nothing at all? Not my hand?" She waved it in front of the binoculars. "Or my face? Or those weird shapes and colors?"

"Shapes and colors," he said. "But nothing else." He held the binoculars toward her. "Here. You try."

"Nuh-uh," Tannis said, shuffling back. "I'm not looking."

"Why?"

"I'm with Riley on Team Chicken."

"I'll look," I said, like it was nothing. "Curiosity's been bugging me, too."

But Tannis stepped between me and Trip before he could hand them over. "Hold it." She put her hands on my shoulders, turning me to look her in the eye. I shook her off, irritated at being maneuvered like a rag doll. "I thought you weren't going to," she said accusingly. "You're not trying to win a pissing match with Trip, are you?"

"I can out-piss him any day."

"Whatever, Riley," she said, her voice dropping. "You're not doing this to impress us—or any certain one of us?"

"Of course not," I said levelly, but inside I was a swirling mess of emotion. I *didn't* want to look again, but I'd been caught off guard by the profound letdown when Trip had said there was nothing. I *wanted* there to be something. I'd been going over it again and again this past week, just like Tannis had. Me in a dorm room. At college. With Sarah. My future: As impossible as it seemed and as wrong as it was, I wanted that.

Tannis eyed me for an extra second, then reluctantly stepped aside, letting me take the binoculars from Trip.

I toyed with the dials for a minute, then took a deep breath and lifted them to my eyes.

And saw immediately that Trip was full of shit.

The shapes and colors swirled and blended, blurring the outside world just like the first time. Then the image, figures and objects emerging from the miasma.

It was different.

It was my mom.

I only recognized her because she was in our living room. And I only recognized *it* because of the stairs curving slightly at the bottom and the small window in the wall. Everything else had changed. The carpet, the wallpaper, the pictures. They were all cleaner and newer. Better.

But my mom looked old. Her hair was a steely gray, piled in a bun like my grammy used to wear. She was smiling at me, but it wasn't her usual smile. It was droopy, lopsided, her left eye half-shut. A heart-stabbing bolt of fear shot through me—I knew these symptoms—and then I saw the man next to her, holding her hand.

He was looking at me too, something really familiar about the way he smiled, cocked his head. Probably because I'd just seen him doing it an hour earlier.

Holy shit. It was *him*.

Trip's dad.

I whipped the binoculars from my eyes, my pulse racing. Had Trip tricked me into looking?

"What?" he asked eagerly. "Did you see something?"

No, he hadn't tricked me. Not unless he was the world's best actor.

There was no way I could tell him. Trip idolized his dad, God knows why. After all the years I'd spent hiding that asshole's secret, I sure as shit wasn't going to have it unravel like this.

It was pure dumb luck—or un-luck—that I knew. It had been the end of eighth grade, seven months after my dad died. I'd been sent home sick from school, and I remember thinking it was weird to see Mrs. Jones's car in the driveway. She didn't really come over anymore then. I walked into the living room expecting to see her, but the room was empty.

Everything seemed normal. Bits of dust floated in the sunlight, chairs were where they should be, lamps off.

Still, hairs prickled on my arms and the back of my neck.

I heard them just before they came down the stairs.

My mom first, giggling. Then *him*. They stopped when they saw me, the three of us frozen like it was a game of statues. First one to move loses. Finally my mom came toward me. "Riley . . ."

Bzzz! my brain said. *You're out!*

My feet were already crossing to the stairs, moving past Trip's dad—*in a bathrobe!*—up two at a time, my head buzzing nonsense and the bits and scraps that had stuck there year after year. Marshmallows. My dad's drinking. I slammed the door and dove for the bed, closing my eyes and jamming in earbuds.

At some point my mom came in. I'm sure she knocked. She'd never just barged in before. *Never been caught with a married man either!*

"Can we talk?" Her voice was tiny, a bug's cry, through the music.

I shook my head, volume still full blast. "*No one knows what it's like . . .*"

"Riley . . ."

I shut my eyes, blocking out the rest, melting into *Behind Blue Eyes*. I felt her touch my shoulder, and shook it off.

Finally she left.

I sat on that bed, Roger Daltrey screaming at me for another hour, the visual coming back over and over. *What am I supposed to do with this?*

We never talked about it. I wouldn't let her. I tried to pretend it never happened, not that the memory faded even the tiniest bit. I certainly never told Trip, and I didn't want him to find out now—after all this time—that his dad wasn't who Trip thought he was, and maybe neither was I.

"No, I didn't see anything," I said to Trip. "I just . . ." I shook my head, grasping for an answer. "It's so frustrating," I blurted. "I don't get why they worked before and not now."

"That's good, isn't it?" Tannis said. "It means what we saw that night was just what you first thought. A hallucination or something. Not the future. There's nothing special or freaky about these." She waved at the binoculars, still keeping a careful distance.

"Right." I mustered everything in me to sound convincing. "Of course not."

"So what does that mean for Nat?" Tannis asked.

"It means these had nothing to do with what happened to her dad," Trip said. "I mean, are you guys positive that even happened? That you really saw something?"

Tannis looked unsure, but I didn't feel the least bit that way. Of course we'd seen something. Obviously there *was* something in the binoculars. What did *that* mean for Nat? For me?

I glanced at Sarah, who hadn't spoken at all. Our eyes met, and I was struck by the sudden and complete certainty that she could read me like a book.

And knew I was lying about the binoculars.

CHAPTER 11

WE FINALLY SAW NATALIE ON WEDNESDAY. HER DAD'S FUNERAL.

Everyone from school and half the town went. My mom had to work. "The nursing home doesn't shut down for a funeral," she'd said ruefully. That she couldn't afford to take the day off went without saying. I recognized lots of people from the mountain and the ski shop. The grocer was there, and people from the hospital. Plenty from the restaurant, too. Moose was at the edge of the crowd by himself. I nodded to him, and he scowled. Still pissed at me. I felt guilty, then angry about it. *He's the idiot using drugs*, I thought. *Not me*. Bill Winston was conspicuously absent. So was Natalie's mom. At least that was the rumor. I wouldn't have recognized her or any of Mr. Cleary's girlfriends, though I saw plenty of skanky-looking women who might have qualified. I wondered if the police had questioned all of them.

Or if they were taking notes as they stood on the fringe of the crowd, a buffer between us and the reporters cordoned off by the roadside, where the police had ordered them to stand. Their numbers had increased tenfold as the story had lingered. The official press release was that it was a murder investigation, daughter left unharmed, persons of interest being questioned.

That Natalie was one of the persons of interest had become common knowledge in the underground whispers, though the police had yet to confirm it.

It was the first time we'd seen her since the day he was killed, and she looked terrible, standing somberly beside her Social Services case worker.

"How's she doing?" John Peters asked quietly as he came over to stand beside us.

"Don't know," Trip answered. "None of us have been able to talk to her since that night at your house."

He nodded. "My dad says they were pretty tough on her." He shook his head angrily. "So unfair."

Trip looked at him, surprised. "You don't think she did it?"

"Of course not." Trip nodded approvingly as John went back to his family.

The service sucked. Randall Cleary had given up on church ages ago, but I guess the church never gives up on anyone, even people like him. A priest gamely gave the eulogy, doing his best to gloss over the details of Nat's father's life and give it some sort of meaning. They'd obviously never met.

I watched Natalie throughout, still finding it hard to believe she'd done it. But I could see lots of other people looking at her with plenty of suspicion. It didn't seem like she noticed it. Or much of anything else.

We stood in a line by the coffin to pay our respects, but more because it was the only way to get close to Nat. The four of us formed a protective cluster around her when it was our turn. Sarah was the first to speak.

"I'm so sorry, Nat," Sarah said, hugging her. "We wanted to see you, but no one would tell us how."

Tears welled in Natalie's eyes, and then spilled over immediately, and I recognized exactly where she was—that state where you're able to hold it together as long as absolutely no one talks to you or touches you with any amount of sympathy. "They had me there for days. Asking questions, doing tests . . ." She took a ragged breath. "It was horrible."

"When do you get to come back?" Tannis asked.

"Now," Nat said. "I'm back."

"You are?" I asked, surprised. "So the police . . ." I hesitated, not sure if Nat realized she'd been a suspect.

"Yeah," she said darkly. "They've finally realized I had nothing to do with it."

"Idiots," Trip spat.

She looked at him gratefully and almost smiled. “Thanks, Trip. I couldn’t agree more.”

“Natalie,” Sarah said. “What happened? That night . . .”

Nat’s eyes shifted to her handler, standing discreetly to the side. “I don’t know,” she said simply. “That’s what I kept telling them. My dad was wasted. Worse than at the mountain. Much worse,” she said quietly. “I went to my room, locked the door, and put on my headphones, the ones Lu gave me?” We all nodded. Lu was her coach, and the headphones were noise-canceling, to help her concentrate before races. Trip had seen them in her bag one day at school, and we’d taken turns wearing them at lunch, trying to read each other’s lips. Tannis had made these ridiculous faces at me, mouthing something I couldn’t understand. The others had been cracking up, and later I’d found out it was *I want you*.

Nat continued, “I woke up just after three in the morning, my lights and headphones still on. I got up to brush my teeth and was going to get a glass of water from the kitchen.” Nat stopped and took a few quick breaths. I could feel my heart beating hard and fast. “I knew something was wrong right away,” she said. “There was a funny smell, and I had the weirdest déjà vu, walking down that hallway.” My skin was prickling. I saw Sarah’s hand slide involuntarily to clutch the other one. “Instead of turning into the kitchen, I kept going. Into the living room. And it was—” Natalie stopped, brought her fingers to her mouth, bit hard like she was holding something in.

"You found him," Trip finished softly.

Natalie nodded, fingers between her teeth for another second. Then she dropped her hand. "It was exactly what I saw in those binoculars," she whispered in a rush. Her eyes darted to Trip, then Tannis, then me. *"Exactly."*

My insides felt cold.

"No." Tannis was shaking her head. "Impossible. We went back and looked. There's nothing there, Nat."

"Nothing where?"

"In the binoculars," Trip said. "We went back up to the cave," he explained quietly, glancing toward Nat's handler. "Monday night. We were worried about you and that you'd . . . you know . . . seen this. We didn't know what it meant. But it's like Tannis said: There's nothing in them. It's just a kaleidoscope. They didn't have anything to do with this."

"So what happened that night?" Nat demanded. "I'm telling you I saw it. Exactly what happened."

"Hallucinations," Tannis said firmly. "If anything."

I looked at her, the tight set of her jaw and eyes, clearly ready to challenge anyone who disagreed. I was struck by how completely she'd latched on to the idea that the binoculars were nothing more than a fancy toy. There's no way I'd have believed Trip without looking for myself. Maybe I'd have felt differently if I'd seen something I didn't want.

Natalie's handler came over then. "I'm sorry, kids," she said, actually looking like she meant it, "but I have to ask you to move on."

The four of us closed in on Nat again, a football huddle with Natalie safe in the center. "We're here for you, Nat," Sarah whispered, hugging her tight. Natalie hugged back, each of us with an arm around her and Nat holding on like we could somehow whisk her away from everything.

We stood at the edge of the crowd for a little, watching people. I could feel the others studying faces too. Watching how Natalie greeted them, how they mixed and mingled and talked among themselves. I wondered if the same question was on all of our minds:

If Nat hadn't done it, who had?

CHAPTER 12

I HAD DINNER WITH MY MOM AND TOLD HER ALL ABOUT THE FUNERAL.

Well, not all.

I didn't mention all the seedy characters who'd been there, or how Bill Winston hadn't been and what had happened between him and Mr. Cleary at the Dash, or any of the other things I'm sure she'd hear or already had heard through the grapevine.

I also didn't talk about all the reporters. I didn't want to remind her of when my dad had died.

"There were a lot of cops there," I said. "And Nat was a mess."

She nodded. "That poor girl."

"The police finally cleared her," I said.

"She was a suspect?" Maybe my mom's link to the grapevine was broken.

"Yeah."

"So who do they think did it?"

"Dunno," I said. "The police have been asking around about who Mr. Cleary's enemies were."

My mom snorted. "Anyone on the tourism board, after the stunt he pulled at the Dash."

"You heard?"

"Who didn't?' She tapped her lips thoughtfully. "Or what about the family of that girl who died last year?"

"The one who OD'd?" My mom nodded. "What does she have to do with it?"

"Where do you think she got the drugs? Sally at the Manor knows them, said the dad was out of his head when it happened."

"Huh." I wondered if maybe *my* link to the grapevine was broken. My mom started clearing dishes, and I flipped absently through the mail. Bill, bill, junk, bill.

"They live up that way too, I think," she added.

A postcard about the SATs, "FINAL REMINDER" in bold red letters.

I stared at it for a minute, my hand stalled between the stacks I'd been sorting envelopes into. Not a bill. But I couldn't bring myself to call it junk, either.

"What's that?" My mom peered at the postcard as she collected my dishes.

"Nothing," I said, wishing I'd tossed it into trash pile,

where it belonged. "Just came with the mail."

But her face told me she got it. It wasn't *nothing*, just nothing we could use. The SAT notices had started coming last year, sandwiched between glossy flyers and fancy college booklets I'd never sent for. I'd paged through them, imagining myself on those campus paths or in the lecture halls. Then I'd read the tuition and swept them into the trash can, along with the local paper and whatever other crap had come that day. Each notice about the SATs had gone with them. Why waste forty-three dollars to take the test? There was no way I could go to college. Believe me, I'd racked my brains.

Community college? The closest was over an hour away, and we only had one car.

Living and working on campus? I'd never make enough for tuition, dorm, books, food, *and* sending money home.

Financial aid? We didn't qualify for enough government aid, and our credit was too shaky for anything else.

Scholarships? No one was giving out free rides these days, and even if I won half a ride, it wasn't enough.

And the biggest unknown, always looming—what if things with my mom got worse?

But I wanted to go. So bad I could taste it.

We finished our dessert in silence. My mom stood to rinse her dish, then turned to me. "I've gotta run," she said. She came closer, smoothed my hair the way she had since I was a kid. "You're a good boy, Riley." She kissed my head lightly, the smell of bleach and her perfume surrounding me. "Somehow we'll work things out."

I listened to the car crunch out of the driveway, then shoved the postcard into my jeans pocket and headed upstairs to start on my homework.

CHAPTER 13

NATALIE CAME BACK TO SCHOOL FRIDAY. WE ALL WALKED IN together, me on one side and Trip on the other. A hush fell over the hallway as everyone turned to stare.

"You okay?" Sarah asked Natalie softly when we paused outside the office. Her voice carried in the silence.

Natalie nodded, tense and uncomfortable. "See you at lunch." She pulled open the glass door and slipped inside.

As soon as it closed, Trip whirled to face the eyes of at least twenty of our classmates. "Give her a break, people, you know?"

A few people nodded, shuffling off. The rest stayed, apparently transfixed by the prospect of watching Natalie Cleary fill out paperwork. Everyone knew by now that the police had cleared her. Forensics and all. But having one of your classmates orphaned by a murder in a town of twelve hundred was still a big effing deal. Trip shook his head in disgust, muttering "Losers," and stalked off.

Behind the glass Principal Miller ushered Natalie and some other people, including Lu Kresbol, Nat's coach and head of the ski program, into his office. Technically Natalie was a ward of the state until she turned eighteen. But that was two months away, much sooner than anyone would get through the paperwork needed to assign her somewhere. So, untechnically, the local Social Services staff—including Matty's mom—had signed off on her staying with Lu. By the time anyone from the state figured out what was going on, Natalie would be legal to be on her own anyhow.

We stayed in the cafeteria for lunch. It felt like we were in a bubble, the silence surrounding us palpable, but it was just too damn cold to go outside.

"How's it going?" Sarah asked Nat after we, too, had sat in silence for a while. "You hanging in?"

Nat nodded. "It's exhausting, honestly," she said. "I can see everyone thinking about it and no one talking about it. Like they're afraid I'll break if they bring it up, even though watching them think about it is worse."

We nodded, none of us sure how to handle her either, and we were her closest friends.

"You don't remember anything at all, Nat?" Trip asked

softly. “Other than . . . you know, what you told us before? You didn’t hear anyone come in?”

Her jaw tightened, and I thought Trip had been wrong to ask that. She shook her head. “No.” Her voice was hoarse.

“Do you know who usually came by?” he pressed.

Natalie looked up. “You mean who his customers were?” He nodded. “Not all of them.” Her eyes darted away from us, taking in some of the nearby tables, filled with our classmates. “But you’d be surprised who I’ve seen at the house.”

I definitely would be, I thought. Nat never talked about it, but I’d sensed it a couple times, the weird dynamic between Nat and people she’d never cross paths with otherwise. Kids like Moose gave her an extra wide berth, treating her a little differently from how he treated the rest of us. Not like they were friends or co-conspirators but like she had them by the balls. Which she did.

“Do they know?” Trip asked.

“Some do,” Nat said cryptically. “Some probably don’t.”

“Did you tell the cops?”

“Of course.”

He hesitated a second, then asked, “Did you ever see Galen Riddock?”

“Yes.”

“How about that night?”

She stared at him. “Why?”

Trip hesitated. "I don't know," he said. "Just . . . he was asking. About stuff. At John Peters's party. I just wondered if he . . . you know, followed up on it."

But of course there was more. Trip called me around five thirty. I was in my room doing homework, and he'd just finished practice. I could hear him breathing hard, imagined him crossing the lot to his car.

"I've been hearing things," he said.

"Maybe you should see a doctor."

"Not that," Trip said. "I *like* the voices in my head. This stuff is about Nat's dad. And that night."

"What kind of stuff?"

"I'll tell you when I get there."

Great. Like I could concentrate on physics now. And I'd already finished all my mindless homework.

I gazed at the textbook for another five minutes or so, but after reading the same paragraph for the third nonsensical time, I gave up, tossing it onto the floor beside my bed.

It was quiet in the house with my mom asleep. I could hear the hum of the boiler, the tick of the clock in the living room.

I thought of the binoculars in my drawer, where they'd been since the night we'd gone back to the cave. I hadn't wanted them here but definitely hadn't wanted to leave them there, either. And no one else would take them. Not that I could have let them anyhow. Now I got the strongest urge to take them out, remembering Nat's words: *It was exactly what I saw*.

What would I see if I looked again?

I had my hand on the knob of my top dresser drawer when the SAT postcard caught my eye. FINAL REMINDER.

I picked it up instead, turned it over absently. Seventy-three dollars. It would have been forty-three a month ago, but this was a final warning, rush reminder. The only time they were offered locally. My last chance. I knew without looking that we didn't have the money, couldn't remember the last time we'd had that much to spare.

But you couldn't get into college without taking them. How could that be my future if I didn't take the test?

Maybe I was wrong about the money. Maybe I could somehow squeeze out enough.

I took the postcard to the living room, searched out the checkbook and the overdue bills to be paid this week. Then I called the bank. My paycheck was in, bringing our available funds to $133.12.

It was enough for the SATs or the bills. But not both.

So unfair.

I studied the payment slips, wishing they would morph into different dates or amounts. *They aren't* that *overdue*, I thought. *There are grace periods. Payment plans.*

I walked up to my room, dug through the stack of

papers beside my bed, and finally spotted the one I wanted. I'd gotten the SAT registration forms from the guidance counselor a few months back when I'd planned to sign up.

Before I could second-guess myself, I wrote it all out. The registration, the check. I put the stamp on the envelope just as Trip beeped outside.

CHAPTER 14

I SLID INTO THE PASSENGER SEAT, STILL HOLDING THE ENVELOPE.

Trip glanced at it. "Need to drop that off?"

"Yeah."

"Writing to Justin Bieber again?"

"Something like that." Trip pulled away from the curb, turning toward town, and I asked, "Where are we going?"

"To see Galen Riddock."

I wasn't surprised. I'd suspected Trip's questions at lunch hadn't been random. "What's the deal?"

"Remember at the Dash party when he was looking to score something?" I nodded, and Trip continued, "One of the guys told me he did. Late night."

I whistled, low. "So he'd have been the last person to see Nat's dad alive."

"Maybe the very last," Trip said grimly. "He was drinking

when we saw him. I could smell it. And he's kind of an asshole when he's drunk."

"And when he's sober."

Trip pulled over by the post office. I hopped out, hesitating only a second before tossing the envelope into the black slot. No turning back. I climbed into the car, asking, "Do the cops know?"

"I don't think so."

"So tell me again what we're doing?"

"We're going to go ask him about it."

I stared, incredulous. "And you think he's just going to tell us?"

"I don't know," Trip said. "I guess I thought we'd just . . . figure something out from how he reacts."

"Maybe," I said doubtfully. "But I think you'll do better on your own. Galen and I aren't exactly pals."

Understatement of the year, but Trip didn't know how much I really hated Galen Riddock. I'd never told him about the day in eighth grade when I'd overheard them by the lockers. My parents had had a humongous blowout fight over the weekend, and when I'd gotten up Sunday morning, it had been just me and my dad, one of the last times we were together, I realized later.

"Where's Mom?" I asked softly.

"Beats me," he said, barely stirring on the couch.

"Did she go to the store?" I knew she hadn't.

"No," he said, not looking at me.

She still wasn't back Monday, and I needed to find Trip. Maybe she'd gone to his house. Or told his mom where she was. I heard Galen's voice just before I rounded the corner.

". . . follows you around. Tell us the truth, Trip. Is he your boyfriend?"

I froze, heard Trip say, "C'mon, guys—"

"No, really," Galen persisted. "I think there's something going on. Do you guys have sleepovers? Stay up late reading, like, science magazines and shit? Share a sleeping bag, maybe?"

Then I heard Trip, angry, "Look, it's not like I have a choice. Our parents are friends, so I have to be nice to him or my mom'll flip out."

I turned, walked quickly and quietly away, the sting of his words sharp. They weren't true, I knew. Galen had backed Trip into a corner. Hadn't he?

It had been football and high school and my dad's death and our parents' drifting apart that had made Trip and me drift apart too. But in my mind Galen Riddock had always been wrapped up in it.

Now Trip considered what I'd said about us confronting him. "Yeah, okay," he agreed. "But come anyhow. Wait in the car."

"In case he admits it and whacks you, too?"

"Something like that," Trip said, only half-kidding.

* * *

The Riddocks lived in an old clapboard house about a mile from school. I saw Galen's blue Toyota parked in the gravel driveway but no other cars. There was an assortment of crap on the porch. A spare tire, an old high chair, a few boxes. It was a bad habit shared by a lot of people in Buford, the public display of accumulated junk, half hoarding, half laziness.

Trip pulled up across from the house. "Get down," he instructed, "just in case he looks out the window."

"This is ridiculous," I told him, scooting down in my seat.

"It's almost dark," Trip said, shutting off the car. "He won't notice you unless you're obvious."

"Yeah. Until you open the car door and I'm spotlighted by the overhead."

Trip reached up and clicked the light off. "Better?"

"No," I said, feeling completely stupid. Trip slammed the door, and I heard his boots crunch up the gravel driveway. He'd left his window cracked a tiny bit. *Like you do when you leave your dog in the car*, I thought. How long was I going to have to sit like this?

I heard a screen door slam shut across the street a minute or so later and lifted my head a bit, figuring Trip had gone inside. Instead I saw the shapes of them, sitting on the front stoop of Galen's porch. I wished I'd had the sense to at least adjust the mirrors before Trip had gone over there. I could have watched them if I'd gotten the angles right. As it was, I could only catch a hum of voices every now and then. A bark of laughter.

Being there, waiting helplessly, reminded me eerily of that night I'd met Natalie's dad. Thankfully, I didn't have to retrieve Trip.

After about fifteen minutes the screen door slammed again, something I'm sure the Riddocks' neighbors loved, and I heard Trip's boots coming closer. He slid into the car and puffed on his hands as the engine warmed back up.

"So?" I was still slumped beside him, just in case Riddock looked out the window.

"He says he didn't go up there," Trip said.

"At all?"

"Not that night." Trip shook his head, pulling away from the curb. "Said he thought about it but ended up driving Warrick and Douglass home and didn't feel like going back across town and up the mountain afterward."

"Well, so there it is." Trip turned the corner, and I pushed back up to a normal position. "I guess you got bad info. Who'd you hear it from?"

Trip hesitated. "An unnamed source."

"What?" I looked at him. "You're not going to tell me?"

"He didn't want word getting around."

"Trip. For God's sake, who am I going to tell?"

He shot me an appraising look. "You better not, Ri. If word gets back to Galen—"

"I'm not going to," I said, exasperated. "Who was it?"

"Richie."

"Milosevich?"

"Yeah," Trip said, and then added, "and he's not the type to make shit up."

Especially not something like that. Richie Milosevich was a quiet mousy kid who'd somehow scored the spot of kicker on the football team. It'd be a big risk for him to rat out someone like Galen Riddock. But even bigger to do it if it weren't true. "You think Riddock's lying?"

"Definitely possible," Trip said.

"How'd it even come up?" I asked.

"Richie pulled me aside," Trip said. "Knew I was friends with Nat."

"But how'd he know Galen was up there?"

Trip thought for a second. "He didn't say. I guess I assumed he'd overheard someone talking about it. I think he lives up that way. Maybe he saw him?"

"At, like, two in the morning?" I asked. "His sister's the one who—"

"Overdosed last year," Trip finished. "Yeah."

I remembered what my mom had said, about Richie's dad flipping out after his daughter had died. But how did all that fit with Galen and Nat's dad?

"Why'd he tell *you*?" I asked finally. "Why not go to the police?"

Trip cocked his head. "That's a good question," he said thoughtfully. "Maybe he's over them, after the stuff with his sister last year?"

"Or maybe he saw your heroics at the Dash—with Nat's dad—and figured it was right up your alley."

"Maybe," Trip agreed. He turned toward town. "Let's keep it to ourselves for now. I don't want people talking or Nat getting all tweaked up about nothing. Want to go grab a bite at the Hull?"

"Nah," I said, knowing I had exactly one dollar in my wallet. "I probably shouldn't." But it was like Trip could read my mind.

"It's on me, Ri. Don't be lame." He turned down the street toward the Hull without waiting for my response. "It's Friday night and I'm starving."

CHAPTER 15

I DIDN'T EVEN REALIZE I WAS LOOKING FOR RICHIE MILOSEVICH the following week until he was there, two feet ahead of me, walking down the hallway toward art. He was one of those kids I probably passed twenty times a week and never noticed. And vice versa. We just weren't on each other's radar. Until now.

He stopped to talk to a guy who was in my history class, and I paused, pretending to be looking in my backpack for a book.

"Didja see his goal against United?" Richie asked.

The other guy nodded. "Sick, right?"

They yammered on about soccer, a sport I, and the rest of Buford, couldn't have cared less about. Vaguely I remembered Trip telling me that was how Richie had wound up playing football. The soccer team had disbanded because they hadn't been able to field a full squad. Richie and the other guy chatted for another few minutes, then moved on. I zipped my bag up, sticking with Richie, even though he was walking away from the lunchroom, where I meant to go.

He was tall and skinny, pale like most of us Northerners. I tried to remember if I'd ever had a conversation with him, or even heard his voice—deeper than you'd expect—before eavesdropping on him. I didn't think so.

We turned down another corridor, leading toward the back door, and I stopped, seeing Moose and his gang of thugs at the other end. He was still angry, had spent a good part of this weekend at work giving me the evil eye. I really wasn't up for any more of that and was about to turn back toward the lunchroom, when I saw him wave to Richie.

I leaned against the wall, watching, hoping they wouldn't notice me as Richie went over to talk to him. Their conversation was short. A few sentences, a smile. A fist bump.

Not at all what I'd have expected.

I walked into the lunchroom still wondering about Richie and Moose. Tannis and Sarah were already at our table. "Hey," I greeted, turning to slide in next to Tannis.

"Hold it," she said. "That one's reserved."

"Oh." I started to get up. "For who?"

"Tom Brady. Have you seen him?" She eyed the cafeteria doors. "He's very late."

"And very married," Sarah added.

"Maybe that's the holdup," Tannis said. She shoveled in a mouthful of food.

I sat back down, elbowing Tannis. "You're a dork, Janssen."

Across the room Trip and Natalie came in, and a slight hush fell over the room as people stared. I watched them weave through tables, knowing by the wooden way Nat walked and how Trip stayed so close that something was wrong.

Sarah did too. "What happened, Nat?"

"The police called me this morning," Nat said, dropping her lunch bag onto the table.

"They didn't change their minds about clearing you, did they?" Tannis blurted.

"No." Nat scowled. "They're 'pursuing leads,' whatever that means."

"That they still don't know jack," Trip said.

"I guess," Nat said, sitting. "But they're done with the house, and they're releasing it to me." Her hands were visibly trembling. "What am I supposed to do with it?"

I was surprised the police would do that, just turn over the place where her dad had been murdered. But I guess they couldn't keep it, and Nat was the sole beneficiary, not that there was much benefit to it.

"What do you want to do with it?" Trip asked.

"Burn it?" Nat made a sound halfway between a sob and a snort.

"What about your things?" Trip asked.

Natalie waved a hand dismissively.

"Nat," Sarah said gently, "I know you don't care now, but you've got to get your stuff."

Trip chimed in. "Your trophies and medals are all there."

"And your scrapbook," Sarah added. "Your dad's stuff too. I know it's the last thing you want to think about, but someday you're going to want it. All of it."

Nat's face was a grimace of sadness and anger. She tried to stifle it all behind her hands, but the tears ran over.

Sarah put an arm around her, tugged her close, squeezing. "We'll help," she said. "We'll all go together."

CHAPTER 16

I HAD CHILLS AS I WALKED UP THE WEED-CHOKED PATH TO NATALIE'S front door. I thought about the last time I'd been here—police everywhere—and the time before that, with Moose.

"You okay?" Tannis whispered.

I don't know if I'd flinched or stopped or what, but I knew I looked a little queasy. "Not really."

She nodded. "Me either."

I gave her a half smile, and she rewarded me with a punch on the shoulder that, in light of what we were about to do, actually felt good. Normal.

The five of us stopped by the single front step. Yellow police tape was still strung across the door.

"You're sure this is okay?" Trip asked Nat.

"They said it was mine," Nat said dully, making no move to touch the tape.

"I didn't mean that," Trip said. "I meant you. Are *you* okay to go in there?"

Natalie shook her head. "No." She took a deep breath. "Let's just try to do this quick, okay?" She gritted her teeth, then swiped away the yellow tape and reached for the handle. Locked. Nat fumbled in her purse for the key, found it, dropped it, picked it up. But she was shaking too hard to get it into the lock.

"Hey." Trip put his hands over hers. "D'you want me to go in first? You take a minute, maybe catch your breath?"

Nat nodded quickly, handing him the keys, and bolted for the front yard. Sarah followed and put her arm around Nat, talking quietly to her.

"Maybe this wasn't such a good idea," I said to Trip.

He was watching Nat and Sarah. "Maybe," he said, turning to me, "but we're here now, and I don't really want to come back. Let's just get her clothes and ski stuff and the other things she asked for."

"Right," I agreed.

Trip fit the key into the lock and pushed in the front door. I was completely unprepared for what we saw.

The walls were splashed with blood and the sofa cushions dark with it. Numbered Post-its were everywhere—taped to walls, laid on floors. Faint dust from what must have been fingerprint kits covered the flat surfaces of the table and window frames. "Holy shit," Trip murmured. It was like the police had closed the door behind them the night of the murder and never come back. Which, I guess, is pretty much exactly what they'd done.

"Are you going in or what?" Tannis said impatiently. She was too far away to see inside, standing below the step with Sarah, who'd come back over to us.

I couldn't believe the police had given the trailer back to Natalie like this, without any kind of warning. What if she'd walked in first? I swiveled my head, suddenly afraid that she was behind me, able to see this mess, but she stood by the edge of the road, looking out across toward the spot where I'd waited for Moose and Wynn way back when.

Trip turned to me. "Dude."

"I can't believe they didn't tell her," I said quietly.

"Tell her what?" Tannis all but yelled.

"Shhh!"

But Nat had heard. "Tell me what?" She started walking toward us.

"Nat . . . ," Trip began, then faltered.

"Stop," I said. I was so afraid she'd come closer. I was barely keeping my lunch down. She couldn't see this. I felt a white-hot anger at the police. Bob and Lincoln. *Idiots*, Trip had called them. Understatement of the year. How could they? I struggled to keep my voice even. "You don't want to go in, Nat," I said. "It's not . . ." I took a breath. "It's still a crime scene," I said. "Like that night."

She blanched, took a step back like I'd hit her or like the truth had suddenly billowed out from the cracked-open door, pushing her away.

"Why don't you just . . . I don't know . . . take a walk or sit a little? And we'll grab your stuff. . . ." I was trying to sound as confident and in-charge as Trip had when he'd taken the keys from her, but my voice was high and thin, the words bubbling up, on the edge of nonsensical. Natalie looked like she was on another planet. I don't think a word I said after "that night" got through. I felt Tannis beside me, pushing past to look inside.

"Oh. God," she whispered, placing a hand on the door-frame to steady herself.

"You okay?" I asked.

She shook her head.

"Tannis?"

She threw up.

"Oh, Jesus," Trip said.

The four of us stood there watching her retch over the side of the front step. Natalie looked like she might join in.

"Hey." Trip put his hand gingerly on Tannis's back. "Why don't you go out there too? With Nat?"

"Uh-huh." Tannis nodded, stumbling down toward Natalie, who stood, motionless, in the yard.

Sarah came forward. "Let me see."

Trip opened the door and stepped inside, letting Sarah

peer past him. She sucked in her breath as she got her first view of the room.

The walls looked like a much angrier version of the physics closet. Like Jackson Pollock on a rampage. Splatter painting, my mom used to call it. Except this wasn't paint or ketchup or whatever Mr. Ruskovich had used at school. It was dark, much darker than I'd imagined and than they showed on TV. Brown. If you didn't know better, you'd think someone had thrown a bucket of mud against the wall. Reddish mud, like I hear they have out West somewhere.

I followed Trip in, my knee joints feeling loose and saggy. I had to stop and lean against the wall by the door after checking to be sure it was clean.

I couldn't stop looking at it.

The remains of that night.

Of Natalie's dad.

Not really, of course, because his real remains were underground. But this was all that was left up here.

I was having a hard time reining in my thoughts, much less controlling my body.

"What's wrong with the cops?" Sarah's voice was low and furious. "How could they send her back here? Why didn't they clean this up?"

"Exactly," I said weakly.

"I don't think the cops do that," Trip said. "I saw it on TV. The family has to hire, like, a special cleaning service or something. But I can't believe they didn't tell her that. They're obviously bigger morons than we gave them credit for. Let's just grab the stuff and leave," Trip said. "Before she decides to come in. I'll find Nat's room and get her trophies and ski stuff. I'll know what's important."

"I'll come with you and grab her clothes," Sarah said.

"So I guess I'll . . ." What? Vomit? Leave? I was pretty sure neither was the right answer but I couldn't come up with much else.

"Why don't you find the other stuff Nat asked for?" Trip suggested. "Her mom's vase, the boxes in her dad's room, the picture she wants. Just see if there's anything else . . ." He surveyed the living room, finally realizing how Nat had lived. And that a drug den wasn't the type of place where you generally found a lot of memorabilia. "I don't know. Just look for, like, anything important."

I scanned the living room quickly after they walked away, but it was pretty barren. Chairs, a few tables, a TV stand. I looked at the sofa and the blood-sprayed wall again, thinking about Galen Riddock. Trying to picture him there, pointing a gun. It was hard to imagine.

I wandered over to the window, paused to watch Nat and Tannis. They'd moved over to the shed by the woods. Natalie was fiddling with the lock, and Tannis was kind of leaning against the little building. On the road a car slid into view, and I felt an electric jolt, immediately recognizing it.

It had been cruising slowly but sped up as it drew abreast of Trip's car.

Moose.

What the fuck was he doing up here?

There was no one to see. No business to conduct.

He'd been here that night, had told me so himself. Holy crap. We'd gone to question Galen, but what about Moose?

I tried picturing him shooting Mr. Cleary—fidgety, scrawny Moose. I couldn't do it. Plus, I knew the cops had already grilled him and let him go.

Down the hall Trip and Sarah were opening and closing drawers. I pulled myself away from the window, remembering that I was supposed to be doing . . . something.

I peeked into the dingy kitchen, then a small bathroom where Nat would have been going that night, just as she realized something was wrong. I saw Trip and Sarah working in Nat's tidy little space. Then I found her dad's room.

Clothes were in heaps on the floor, a lot of them visibly dirty. Dresser drawers hung open; the bed was unmade, with sheets that looked badly in need of washing. I didn't want to think about that.

Some of the mess in the room might have been from the police—their little notes and numbers and fingerprint dust were everywhere—but I guessed most of it was probably just the way Nat's dad had lived.

I sifted through some stuff on the nightstand, then

opened the drawer. There was a picture of Natalie in there. I picked it up, realizing my mistake as soon as I saw the clothes. Not Natalie, just someone who looked nearly identical. Her mom. It had to be. She was standing beside a muscle car, had her hand on the hood, was laughing into the camera. She was little like Nat, petite but not fragile-looking. She looked sweet. Not like someone who'd abandon her daughter. Don't judge a book by its cover, I guess.

I slipped it into my backpack and opened the closet. More clothes on the floor, empty food cartons. There was a cardboard box toward the back. The police had dusted and opened it, I saw. I lifted the flaps and realized what the cops must have—this hadn't been touched in at least ten years. It had nothing to do with the crime but held just the things Natalie would probably want to keep. Letters from her dad to her mom. Pictures of their wedding.

I checked the rest of the room but figured Nat wouldn't want any of the trash or filth or the random pair of women's underwear I found. I tossed the photo of her mom into the box, along with another of the three of them at Christmas that Nat had asked for. I didn't see the crystal vase she wanted anywhere, and I could feel my lunch threatening again, so I hauled everything out and joined the girls on the front lawn, waiting for Trip and Sarah to finish.

CHAPTER 17

WE LOADED THE BOX AND TWO TRASH BAGS FULL OF NATALIE'S stuff into the trunk of Trip's car and drove to Lu's town house at the mountain.

Trip carried the box and I grabbed the bags when we got there, following the girls in. There weren't a lot of people in town who could afford to live in the complex right at the base. Mostly weekenders owned the homes there, using them only when the snow fell, but Lu's family had some kind of fishing company back in Sweden they'd run for generations. She was a shareholder or partner or something, which gave her more than enough money to buy pretty much whatever she wanted in Buford. She was also one of the hardest-working and nicest people in town. It hadn't surprised anyone when she'd insisted on taking Nat in, not because Nat was the team's star skier but because Lu had known Nat since she was six, and it was just the kind of thing she'd do. Lu had driven to the police station as soon as she'd heard about Mr. Cleary, and hadn't left until they'd turned Natalie over to her.

Inside, it was bright and warm, all the lights in the living room on and Lu tucked into a corner of the sofa with a book. She stood when she saw us.

"Hey, hot stuff," Trip said. He could get away with that, having skied for Lu until he was twelve.

"Hey, yourself," Lu answered, walking immediately to Natalie. "You okay?"

Nat nodded and then burst into tears.

"Shhh," Lu soothed, enveloping Nat in a hug. She stroked Nat's back, raising her eyebrows questioningly at us.

Trip shook his head solemnly. Lu nodded and led Natalie to the sofa, folded her into the corner.

"Stay here, hon," she said. "Trip and . . ." She looked at me.

"Riley," I supplied.

She nodded. "Let me show you where to put Natalie's things. If one of you girls wants to make her some tea, it's in the cupboard over the stove," she told Tannis and Sarah.

We followed Lu up a flight of soft carpeted stairs while Tannis headed for the small kitchen and Sarah took a spot beside Natalie.

"What happened?" Lu asked once we were in the room where Natalie was staying. It was just as clean as her room at the trailer, but soft and new and inviting. I was glad Natalie had somewhere like this. It felt safe and about a million miles removed from where we'd just been.

"The police hadn't cleaned up anything," Trip said.

Lu's eyes went wide. "No."

Trip nodded.

"That doesn't sound like Bob Willets," she said. "He's got more sense than that."

"I'd have thought so too," I agreed. "I don't know who Nat actually talked to."

"Bureaucratic oversight?" Lu asked.

"Maybe."

"Well, it's a pretty damn huge one." Lu set her mouth in a grim line. "Okay. Let's get her mind off it."

We played Yahtzee and Scrabble for hours. Lu kicked everyone's butts. Tannis came in last because she was stuck with a tray full of *E*s, at least according to her. Lu made us all hot chocolate, and by then Natalie looked a lot more relaxed.

So of course Tannis had to ask, "Did being there—back home—jog your memory at all, Nat?"

Nat blanched, and I saw her hand tremble. Lu frowned at Tannis, but she was oblivious.

"I don't know," Nat said softly. "I keep trying to remember stuff . . . but there's just . . ." She shook her head. "Nothing. Obviously *someone* was there. But I don't know who."

"It's probably good you don't," Sarah said.

"What do you mean?"

"Well, if you had come out . . ."

"Oh!" Nat clapped a hand to her mouth. "You mean I might have . . ."

Sarah nodded. "Been a victim."

"God," Natalie said. "I didn't even think of that."

"Do you think she's in any danger?" Tannis asked.

"What kind of danger?" Lu said.

"Well, everyone knows now that she was there. What if the killer thinks she knows something . . ."

"I think you've been watching too much TV, Tannis," I said.

Trip cocked his head. "I don't know. I mean, I think if someone were after her, she'd already know it, don't you?"

"Yes," Lu said firmly. "I think that's true. Natalie's perfectly safe. And will continue to be."

We all nodded, and I couldn't help feeling that, regardless of a killer lurking in Buford, Lu was right. Nat Cleary was probably safer now than she'd ever been before.

CHAPTER 18

I WAITED UNTIL THE END OF PHYSICS ON WEDNESDAY TO TALK to Mr. Ruskovich. The closet was still firmly locked, though Mr. Ruskovich had said he was considering reopening it, if we felt up to it. Everyone had nodded and Matty added an enthusiastic, "Definitely!" Our physics lessons over the past week had been uncharacteristically boring. Matty and Chuck practically ran out of the room each day when the bell rang. I hadn't asked Matty about Tannis again, and he hadn't asked me about the SATs—an unspoken truce. I almost wished he *would* ask so I could tell him I'd finally registered, though I still felt guilty enough about it that I hadn't even confessed to my mom. I was hoping she wouldn't notice.

Sarah lingered after the others had gone, shooting me a questioning look before finally gliding out the door.

"Yes, Mr. Larkin?" Mr. Ruskovich asked as soon as we were alone. He'd been shuffling papers, clearly aware that I was stalling. He put them aside now, leaning on his desk. "What can I do for you?"

I was nervous about asking him, but I couldn't stop wondering about the binoculars. Trip, Tannis, and Sarah were all more worried about who'd killed Nat's dad. It's not that I wasn't, but to me the binoculars felt bigger. Definitely more personal. I'd been thinking about them more and more, feeling them like a constant thrumming pulse in my drawer. My very own telltale heart. It occurred to me that maybe Mr. Ruskovich could help. Maybe there was a science behind them and what they did. Maybe he could tell me if what I saw really was—could be—my future.

"Natalie Cleary said something I wanted to ask you about. In confidence," I added.

"Of course."

"She thinks she saw her dad's murder before it happened."

Mr. Ruskovich eyebrows shot up. "A premonition?"

"Or a vision." I hesitated, dying to tell him the whole story. I trusted Mr. Ruskovich. He was my favorite teacher. But I didn't really *know* him. And what if he wanted to *see* the binoculars?

"So your question is . . ."

"Whether that's possible," I said, deciding to play it safe. "Is there a scientific basis for seeing the future?"

Mr. Ruskovich frowned. "I'm not sure I can tell you that, Riley."

"Oh."

He read my disappointment. "You thought I'd have a better answer."

I nodded. "Last year when we were talking about time machines and how matter moves . . ." I shrugged. "I guess they're not really related."

"Ahhh, I see where you're going with it." Mr. Ruskovich nodded. "That's reasonable. Well, as far as science knows today, time travel is impossible. Matter cannot travel through the space-time continuum. But can we somehow have knowledge of future events? That's a different discussion, and yes, I'd say it's possible."

"How?"

"'Why?' is probably the better question," he corrected. "Some things *can* move through the space-time continuum."

"Like?"

"Energy," Mr. Ruskovich said immediately. "And I suppose it's possible that energy from the future could travel through time."

"Could you make a device that made that happen?"

He raised his eyebrows. "Channeled that energy?"

I nodded.

Mr. Ruskovich thought about it, then shook his head slowly. "I suppose so," he said, "but I can't really imagine how.

It seems very far-fetched." He cocked his head. "Natalie Cleary told you she'd seen her dad's murder in some kind of device?"

"No," I said, backpedaling quickly. "Not that. I was just thinking out loud. About premonitions and the science behind it and whether, you know, there were any practical applications or . . . anything." I finished lamely.

"Uh-huh." Mr. Ruskovich checked the clock, then stood, collecting his papers. "I don't know about practical applications, but I think the lesson science fiction writers have been teaching us for generations is that knowing the future is a dangerous thing." He looked at me. "Wouldn't you agree?"

"Yeah," I said, thinking that not many good things had happened since we'd looked. "I guess I would."

I wasn't two steps out the door before Sarah fell into step beside me. I nearly jumped out of my skin. "Why'd you ask him about that?" she said.

I felt my face turning red. I should have known by the way she'd watched me that she'd known I was up to something. I never felt like I could put anything past her. "It's been bugging me," I said, not looking at her. Hoping I sounded nonchalant. Knowing I didn't.

"But we went back," she pursued. "And you guys didn't see anything."

"Uh-huh."

Sarah stopped, grabbing my arm so I'd have to stop too.

I felt her hand, warm on my biceps, and resisted the urge to flex. I gazed down at her, so close I could see faint freckles across her nose. "Riley."

"Sarah."

She studied me an extra second. "You saw something the other night, didn't you?"

It was barely a question, and I thought about lying but could tell she already knew. Her eyes were so intense, like she could read every blink, every muscle twitch. I nodded.

"I thought so," she said. "That's why I—"

Suddenly her phone interrupted, blaring. *Sexy and I Know It.* Trip. He'd programmed it himself. She held up a finger.

"Hey," she said into it. "I'm on my way." I picked at a loose string on my backpack, trying not to listen to the rest of her conversation but perfectly able to fill in Trip's side. I watched her face soften and smile, and felt a stab of completely irrational jealousy. Then her eyes flicked to me. "Hang on," she told the phone, pulling it away from her ear. "Nat wanted to know if you took anything out of her things from the trailer."

"Of course not."

"Where's the vase? The crystal one that was her mom's?"

"It wasn't there," I told Sarah. "I looked on the living room shelf where Nat said it would be. And around the rest of the house . . ." Until I felt like I might puke. "Nada," I finished.

She conveyed that to Trip. After she hung up, Sarah told me, "Nat said it should have been there."

"Maybe her dad gave it away." *Pawned it*, was really what I was thinking.

"No. Nat remembers seeing it that night when she got home from the Dash party."

"Maybe the cops have it."

Sarah shook her head. "John checked with his dad, and they don't."

We looked at each other, and finally I asked, "So what does that mean?"

"Exactly what you think," Sarah said. "That either it's there and you didn't see it . . ."

"Or someone took it between when Nat got home that night and when we were there," I concluded.

The phone rang again. Trip. "I'm coming!" she said, not waiting for a response from him before hanging up. "Sorry," Sarah said. "I told him I'd meet him before his math test. He needs help."

"True, dat," I agreed.

She snorted. "Oh my God, you are so white. Listen," she said, her voice turning serious, "I want to talk to you about them."

"Nat and Trip?"

"No. The binoculars," she said impatiently. "Can you come over later?"

"Tonight?"

"Well, that would be most convenient," she said. "But if you're booked, maybe next week or a month from now . . ."

"No, tonight's fine. When?"

"I have to go to the Hull with Trip. Can I text you when I'm home?"

I nodded mutely.

"Great. Thanks." She put her hand back on my arm and squeezed gently before walking off. A few steps away, Sarah turned back. "And, Ri?"

Her voice was husky, and I could still feel the warmth and tingle where her hand had been. "Yeah?"

"Bring them with you. The binoculars," she added. "Not Nat and Trip." Then she jogged away, down the hall.

CHAPTER 19

I SAT IN THE LIVING ROOM, WILLING HER TO TEXT ME. IT WAS past eight, and I'd been there for over an hour, fiddling with the binoculars, wanting badly to look into them again. Just in case I'd see what I did that first time. Get to feel her bare skin.

I'm sure it seems pathetic, my puppy-dog crush on my best friend's girl.

The thing was, she wasn't his girlfriend when it started, sometime between Kelly Lipman's party and when Trip asked her out last year.

At first she was just this girl I was kind of amazed by. She'd smile at me in the hall sometimes, and I'd smile too, feeling a twelve-year-old's embarrassment. I wanted to talk to her but had no idea what to say. By ninth grade most of the girls had started wearing makeup, crimson lips and heavy-ringed eyes, but not Sarah. Her face stayed fresh, dark eyes striking against that powdery skin. I realized sometime that year that I liked her, but I was still so consumed with the awfulness of the previous twelve months—my dad dying, shit with my mom, Trip and me hanging out less and less—that doing something about it was the last thing on my mind. It took till the start of junior year for me to finally work up the nerve to ask her out.

"I've been thinking about that stupid dance next weekend," I told Trip one day. We were walking into town ten days before homecoming.

Trip and I had started hanging out again that summer, as randomly as we'd stopped. One June day he'd just showed up at my house like we hadn't spent the past two years barely speaking. I'd gotten used to it by then—us not being friends—chalking it up to some combination of sports and cool kids who were a lot more fun than the mopey kid with the dead dad. Even if that kid used to be like a brother to him.

I was distant with Trip at first. Not putting too much faith in whether he'd come back the next day or show up when we had plans. But for the most part he did, and as that summer wore on, I remembered what I'd always liked about him, what I'd missed. It felt like a piece of me had come back.

A couple times I thought of asking him about it. Why it

was okay to hang out with me now. But why bother? What was the point in acting like a jealous needy girlfriend? Trip was just Trip. Capricious, fearless, self-centered, fun, charismatic, loyal when he wanted to be. Instinctively I knew I either took him as is or not at all. He wasn't going to change for Riley Larkin.

"Yeah, I've been thinking about that dance too," Trip said, kicking a pebble that skittered into the gutter. We were going to the library to work on a research project for history. "You know who I think I'm gonna ask?"

"Who?"

"Sarah McKenzie."

And just like that I lost my chance. Unbelievable. I stared at him, trying to figure out how to fix it. What could I say? *She's mine? I thought of it first?* Ridiculous.

"How about you?" Trip asked. "What are you thinking?"

I'm thinking how much I wish we hadn't started this conversation. And that I'd had the guts to ask her out last week or the week before or two years ago when I realized how into her I was. I'm thinking how irritating it is that you always one-up me like this. Even when you're not trying and probably don't mean to.

"I'm thinking I'm going to skip it," I told him. "It'll probably be lame anyhow."

"Yeah," Trip agreed.

And the rest, as they say, is history. Trip went with her, I stayed home, and from then on I got to watch the two of them—my sometimes best friend and the girl I'd been crushing on—fall in love. Un-fucking-believable.

Around nine I finally heard from Sarah. *Home*, she texted. *Sorry it's so late.*

No prob, I wrote back right away. *Want to talk?*

Yes, can u come over?

Be there 15 min. It'd be more like twenty-five, I thought, pulling on my hat and gloves and steering my bike out to the road. But if I pedaled hard, I might make it sooner.

The air whipping past was bitter, but at least I wouldn't be a disgusting sweatball by the time I got there.

I made it in just over twenty minutes, pausing to catch my breath and tame my hair before ringing the bell, my inner fourteen-year-old crowing, *Alone with Sarah! Just her and me!*

The door opened, and Sarah smiled, making me feel every bit like a fourteen-year-old who had no idea what to say or do with girls, instead of the . . . well, seventeen-year-old who had no idea what to do with girls. She ushered me in, glancing up and down the block.

"Where's your car?"

"Right there." I pointed to my mountain bike lying in the shadows beside her house.

"You *biked* here?" She shook her head. "Oh God, Riley. I'm such an idiot. I'm sorry. I didn't even stop to think—"

"Sarah," I stopped her. She looked so upset that I felt

bad. "It's no big deal. Really. It's what? Two miles? This is Vermont; we're outdoorsy here."

Sarah smiled gratefully, then closed us into the small, warm living room. I took in the white walls hung with old posters and tie-dyed tapestries, the mismatched sofas and blankets, and scattered everywhere—plants. Lots of them, their greenness surprising after weeks of seeing only the browns of dead grass and mud. The walls between the plants were lined with books, and boxes of more books were piled haphazardly beside half-filled shelves, like Sarah's parents were still unpacking.

"You guys going somewhere?" I asked.

"Oy," she said, exasperated. "The boxes. Always the boxes."

"Your house is really nice," I told her.

"You've never been here?" I shook my head. "Well, thanks," Sarah said. "It's not fancy, but it's home."

"It feels like one," I said. "That's a compliment. It's really comfortable and . . . nice."

She gave me a half smile. "That's very sweet." Sarah took my coat and hung it on a hook by the door, her slippers scuffing across the wood floor as she walked.

I wandered over to a table where a sculpture of a windmill sat. It was made out of what looked like old bicycle parts and an erector set. There was a single bare lightbulb beside it.

"What's this?" I asked.

Sarah came over and fitted something onto the arms of the sculpture, and it started to spin. After a few seconds the bulb began glowing with a soft red light.

"Whoa!" I studied the thing, realizing they were magnets she'd put on and that there were wires snaking from the center of the sculpture to the bulb, making it a mini-generator. "That's really cool. Where'd you get it?"

"My mom made it," Sarah said.

"Really?"

Sarah smiled. "Her hobby. Tinkering, she calls it."

She motioned me toward the sofa. I gave the machine another glance, then sat, trying to look at ease, though I felt anything but relaxed. It was quiet in the house, like it really was just me and Sarah.

"So, um, where are your parents?" I asked.

"My dad's down in his office in the basement," she said. "And my mom's with the jerk she ran off with, somewhere in Florida."

"Oh . . . uh . . ." I racked my brains, trying to think if I'd known that. How could I not have? I smiled sheepishly. "Open mouth, insert foot. Sorry."

She smiled back, mostly clearing the cloud that'd passed over her face. "No worries, Ri."

She sat and leaned forward, getting right down to business. "Why didn't you tell us the truth?"

I wasn't surprised—Sarah was a pretty direct girl, and she'd told me she wanted to talk about the binoculars. But I wasn't quite ready. "How did you know?" I stalled.

"I can usually tell when you're hiding something." She smiled. "Don't take this the wrong way, Riley, but you're not a very good liar." She added, "That's a compliment."

It didn't feel like one. My face burned. I wondered how much else she'd figured out. She was still waiting, delicate hands dangling between the worn parts of her jeans.

"Partly it was Tannis," I said. "She was really twisted about what she saw, thinking the kids meant she'd never race."

Sarah nodded. "She lost it with me one day too." She paused, then added, "That hit close to home for you, didn't it? The things Tannis was upset about . . . being stuck here?"

I raised an eyebrow. "I didn't realize we'd be psychoanalyzing me tonight."

"Sorry." She smiled. "My dad's a shrink. Can you tell?"

"Well, it explains your deliberate pauses and penetrating stares," I said. "Anyway, when Trip didn't see anything, Tannis was so . . ."

"Relieved?"

I nodded. "And if I'd told her I *did* see something . . ."

"She'd keep believing that what she saw was her future," Sarah finished.

"I didn't see any benefit to that."

"That was really thoughtful of you," she observed. "I didn't know you had such a soft spot for Tannis."

"I don't. But seeing her cry was like . . . snow in July or a plague of locusts—"

"Signs of the apocalypse?"

"Right. I didn't really want to deal with that."

Sarah nodded. "But you *did* see something?"

"Yes."

"What?"

Which of course was the *real* reason I hadn't said anything. "I can't tell you." Seeing her disappointment, I added, "It's not you, Sarah. It's just that it involves other people." It was my mom's and Trip's dad's secret. And Trip's, even though he didn't know it. "I'm sorry."

She was trying to figure it out—I could tell in how she studied me. But there was no way she'd guess this one. "Any of us?" she probed.

"Not really."

"Is it something bad?"

I thought about that scene, my mom with Trip's dad, her droopy eye and what I knew that meant about her sickness. But she'd still been in our house, which looked nicer than it ever had before. "Good and bad," I answered.

"Do you think it's the future?" she asked quietly.

"I have no idea," I said. "I mean, how could that even be possible?"

She didn't answer, didn't ask me about the stuff Mr. Ruskovich had said. Instead she rubbed her forehead, anxious. "I need to look into the binoculars, Riley," she said finally.

"What?" I hadn't expected that. "Why?"

"The same reason you did. So I'll know if it's real that you really saw things."

There it was again. "You," not "we."

"I just told you I did," I said, wondering what she'd seen and why she needed to hide it.

"Would you have believed Trip if he'd looked and seen something? Would that have been enough for you?"

"I'm not sure. I think so," I lied.

"You didn't believe him when he said there was nothing," she pointed out.

"Yeah, but—"

"I think there are just some things you have to see for yourself," she said. "Right?"

"Maybe." She was right, of course. But I didn't want her to look again. I wasn't sure why. Mr. Ruskovich's warning, maybe.

"Where are they?" she asked softly.

"In my bag." She looked at me expectantly. I unzipped it but didn't take them out.

"Sarah," I said. "I have to tell you something."

She looked at me warily, and I took a deep breath. "I

know you looked before. I saw you. Outside the cave that first night."

Her eyes widened. "Why didn't you say anything?"

"It seemed like you wanted to keep it secret." I watched her carefully. Was it wrong for me to hope that her vision had been like mine? About her and me? Because that was what I was hoping. But I couldn't tell anything; her eyes gave nothing away. "I guess I wanted to respect that," I finished.

She didn't say anything right away, so I asked what I really wanted to know. "What did you see?"

CHAPTER 20

FOR A WHILE SARAH SAID NOTHING. I TRIED TO READ HER BODY language like she seemed able to read mine. She stood, walked a few steps, hands shoved into jeans pockets, which made her shoulders hunch together. She looked tiny, like a little wisp. If you saw her quickly, you might mistake her for a child, ten or twelve. Until you saw her face.

"I'm with someone," she finally said, "a guy." She looked back at me just long enough for me to see something in her eyes, like she was afraid to say it.

"Me?" I asked softly.

"You?" She raised her eyebrows. Her voice was amused and sad together when she said, "No, it isn't you, Riley."

I felt like a total idiot. "I just thought . . . the way you were saying it . . ." Oh God, could the floor swallow me up, please?

Mercifully, she continued. "I've never seen him before. We're in a park, walking. There's a dog with us. We're holding hands. I don't know the park or the dog, either. The guy is older." She paused. "Maybe I am too."

How much older? I wanted to ask. *Before or after my vision, when we're in bed together?* Suddenly I didn't want to hear any more.

"Even weirder . . . ," she said, looking toward the window wistfully, "I'm in love with him. I don't know how I know that, but I do."

Something hot and sharp was in my chest. *Jesus, I'm jealous. Of a guy Sarah doesn't know, who might not even exist.*

"I feel like he's my . . . soul mate?" she said, mostly to herself. "It's the strangest feeling." She gave me that half-sad smile again. "The connection I feel to this guy. And now I keep wondering, what if I never meet him?"

I tried to think of something funny to say to break the mood, but I didn't feel funny. This felt wrong and bad and not at all the way I wanted it to.

She looked down at her hands. "The worst part—" She stopped.

"What?" I prompted.

She shook her head.

"Whatever it is, Sarah, it's between us."

She glanced up with just her eyes, head still bowed, then sighed and looked back at her hands. "The worst part is what it's done to how I feel about Trip. I used to think I loved him. Now I know I don't."

And—shitty, awful, back-stabbing friend that I am—I felt happy. *She doesn't love him.*

"So I want to look again," she said more firmly. "I need to know. If I don't see anything, maybe I can just forget about what I saw, you know? Maybe I can believe that the binoculars are nothing. I can believe that they didn't predict what would happen to Nat's dad. Or you. Or me."

"And what if you see something?" I said. "Wouldn't you rather just not know?"

"No," she said immediately. "Just like you wouldn't."

I couldn't argue with that.

Sarah came back to the sofa, where I still held the box. She reached over and took it from me, her skin softly brushing mine. She unlatched the case, took out the binoculars, and hesitated only a second before bringing them firmly, surely to her eyes. I watched it all, powerless. Her body suddenly got still, shoulders stiff, knuckles turning white.

I knew she was seeing something, and my nerves thrummed with anxiety.

"Sarah," I called gently. She didn't answer at first, but then slowly she brought the binoculars away. I was scared by how she looked. Probably how I'd looked after the things I'd seen. Like she knew something much bigger than anyone should.

"Well, now I know," she said dully.

"Did you see something? The same thing?" I pressed when she nodded, "That . . . guy?" It burned to say it.

"No. I was older," Sarah said. "Much older. I don't know how I know that . . ." She trailed off.

I waited. "And?" I prompted. "What did you see?"

"Houses. Cars. All of them different. Newer than anything around today," she said thinly. "I'm looking out a window at them, at life out there, passing by. And I'm thinking." She paused, swallowed, searched out my eyes. "I'm thinking something good. Happy. But also sad."

"Bittersweet?"

"Yeah," she said. "And I feel tired."

I saw tears welling in her eyes.

"Sarah?" I reached over, gently touched her arm. "What?"

She shook her head. "Nothing. Oh my God. Just . . ." She put her hands to her face, blotting the tears, and breathed in deeply. Swallowing like she could push away the stuff she was feeling. "I could see my hands," she said finally. "I guess that's how I know I'm old. They're all veiny and frail." She looked at her smooth, delicate hands, turning them wonderingly. "I'm old in it, Riley. Really old. And I feel . . ." She hitched a breath, struggling for control. "Lonely."

I reached for her, folded her into my arms, and she let me. I felt the shiver of her slight body, hesitated for a second, then put my hand on the back of her head. The coarseness of her hair was just like I remembered it from the binoculars.

We stayed like that for a minute. There were so many things running through me with her this close—excitement, tenderness, and worry. I was intensely conscious of where every part of her touched me, her legs pressing against my thigh, her head on my chest, breast inches from my arm. Maybe Sarah felt it, because she pulled back a little, looking up at me. Her face was serious.

I thought she was going to tell me more about what she'd seen, but instead she said, "You like me, don't you, Riley?"

"Sure," I said. I tried to drag my eyes away, my heart racing. "Of course."

"No," Sarah persisted. "Not like 'we're buddies.'" She held my gaze, the sound of her voice, low and raspy, raising goose bumps on my arms. "Like a boy likes a girl."

Holy crap. I could barely think, my eyes drawn to her full lips, parted and moist. I shivered, knowing she already knew the answer. "Yes," I answered thickly.

"For a long time?" she whispered.

I nodded, barely, and then—I couldn't help it—I kissed her. I don't even remember leaning in, but I must have, because our lips brushed against each other softly, the feel and taste of her making me dizzy. I pressed harder, felt her teeth, her tongue. My hand was in her hair, tangling about those thick coarse strands. Her breath came short and fast, her hands on my chest. And then she pushed away, eyes wide, gasping,

"My dad."

Dimly I heard the clomp of footsteps, my sluggish brain processing what she'd said. And what I'd done. "Oh, shit." I was breathing hard, drunk with how it had felt to touch her. "I'm sorry." I moved to the far side of the couch, not trusting myself to be any closer, trying to smooth out my clothes and compose myself.

She looked down. "Don't be," she mumbled, straightening her shirt, brushing at her face. "It's not your fault."

Her father pushed through the door then, looking as flustered to see us as we were him.

"Oh!" His gaze shifted from Sarah to me and then back. "I didn't know you had a friend over."

"This is Riley," she said, gesturing to me. "From my physics class. Riley, this is my dad, Dr. McKenzie."

I stood, holding the binoculars case—the first thing I could grab—in front of me as I crossed to shake hands with him. "Nice to meet you, sir," I said, wondering if anyone in the history of man had ever been as embarrassed as I was right then.

His hand was dry and papery, especially compared to my hot, sweaty one. "Jim. You can call me Jim," he said, oblivious to my flaming embarrassment.

"Uh, okay. Thanks. Jim."

Sarah looked ready to burst out laughing, not oblivious

at all. Which, despite my mortification, was a nice change from how she'd looked after the binoculars. "You done working for the night, Dad?"

He nodded absently, and I noticed his rumpled shirt and messy hair. Maybe he'd been making out with someone too. *Ugh, why does my brain think stuff like that?* "What are you two doing?" he asked. "Studying?"

"Yup," she said breezily while I nodded along.

"Good, good," he said. "Okay, well I'm off to bed. Don't stay up too late," he told Sarah, glancing at me. "School night and all."

"I was just going," I said, starting to collect my things as he climbed the stairs. "Nice to meet you."

"You too," he said, waving without turning around.

I could feel Sarah watching me from the couch, but I didn't dare look at her as I stuffed the binoculars and case into the backpack. Finally, when I couldn't avoid it, I met her eyes. "Well," I said.

"Well," she said back, smiling.

"This is awkward."

She nodded. "We shouldn't have done that."

"Right." I tried to read her face to figure out what she was feeling, but I was no good at that. So I asked, "What do we do now?"

Her eyes sharpened like a hundred thoughts were running through her head. "I think we pretend nothing happened," she said finally. "I don't think we want to tell anyone about the binoculars. Like you said, how could that help?"

I nodded.

"And I definitely don't think we want to tell them about . . . you know . . . the other." She blushed, which was unbelievably cute.

"Right."

"So . . . we just forget about it."

"Okay," I said, knowing there was no way in hell I could forget it. I was already replaying it and would probably keep it on repeat all week. And the way she'd kissed me back, her breathing shallow, I doubt she'd forget it either. Which made me feel like a bit of a studmuffin, as Trip liked to call himself.

I pedaled home, not thinking about the future. Not feeling the cold or the burn in my muscles or even the crushing guilt that should have come with making out with my best friend's girl.

CHAPTER 21

THE GUILT CAME THE NEXT MORNING. WHEN TRIP PICKED ME UP.

"I tried calling you last night," he said. "Where were you?"

"What're you, my mother?" I said, but my heart was beating triple time. Did he *know*? I hadn't even checked my phone. I pulled it out now. Four messages from Trip. Jesus, what was wrong with me? "Sorry, man," I fumbled. "Is everything okay?"

"Yeah," he said shortly. "I just wanted to tell you something. No big."

"What?"

"Why don't you listen to the messages and find out? Unless you're too busy."

"Come off it, Trip." I remembered him telling me once that the best defense is a good offense. "You're acting like a jilted girlfriend." I winced. Poor choice of words.

"'Jilted?'" Trip said. "Were you playing Scrabble at the nursing home last night?"

"You got me." I clicked through the prompts on my phone, held it to my ear, and felt my eyes go wide. "Holy shit," I said. "They arrested Galen?"

"Sort of," he said.

He was going to make me work for it, I realized. He really did act like a girl sometimes. "What does that mean? What happened?"

"Nat found her vase."

"At Galen's?"

He shook his head. "She and John Peters were in town yesterday, walking to the library, and there it was, sitting right in Morris Headley's window at the antiques shop."

"Holy shit," I said again. "What did Galen have to do with it?"

"They went in," Trip continued, "and asked Morris where he got it. Which of course he couldn't remember because he's half-senile and doesn't remember his name most days of the week."

I nodded. During high season Bob Willets had gotten into the habit of dropping in on Morris in the mornings, just to make sure he hadn't opened the shop wearing only his boxer shorts, like he had one day last summer, scaring a busload of Red Hat ladies half to death.

"Nat said he spent, like, an hour flipping through papers, finally coming up with the ticket."

"And Galen was the one who'd brought it in," I guessed.

"Exactly."

It was all the talk that morning at school. It had been scandalous that Nat's dad had been murdered, doubly so when she'd been held for questioning. And now one of her classmates had been hauled in? OMG, as the cheerleaders might—and did—say. The hallways were buzzing. I bumped into John Peters on my way to physics, so I heard the biggest piece of news first.

"My dad said they released Galen," he told me, phone still in hand.

"What? Why?" I said.

"He swears he didn't take it from Natalie's house. Or give it to Morris Headley."

"But you were there with Natalie," I said. "You saw the ticket, right?"

"I did. And it was definitely his name on there." John nodded. "But I guess they did a handwriting sample and compared it to the ticket and some other, older things Galen had signed. It didn't match."

"So someone forged it?" I said. I was having a hard time following this. Galen was at the house, not at the house. Took the vase, didn't take the vase. My head was spinning.

"Seems that way," John said.

* * *

Mr. Ruskovich called me up to his desk when I walked in. I didn't even hear him at first; I was still trying to unravel the things with Galen Riddock.

"I'm planning to reopen our unit on forensics today," he said quietly. "I've already spoken to Sarah McKenzie but wanted to double-check with you also, since I know you're close to Natalie. We can always come back to this unit later in the year." He watched me carefully, adding, "There's no shame in being affected by what's happened."

I nodded. "I know," I told him. "I'm okay with it, though. Really. It's an interesting lesson."

Which it was, but sitting at my desk as he explained the formula for determining the angle of impact felt surreal. I knew that when he finished, he'd walk across the room and open that door. I kept picturing him doing it and finding myself suddenly back in the Clearys' living room, like the physics classroom was somehow a portal to that nightmare.

Mr. Ruskovich split us into teams of two, pairing Matty with Chuck and me with Sarah. Maybe he thought that was a good idea, us both being friends with Nat. But it was really, really awkward. I'd barely been able to look at her today, dreading our shared class as much as I couldn't wait for it. And now she slid into the desk beside mine, pulling it close enough for us to both see the notebook. I felt her in my space like she was coated with something radioactive.

Sarah stared at our notes, biting her lip nervously. She glanced at me, then quickly back down, her cheeks flushed pink. "Let's use this one," she said, pointing to the length and width measurements of the first of our three splatters, labeled *D*. "One of them is a whole number, so it'll be the easiest."

"Okay," I said, trying to focus but really more concerned with making sure I didn't accidentally touch her. Mr. Ruskovich sauntered across the room toward the closet. I watched as he plucked the key and inserted it into the knob. Sarah tensed beside me as the door clicked open.

Seeing it again was a huge relief, because the truth was that it didn't look much like the real thing at all. The drops on a blank white sheet were a world away from seeing them in your friend's house where you'd once met her dad in pretty much the same spot where he'd been killed.

"How you doing?" I asked Sarah softly. She met my eyes, and I tried to ignore the connection between us, so strong it felt almost visible.

"Okay," she whispered. "It's weird. But I think we can do this. Right?"

I nodded with much more confidence than I felt. "Yeah," I said, not sure if we were talking about physics or us or both. "We'll concentrate on the equations. It's just math."

We were about halfway through the first problem when Chuck and Matty stood to start mapping their calculations. I knew they'd get in there before us, which was fine, except for Matty's smug grin and the *L* he flashed me before they went in.

Mr. Ruskovich was having us work with six splatters—three for them and three for us—and we were taking turns mapping them. The only problem, as Mr. Ruskovich explained, was that by the end we'd be maneuvering around lengths of string taped across the closet, like the laser beams you see in heist movies when the thief has to make off with a priceless statue.

"And it's critical you don't touch or move any of them," he stressed. "Precision is key. Your convergence point needs to be as exact as possible, because you'll also use it and the angles you've figured out to determine the height of the suspect. You don't want to imprison the wrong person because you contaminated the crime scene."

Pretty unlikely here, since Mr. Ruskovich had built in a wide margin of error, with suspect heights ranging from the extremely petite four-foot-tall Miss Scarlet to the gargantuan Mr. Green at ten feet.

"What is he, the Jolly Green Giant?" Chuck had asked.

"Or the best new prospect for the Celts," Mr. Ruskovich suggested.

"They need it," Matty muttered.

We'd started on the third problem by the time Matty and Chuck returned to their seats. Sarah was flying through the equations.

"I didn't know you had such skills," I told her.

"Oh I got skills, boy." She smiled, and I flushed, reading double entendres into everything she said. "It's actually really cool if you can forget about . . . you know, the other stuff."

By the time we got into the closet with our string and tape and protractor, I'd done a passable job of forgetting the real-life crime scene. We taped one end of string to splatter *D*, and Sarah used the protractor to measure the angle, directing me on how to position the other end. "A little higher, higher, lower." When she was satisfied we'd gotten it just right, I taped the string to the far wall. Sarah double-checked the angle, pronounced it good, and we started on the next, me doing the protractor work this time, both of us careful not to disturb anything as we taped our second string. It met up with our first one and the ones Matty and Chuck had done at nearly the exact same location. We stood back and surveyed the scene.

"Cool," Sarah said, eyes gleaming.

She took a quick measurement of the height of the probable point of impact. "We should be able to figure out who it is already." Sarah slid into her seat and worked through some inscrutable set of formulas while I started on splatter *F*, our final one. After a few minutes she nodded. "Matty was right. It's Professor Plum."

I raised my eyebrows. "How can you be sure?"

"Look at the angle of impact of the two we've already

done, the point where it happened, and think about the direction of spatter and the weapons. It couldn't have been someone as short or tall as any of the others."

I looked at the scrawls on her notepad. "Uh . . . okay." I had no idea how she'd figured that out so quickly. I'd always known Sarah was smart. It was part of what made her so amazing and her thing with Trip so confounding. I watched her toying with the numbers again, her brow furrowed.

She looked up. "What?"

"Uh . . ." I floundered.

"You're still in awe of my skills?" She smirked.

"Actually, yes."

Sarah held my eyes for a second. "Are you thinking what I am?"

Unless she was thinking how unbelievably hot she was, no. "What?"

She cast her eyes quickly over to our classmates and teacher, all busy with their work. "We should use this." She gestured at the paper.

"Use wha—" I stopped, my jaw literally hanging open. "You don't mean at Nat's . . ."

I almost told Sarah no way, but I was finding myself sucked into the whodunit along with all the Buford High gossipmongers, the developments with Galen turning it into a real puzzle. If the receipt at Morris Headley's had been forged, did it mean someone was trying to frame Galen? Or had he just been smart enough to fake his own signature when he'd pawned it, as unlikely as that seemed?

I nodded. "Okay. Let's run it by the others."

It didn't go so well.

"No way," Natalie said immediately. "You can't be serious."

I looked at Sarah, wondering if we'd made a terrible error in judgment.

"Nat," she said calmly. "The cops are getting nowhere. Things keep going around and around. Why shouldn't we look into it a little?"

"I . . . just . . ." She shook her head, tears in her eyes. "No."

Sarah watched her for a second, then nodded. "Okay," she said, soothing. "You're right." She put an arm around Nat. "I'm sorry. We were just trying to help."

"I think we should still get together, though," Trip said. "We can do it at my house and just talk through what we know. There's a lot going on here, and I'll bet you any money we're hearing more than the cops are."

"Not that they'd have a clue what to do with it anyway," Tannis said.

"We'll do it Saturday night. Okay?"

It was a typical Trip suggestion that wasn't so much a suggestion as a command. I could see that Natalie wanted to say no, had had enough of all of this, but instead she asked, "Do you mind if I bring John?"

"John Peters?" Trip asked.

"Duh! Who else?" Tannis rolled her eyes. "He's Nat's new boyfriend, dummy."

"He's not my boyfriend."

Trip raised his eyebrows. "Why do you want him to come?"

"He might be able to help."

Trip thought about it for a second. "Yeah, okay. As long as you think he's not going to be pissed that we're, like, messing in 'police business.'"

After Natalie and Tannis left, Trip turned to me and Sarah. "Listen," he said. "What you suggested to Nat earlier?"

I nodded, anticipating a rebuke.

"I think it's a great idea. Probably stupid to mention to Nat," he added. "I mean, do you really think she wants to go back to the living room and measure her dad's blood?"

"No."

"But you should do it."

"Behind her back?"

"It's for her own good," Trip said. "You still have the keys?"

I did, having locked up when Trip loaded the car the last time we'd been there. I'd found them in my coat pocket later but when I tried to return them to Nat at school, she'd told me to "throw them in the sewer."

"You can't take Tannis, obviously," Trip continued. "She'll just puke her guts out again. I wouldn't even tell her, just in case she decides to tell Nat. I can come, but it'll have to be after practice, which gets pretty late. It's not like I can contribute much anyhow. Let's face it. This is a job for nerds . . . like you two." He smiled broadly.

Sarah stuck her tongue out at him, and he tried to grab it. She shrieked and jumped away, laughing.

I watched them, thinking, *Is this for real?*

Is Trip really flirting with his girlfriend, who I have the hots for—and who I made out with just yesterday—and then sending me off alone with her for hours on end?

I guess he figured there was no chance she'd be into a nerd like me.

But I knew that was just a lame-ass excuse to make myself feel better. The proverbial devil on my shoulder. The reality was that Trip trusted me. He'd never in a million years think I was the kind of guy who'd make a play for his girlfriend.

And I was an asshole for having betrayed that. It wouldn't happen again.

"What do you think?" I asked Sarah directly, vowing to get myself in line, stop thinking about her. I hoped she'd make it easy and back out.

But of course, she didn't. "I already told you I think we should do it," she said. "If you're game, Riley, I'm in."

CHAPTER 22

WE PARKED ABOUT A HALF MILE UP THE ROAD FROM THE CLEARYS'. It wasn't much of a hiding spot, but it seemed better than leaving my car in front like a neon sign, just in case Natalie drove by. Or Tannis or the cops. Or the killer.

Sarah and I walked back downhill to the trailer. Our breath came fast as we picked our way carefully through the front yard.

I dug my hand into my jeans for the ring of keys and then propped the screen door with my hip as I fit the key into the lock, my stomach feeling sour. I looked over my shoulder at Sarah. "You ready?"

She nodded, looking as jittery as I felt.

I opened the door, and a stale, tangy odor wafted toward me, tickling the back of my throat. Neither of us moved for a few seconds. Maybe she was having the same second thoughts I was, but if I questioned it, I had a feeling we'd wind up bolting for the car, so I stepped inside. Sarah followed, pushing the door gently closed behind her.

We stood there staring at the walls, splashed with dark droplets.

"It's just math. Right, Riley?" Sarah's voice sounded high and quavery.

"Right." I let my bag slide to the floor, then knelt beside it. *Focus*, I thought, willing myself to breathe deeply, which might have been a mistake. There was an undercurrent of something rancid. Rotting food, probably. No one had taken out the trash here or cleaned the dishes. The power was probably shut off, with things moldering in the fridge.

"You okay?" Sarah asked.

I nodded, but I really didn't feel okay. She put her hand on my shoulder, and for once I didn't think about how it felt to have her close or touching me. I was too busy trying to stay conscious.

"We can do this," I muttered.

"That's what you told me in physics," she reminded me.

I took another deep breath, feeling the dizziness pass. I unzipped my bag. "Okay, let's get started."

Once we got into the numbers, it was much better. Sarah took the tape measure, leaving me to record.

"This one look good?" she asked, standing just beside the blood-soaked couch.

I glanced over and nodded. She stuck a Post-it with an *A* on it beside a long splotch. It matched the other Post-its left by the police, but with Sarah's distinctive sharp handwriting. She took the measurements, calling them out to me, then started hunting for splatter *B*.

Beside the phone was an ashtray, empty but with the scattered dust of old cigarettes on the bottom. There were rings on the table, overlapping one another like a Spirograph design made by someone who hadn't quite been able to get the hang of it. I guess Mr. Cleary hadn't believed in coasters. Trip's mom would have had a fit. I snorted, the idea of her somewhere like this so ridiculous.

"What?" Sarah glanced over.

I shook my head. "Nothing."

We did the next three splatters the same way—Sarah marking and measuring, me note taking and scanning the Clearys' living room. They'd never bothered to put photos up or hang anything on the walls, except for a bizarre oil painting of a clown. It looked like it had been done with a paint-by-numbers kit, and sure enough, when I got closer, I saw *R. Cleary* scrawled at the bottom.

Opposite the sofa was an old TV on a stand, with books and a few games stacked on the shelves. None of it looked like it had been touched in about fifteen years. I wondered if it was stuff they'd bought for Natalie, maybe even played with her when she was a kid. Or if it had always sat there unused, little Nat left to manage for herself just the way she was now.

"What ever happened to Natalie's mom?" I asked Sarah.

She glanced over at me. "Nat said she left them. Years ago. When Natalie was seven or eight."

"Where'd she go?"

"I don't think Nat knows."

"She hasn't talked to her in all those years?"

Sarah shook her head.

"That's kind of crazy, don't you think?" I asked. "That her mom would just take off like that?"

"Why?" She gave me a funny look, then turned back to the wall. "Happens all the time, Ri."

Oh, shit. I'd forgotten about her mom. "You don't talk to yours, either?" I asked gently.

"Not much. She checks in once a year or so," Sarah said without turning around. "When she can squeeze it in between the five hundred other things she's doing. It's one of the reasons Nat and I clicked right away," she said. "Just us and our crazy dads."

"Your dad didn't seem crazy."

"I'm not sure you would have noticed." She smirked at me over her shoulder. "You seemed a bit . . . preoccupied."

"Maybe," I admitted.

"He's not crazy, of course," Sarah said. "Just eccentric. Absentminded. Shrinks are like that sometimes."

"That's the word on the street."

She shook her head sadly. "You hanging out on the streets again, Riley Larkin?"

"Fo' shiz."

"Good grief," she muttered, leaning in to read the measurement. "Sometimes I think my dad forgets I even live there with him. Like I ceased to exist when she left. Like everyone did."

"He still misses her?"

"She was the life of our house," she said. "Of our family. It broke his heart when she left." Sarah said it simply, without any of the melodrama the words implied. But I could see her fighting for composure. Sarah took a shaky breath as she stepped back, assessing the wall. She set down the tape measure. "Anyway, enough of that. I think we're ready to map it," she said. "You have string and tape?"

I pulled them out of the backpack. Sarah leaned over to turn on the table lamp. Nothing. She frowned.

"Power's probably off," I said.

"It's going to get dark before we're done."

I smiled and pulled a high-powered flashlight from the bag. "I figured."

"You are such a Boy Scout." A chill raced up my spine as I realized that was exactly what Nat's dad had called me. Sarah didn't notice, handing me the end of the string.

"Go that way." She pointed toward the middle of the room.

It took almost two hours of painstaking work to get the strings taped across Nat's living room. When we were done, Sarah and I stood back, taking in the obvious impact point.

"It's kind of amazing how that works, isn't it?" she said.

"Yeah." It was. Because looking at where the strings intersected, you could see exactly where Nat's dad had been when he'd been shot. Standing directly in front of the sofa.

"He must have fallen back onto it, then," Sarah guessed.

I nodded, the huge pool of blood there making it obvious. Without mapping the scene, I'd have assumed he'd been shot sitting there, but the strings made it clear he'd been standing, and I could almost picture it happening, like the ghost of him was there before us.

"So what does it tell us about the perp?"

"'The perp?'" Sarah raised her eyebrows. "Did we just walk onto the set of *Law & Order*?"

I grinned sheepishly. "Okay. The criminal? The shooter?"

Sarah backed up, looking at the strings, the splotches, and the measurements. "Well, if her dad was standing, the angle of spatter would tell us the perp"—she grinned at me—"was taller than him."

I nodded, having come to the same conclusion. "Randall Cleary wasn't exactly a giant."

"No," she agreed. "Lots of people are probably taller than him."

Except Moose, I thought, feeling a huge relief. "Not Natalie," I said aloud. "Unless she was standing on a chair."

"Most people don't look for a podium when they're shooting their parents."

"Yeah, even the police probably figured that out. Maybe that's why they cleared her," I said.

"That and the ballistics tests that showed she hadn't fired a weapon."

"Right."

We stood there quietly, looking at our hours of work, until finally I said, "We have to take this all down, don't we?" I waved toward the string and tape.

She nodded. "For all we know Nat could be missing a piece of clothing or something else she needs. Or decide tomorrow that she really does want to come up here."

I took out my phone. "Is it weird if I take a picture?"

"Yes."

I snapped a few from different angles, then slipped the phone back into my pocket. I pulled down the first of the strings. "So much for all that work."

"Well, you'll always have the photos to remember it by."

It was near nine when we finally tucked everything away. Trip called as we were finishing up. "Do you mind double-checking to be sure we got everything?" she said, already stepping aside to talk to him. I tried not to listen or be jealous or notice the way she looked in her faded jeans.

I scanned the floor, looking for stray scraps of string or tape or anything else we might have left behind. Not that anyone would notice it amid the mess the cops had made, their small numbered cards still propped around the room and stuck on walls. I squatted down to look at them more closely, curious about how the police had numbered and laid them out. It wasn't every day you got to hang out at a real-life crime scene. I heard the jingle of change as everything in my jacket pocket spilled out onto the carpet.

"Shit." I stopped a quarter from rolling away, scooping up a small cluster of nickels and pennies that had landed by my shoe. Then I knelt forward to grab a dime that had rolled toward the sofa and landed by the pleated skirt. In the beam of the flashlight, I noticed something else, mostly hidden behind the tweedy fabric.

I felt my breath catch as I carefully pushed aside the sofa's skirt to get a clear view. I nudged the object gently, and it spun a fraction, the shiny silver top coming out from under the sofa.

It was a lighter. With a silver skull and crossbones, one side of the skull worn away where his hand always gripped it.

It was Moose's.

I'd seen him light his cigarettes with it every weekend for three years. There was no question.

Behind me I could hear Sarah ending her conversation. Without giving it a second thought I pulled my T-shirt down and used it to carefully grip the lighter without having it touch my skin. I slid it into my pocket and stood.

"What were you doing down there?"

"I dropped some money."

We locked up and walked back to the car. It was quiet in the woods, and I imagined the way it must have sounded to Mr. Johnson up the road the night it happened, sirens screeching. I'd have hauled myself out of bed and gone down there too.

Sarah and I talked about physics and Nat and school stuff most of the ride home. When I dropped her off, she paused for a second before getting out.

"Thanks, Riley. For not making it weird."

"That wasn't weird?" I said. "How am I going to top taking you to the scene of a murder? Damn, you're a tough customer, McKenzie."

She smiled. "You know what I mean."

I did. Her. Me.

"See you at school," she said.

I nodded, waved, and watched her walk up the path and slip inside her house. But I was thinking of Moose's lighter and the thing that stayed seared in my mind. How it had lain. Half-hidden by the sofa. On top of a blood spatter—not under.

It had fallen there after Mr. Cleary had been shot.

CHAPTER 23

I DROVE HOME, READY TO FLOP INTO BED WITH A BOOK THAT had nothing to do with school or murder. The house was dark when I drove up, which was odd. My mom should have been getting ready for work. My heart was pounding as I trotted up the walk, knowing something wasn't right.

As soon as I stepped through the door, I knew why. It was cold inside. My stomach sank as I flipped the light switch, already knowing what would happen: nothing.

The power was off. Which was what happened when you spent the bill money on SATs.

"Riley?" I heard her call from upstairs.

"Oh, shit," I muttered. "Yeah, it's me."

The beam of a flashlight bobbed on the wall as my mom came out of her bedroom and picked her way carefully downstairs. She stood at the bottom. "I tried to call you."

"You did?" I pulled out my phone. Three messages. I'd had it off up at the trailer. "Sorry," I said. "It was on mute from school. I guess I forgot to turn it on."

"The power's off," she said. "Do you know what happened?"

I nodded and took a deep breath. "I spent the money," I said. "I'm sorry. I just . . . I was hoping they wouldn't get to us so quickly."

"What did you spend it on, Riley?" she said. She didn't yell, but I could tell she was angry. I'd never done something like this before. It wasn't how we operated, both of us knowing that the only way to stay afloat was by working together.

"The SATs," I said quietly. "I registered to take them."

She didn't move, but everything shifted, her anger draining away. My mom looked sad and tired. The dim light threw shadows into the lines around her eyes and mouth, wrinkles that hadn't even begun back when we'd roasted marshmallows with the Joneses. This was the face I'd seen the last time I'd looked in those binoculars. The start of it, at least.

When she finally spoke, her voice was soft, "Why don't you build a fire, Riley." She squeezed my shoulder. "It'll be okay."

"How?"

"We can go without electricity for a day or so. It'll be like camping." She smiled.

"But we won't be able to pay it until—"

She interrupted, "I'll get the money."

I almost asked where, but I suddenly understood, feeling completely disgusted. Disgust*ing*, actually, since I was the one making her do it. "Mom—" But I couldn't say any of it. About how wrong it was to ask *him* for help, especially for money. Because we didn't talk about that, and this was my fault. I was the one who'd put her in that position.

"It's okay, Riley," was all she said.

I watched her sneakers—less ripped up than mine only because she wore nurse shoes half her waking hours—turn and walk toward the stairs.

I did what she said, crumpling page after page of newspaper until flames lit the room. My eyes were dry by the time she came back down.

"There are candles in the linen closet by the bathroom in case the flashlight runs out of batteries," she told me, pausing at the front door. "Just be careful, 'kay? Make sure they're out and let the fire die down before you go to bed tonight."

"I won't burn the house down on top of this."

"At least we could collect insurance money."

"Mom . . ."

"I'm *joking*, Riley." She stopped me before I could say anything serious, then gave me a peck on the cheek. "I'm worried about you. Don't burn *yourself* down, okay?"

I nodded. "Okay."

After the door closed, I went up and scavenged some candles, planning to do my homework by the fire, since it was the only warm place in the house. I'd just gotten my calc book out and open to the assigned page when the doorbell rang.

I figured my mom had forgotten her house keys along with whatever she'd come back for, but when I swung the door open, my crack about senility faded, because it wasn't my mom.

It was Sarah.

CHAPTER 24

SHE WAS BACKLIT BY THE STREETLAMP BETWEEN OUR HOUSE and the McGintys', the mist making the air behind her foggy and ethereal. It was on her skin too, a fine sheen of moisture.

"Can I come in?" she finally asked, when it became obvious I had no manners.

"Of course. I'm sorry." I stepped aside to let her pass, my heart racing. "I thought you were my mom."

"I didn't realize we looked so much alike."

"No. I mean, she just left for work, and—"

I saw Sarah looking at the fire and the candles. She turned back to me, eyebrows raised. "Am I interrupting something?" She glanced past me, down the hall. "Do you have company?" Her smile faltered. "I had no idea—"

"No one's here," I said. "Or coming over."

"Oh." Her smile faded a little. "Well, I, uh—I hope it's

okay that I stopped by." She paused a second, suddenly nervous. "I had a thought."

"If you were Tannis, I'd say congratulations."

Sarah smiled, looking around for the light switch. She crossed, flipped it before I could tell her not to bother.

Nothing happened, of course.

"It doesn't work," she said.

"Not at the moment."

It only took her a few seconds. "Your electricity was shut off."

I nodded.

"Because you couldn't pay the bill." Her voice was gentle. I had never, ever talked about my financial situation with Sarah, but she wasn't stupid.

"It'll be back on soon."

Sarah swallowed hard. "God, Ri," she said, her voice tight. "I'm sorry."

I wanted to tell her it wasn't a big deal—my own stupid decision—but I didn't want to explain the whole thing.

I saw her eyes sweep the living room. I never minded it much. It was comfortable enough, but to her the water stain on the ceiling and the peeling paint by the mantel must have looked very different. She turned back to me, her jaw set. "How much is the bill?"

"Not much," I said, glancing away from those searching eyes. "It's not a big deal."

Sarah reached out, touched my arm so I'd look at her. My skin tingled with the feel of her hand. "Riley." Her eyes, deep and dark, held mine. "How much?"

"Eighty-three dollars," I said hoarsely.

"Let me float you the cash."

"No," I said instantly. "I mean, thank you. That's really, really nice, but—"

"Look, I'm not going to tell anyone," she said.

"I know." I took a breath, not wanting to say it but knowing it was better than having her pity me. "My mom's getting the money tomorrow." From her boyfriend. Who just happens to be my best friend's married dad.

Sarah's eyes darted around the room again. "Okay," she said hesitantly.

"So . . . you wanted to talk?" I smiled wryly. "Before we were so rudely interrupted by my lack of electricity."

Sarah smiled. "I've been thinking about Galen and who might have framed him."

"So have I," I told her. I watched her for a second, deciding to come clean. "I found something at the trailer."

Her eyes went wide, then sharpened. "On the floor," she said. "Just before we left, right?" I nodded. "What was it?"

"A lighter," I said. "It's Moose's."

"Who?"

"Moose Martin. I work with him. He's in our class."

"How can you be sure?"

"I checked the yearbook."

"No, you dope." Sarah swatted me. "That it's his lighter."

"I just know," I told her. "The way it's worn down . . ."

"Can I see it?"

"Sure. It's upstairs." I turned, not expecting her to follow, but she did, pausing just inside my room while I crossed to the dresser. She shined the flashlight around the small space.

"I like your room," she said. "It's very 'you.'"

I glanced at the walls, blank except for an old Fenway Park poster; my dresser and shelves, stacked with books; the quilt my grammy had made. "Nerdy?" I smiled.

She grinned back. "No. Basic. Solid. The things you need and nothing more."

"Uh-huh." I liked that she thought of me that way. I pulled out the baggie I'd sealed the lighter into. I'd been careful not to smear or touch it but should have left it at the scene, I knew. It was probably worthless as evidence like this.

She studied it, nodding, clearly seeing what I meant about it being recognizable, just like his car.

"I saw him drive by the trailer the day we went up with Nat," I told her. "I'm wondering now if maybe he'd heard the cops had released the crime scene. Maybe he was going back for this."

"But . . . wouldn't the cops have found it?"

"I guess not."

"Did he know Nat's dad?' she asked.

We sat then, Sarah at one end of the moonlit bed and me carefully at the other, and I told her everything. About the time I'd gone up there with him, how I'd told the police at the restaurant and how pissed Moose had been. About how he'd admitted going there the day Nat's dad was killed.

"Wow," she breathed when I finished.

"Yeah," I agreed. "Wow."

"Do you think he did it?"

"I don't know. I hope not," I said, adding, "he's too short, if what we mapped up there is right."

"If," she said.

"Yeah." It's what nagged at me, as much as I didn't want it to. "This is definitely his. And it was on top of the blood."

"Should we tell the police?"

"Probably," I said. "But I'd like to talk to him first. I feel like I already ratted him out once."

"Riley, if he's the killer, it's not ratting him out."

"Yeah, I know. I just . . ." I didn't know how to explain how I felt like Moose always got the shitty break. How George always treated me better at work. The way guys like Trip and girls like Sarah ignored him, didn't even know who he was. I knew what that felt like a little. I'd gotten a taste of it every now and then, growing up with Trip around. I guess I wanted to give Moose a chance on his own. Just him and me. Just in case things weren't what they seemed, because lots of times they weren't.

She nodded. "Okay."

I put the lighter back into my top drawer. Sarah stood, stretching, her hands over her head. It tugged her shirt up, and I could see where her jeans hung loose around her hips, the top of her panties, black and lacy. I looked away, my ears hot.

"The binoculars," she said, noticing the case, also in my top drawer. "Have you looked in them again?"

"I've thought about it," I admitted. "But, no."

She nodded, picking up a picture from the top of my dresser. It'd been there so long, I'd forgotten all about it. "When was this?" Sarah asked, studying it. Me and Trip in front of our tent. The camping weekend when his dad had fed my mom marshmallows. I was surprised I hadn't burned it. Maybe I would now. Just toss it into the fire downstairs.

"A long time ago," I said.

"I can tell." Sarah smiled. "You guys look so cute. What are you . . . ten? Eleven?"

"Something like that."

"You've been friends for a long time," she observed. It made me wonder if Trip had ever talked to her about how we'd grown up together. Or if he'd boxed most of that up with his Pokémon cards and car magazines.

"Since we were born, pretty much. Our parents were friends."

"Are they still?"

"Not since my dad died," I said.

She nodded but didn't say anything, which I appreciated. Some people feel like they have to rush in with "I'm sorry" or platitudes, but it's just better when they act like it's no biggie, because it really isn't. I mean, it *is*, but I've lived with it every day for the last four years. Just because someone's never talked about it with me before doesn't make it new news.

"I've never had a friend like that," she said, flopping back onto the bed. "We moved around so much when I was younger. This is the longest we've lived anywhere."

"How come?"

"Mostly it was my mom," she said. "She was the kind of person who'd have three projects going and still be looking for the fourth, you know?" I nodded. "She was always doing something new, learning something else. My dad tells this story about when he was in grad school. She was an undergrad, double-majoring in engineering and physics."

"Um . . . wow?"

Sarah smiled. "Right. Anyway, he was doing his dissertation on brain function, dormant sections, hypnosis, stuff like that. She got interested in it, but it wasn't like she just asked about it or read a book or two. She read them all." Sarah laughed softly. "By the end, he always says, she could have written his paper better than he did."

"She sounds kind of brilliant."

"She was. Is," Sarah said. "Brilliant and flighty and a little bit nuts. In a good way," she added wistfully.

"I see you got one of three."

"I'm not *that* flighty," Sarah said, grinning.

"Not the one I meant. I've seen your mad skills."

She laughed. "But to get back to your question," Sarah said more seriously. "My mom liked to see new places. Do new things. It was like an itch to constantly go, do, explore. In some ways it was great." Sarah smiled fondly. "When I was little, we were always running off to museums and exhibits and parks. She taught me to bike and swim and play tennis. Or, if we were at home, we'd have a soufflé baking at the same time we were making a sodium chloride volcano." She bit her lip for a second, then added, "But it wasn't great in the way that made us move every time she got bored. I used to wish we'd just stay put, you know? Just for once not constantly have to make new friends."

"I can't imagine you ever had much trouble," I said, grinning.

But Sarah didn't smile. "Please. If it weren't for Natalie, I'd probably still be skulking around the corners of school. You know, Vermont isn't the most welcoming place."

Yeah, I guess I did know that. We all did.

"Of course, if I'd have known that the price for staying somewhere was her leaving, I'd have pulled that wish back in a second," she said quietly. "I'd do anything to have her back."

I didn't say anything at first. I didn't like talking about my dad, but I knew what Sarah was feeling—that intense, hollow gap; the feeling that some vital part of you was missing—and it seemed like she wanted to talk about it.

"What happened?" I asked. "With her and your dad?"

She got that wistful look again. "They were quite a pair," she said. "The absentminded professor and the mad scientist."

"Who was the scientist?"

"She was. It's what she did for work," Sarah said. "But it was also her passion at home. She had botany projects and chemistry, and of course, a spot for tinkering wherever we lived. All those plants in our house?" I nodded. "They were hers. Grown from seed, varieties she'd cultivated . . ." Sarah trailed off. "I've been keeping them alive, because if it were left to my dad, they'd be deader than doornails."

"Why did she . . . like, when she went away . . ." I fumbled for how to ask it.

Sarah knew what I was getting at. "When my mom got into something, she was all in. Like with my dad's dissertation. Unfortunately," Sarah said wryly, "that applied to people, too. She met a guy at work." She looked away and I could see her fighting tears. "And that was that."

I didn't know what to say. Her mom sounded like all the things Sarah had said, brilliant and flighty and a little bit nuts. But not in a good way at all. I knew Sarah didn't see it that way, though. People rarely do when it's someone they love.

"She wanted me to go with her, but my dad wouldn't let me," Sarah said softly. "I think he hoped if I stayed, she would." She shook her head. "After almost twenty years with her, you'd think he'd know better."

"I'm sorry."

"She told me she'd be back." Sarah shrugged sadly. "I guess she's just been too busy with another guy or an important project."

"I can't imagine what would be more important than you." It slipped out before I knew it. The words were right, but I could tell I'd said them too honestly, with too much of my own feeling. I felt my face redden.

Sarah met my eyes. "Thanks, Riley," she said after a minute. "That's sweet."

I didn't know what to say, so I kept quiet. The silence lingered in the stillness of my house. Sarah was close enough that her bent knee touched my leg just barely, but it felt like that spot was lit with a neon heat. I'd been working really hard to ignore the charge between us, the inescapable memories of how it had been to kiss her last time. I was trying to be good, do the right thing.

But then Sarah moved, pressing her leg against me so gently, I might have thought it was unintentional, except for the way her eyes held mine. A tingling raced up my thigh like a trail of sparks. I made some sort of sound, my breath tight and short, and then I was leaning toward her, eyes closing as our lips touched. Everything beyond was gray and dark, my focus totally narrowed to the feel of her cheek brushing mine, breath on my ear making me shiver. We fell back onto the bed, and her hand was on mine, guiding it to her buttons, then moving lower as I fumbled with them, opening her shirt. I sucked in my breath at the sight of her pale skin.

And then I saw her necklace. Light glinted off the locket Trip had given her last year, a picture of the two of them inside.

"Oh God, Sarah." I pulled back, away from her. I kid you not, it was probably the hardest thing I've ever done. "I can't. God knows I want to."

Fool! my inner fourteen-year-old screamed. *How long have you been waiting for this? You're blowing it, you idiot!*

Fourteen-year-olds can be very cruel.

I looked away while she scooted up toward my pillow, buttoning her shirt, then hugging her legs to her chest. Neither of us spoke for a long time.

"Can I ask you something, Riley?" she said finally.

"What?"

"Have you ever . . . done it before?"

What? I hadn't expected that one. "Not in real life," I answered.

She laughed softly. "You know, a shrink might say you use humor to cover insecurity."

"I prefer to think of it as lightening terribly awkward situations."

She smiled. "That too."

I hoped she wouldn't go into what else a shrink might say about my being here with her—Trip's girlfriend—the way his dad and my mom . . . Ugh, I couldn't even think about it.

"Why?" Sarah asked.

"Why what?"

"Why haven't you?" she said. "You're almost eighteen. You're smart, good-looking, nice—"

"You're making me blush."

"You were already doing that," she said, not letting it go. "You must have had the opportunity."

I had, in fact, one night out with Trip. And as far as he knew, I'd taken it. We'd gone to a party at one of the houses on the mountain, some college girls here for the weekend. Trip had fitted their rentals, and one of them had invited him over later.

"Their parents'll be in Burlington for some dinner," he said. "It'll be small—it's not like they know anyone here. They asked me to bring some friends."

Trip knew I hated shit like that. Spoiled rich kids one-upping each other, pretending we were all pals, then laughing about us behind our backs. I told him that, and he said I was paranoid. "They can only laugh at you if you give them a reason to, Riley."

"Come off it, Trip. They'll laugh at us either way. It's sport to them—ski during the day, make fun of townies at night."

"Fine," he said angrily. "Don't come."

But I went, and I think the girls were honestly too wasted to make fun of us. We weren't there an hour before Trip was taking one to the bedroom.

"Good luck, man," he said, and winked.

Her friend, who I'd been kind of talking to, grabbed my hand, tried to drag me up. "Lemme show ya round," she slurred.

I followed her, knowing full well where this was going. We wound up in another bedroom, her beckoning from this massive bed. I went with it, and it got pretty hot, but when it came down to it, I balked. I'm still not sure why.

"You doan wanna?" she slurred.

"I do," I said, because I did. And it would have ensured I wasn't *that* guy, Last Virgin Standing. Not that Trip wouldn't have found something else to rag on me about.

But this girl was a mess. "I just . . ." I hesitated, then told her the truth. "I don't really know you."

She squinted at me like she couldn't believe it, then burst out laughing. "OMG, how *cute* are you?" She sat up, not bothering to straighten her clothes. "So this is where they keep all the gentlemen." Only, it came out "gennelmen." We ended up talking for a while because I didn't want to go back out there and look like a total loser. It turned out she was actually nice, and I was kind of sorry I hadn't done it.

I let Trip believe I had, and he congratulated me over and over on the way home. After telling me in agonizing detail about his adventures.

"It didn't seem right," I told Sarah now.

She nodded, as if that were exactly the answer she'd expected. "Can I ask you something else?"

"I'm not sure," I said. "I'm finding your questions rather forward."

"How come you never asked me out?"

"See what I mean?" I said, hoping she'd drop it and spare me the agony. But of course she just sat there waiting. "You were going out with Trip," I said finally. "I'm pretty sure he wouldn't have approved."

"Before that," she pressed.

I stared at her for a minute, then said, "I've been asking myself the same thing."

Sarah nodded, looking at her hands, then back up at me. "I'm going to break up with him." Which would have been great news if it had been anyone other than Trip.

"I . . . We . . ." I gestured at the space between us. "This still can't happen." Going out with your best friend's ex was almost as taboo as what we were doing now.

"I understand," she said. "It's not about that." Sarah shook her head. "I mean, it is, but—"

"Think about it," I interrupted. "Things are complicated right now. With Nat and everything. I'm not sure any of us are thinking clearly."

She nodded, maybe realizing the same thing I had—that if she and Trip split up, it wouldn't be the five of us anymore.

"I'm not saying you shouldn't. Or that you should," I told her. "Just be sure you know what feels right to *you*."

She stood then, shivering a little in the chill of the room, and looked me straight in the eye. "What feels right is the thing I can't have."

I didn't know what to say to that, so I told her, "I'll walk you down."

"You don't have to."

"Humor me," I said. "Let me be a gentleman."

Sarah smiled sadly. "You're rarely anything but, Riley Larkin."

CHAPTER 25

MOOSE WAS AT THE DISHWASHER UNLOADING A MOUNTAIN OF silverware when I walked in. With all the reporters in town, the restaurant had been extra busy, which I guess was the silver lining of a local murder. If there is such a thing. He grunted when I approached, looking like he was half-asleep.

I had started the day with an ice-cold shower, so was wide-awake but not in an especially good mood. "Nice to see you, Moose," I said, snapping on my gloves.

"Fuck off."

"Hey." I turned to him. "Enough with the attitude, okay?"

He whirled to face me, not that sleepy after all. "No, it's not okay. Thanks to you the cops have been all over me for the last few weeks."

"Thanks to me? I'm pretty sure *you* chose your recreational activities, not me."

"You didn't have to broadcast it to the fucking world."

"I didn't," I said, "but I wasn't going to lie to the cops. I told you that."

"Whatever." He flipped the back of his hand my way. But now I was pissed.

"Maybe I should just give them this." I held up the baggie.

Moose looked shocked, reaching for it, but I pulled it away. "Where'd you get that?" he demanded.

"At the trailer," I said quietly. "By the sofa where Nat's dad was shot."

Moose's eyes went wide. "What?"

"You heard me," I said. "You told me yourself you were up there that night."

Moose glanced around. The kitchen was empty, and I was practically whispering, but I could understand why he was scared. He had reason to be. "I guess I dropped it."

"I guess so." I stared at him staring at me. Maybe I should have been scared myself, but more than anything, I felt massively disappointed. I didn't want it to be Moose, didn't want him to be another deadbeat, go-nowhere Buford loser rotting in jail. But I couldn't change what he'd done. "So," I said finally. "Are you going to turn yourself in?"

"For what?"

"For murder."

"What?" Moose turned white. "No!" He lowered his

voice, whispering furiously, "I told you before, I didn't do it. Why do you keep trying to pin it on me?"

"Moose. I found this up there."

"So?"

"It was on top of the bloodstains. Look." I held the baggie up again, pointing to where Randall Cleary's blood had dried. "It was lying in blood."

Moose frowned, not getting it.

I sighed. "There was blood *under* it, Moose, but not on top. That means it was dropped after the blood," I explained. "After he was shot."

His eyes bugged out, and he held up his hands. "No. No way, man. I told you I was there, but he was definitely not dead. There was no blood—" Moose was babbling, words tumbling out. "You gotta believe me. Maybe I dropped it and someone else kicked it into the blood later or moved it there on purpose. I don't even think I had it that night," Moose said, a weird look on his face. "Maybe I left it somewhere or someone's trying to frame me."

I thought there was a lot of that going around for such a small town. It couldn't all be true. "What were you doing driving past his trailer on Monday?" I asked, switching gears and feeling a little like bad cop Lincoln Andrews doing it.

"What're you, following me?"

"No. I was inside the trailer. I saw your car. Monday?" I said. "Around five?"

He glared at me, angry, then spat, "I was going to the Miloseviches'. I visit them every now and then."

"What? Why?"

"Everyone knew last year," he said bitterly. "I guess most people have forgotten by now."

"I know who they are," I said crossly. "Richie plays football, his sister OD'd."

"Yeah," he said. "That's all anyone remembers about her. But her name was Jessica. And she was my girlfriend."

"Your girlfriend?" I said stupidly.

He nodded, slamming the dishwasher shut and hefting the bucket of silverware and napkins. "Yeah. And sometimes I miss her. So I visit her family 'cause they do too, and no one else seems to give a shit."

He pushed through the swinging doors, probably thinking he was getting away from me. But I followed him.

"Why were you on probation last year?" Moose shot me a dirty look and kept walking. "When the police first came to question us? After Mr. Cleary was killed? You were sweating it out because you're on probation," I reminded him. "Why?"

"Why do you think?" he said. "For drugs. They got me with some last year, around the time Jessica . . ." He trailed off, shrugging.

"But what were you so worried about? If you didn't shoot him and didn't have anything—"

"Look, I stole something from the trailer while Cleary was taking a leak, okay? It wasn't drugs, and I needed money and figured he owed me, you know?"

I stopped, suddenly getting it. "The vase," I said. What did that mean? Had he pawned it? Given it to Galen? Or had Galen been with him?

"How the fuck do you know all this stuff?" Moose asked, incredulous.

"Was Galen Riddock with you?"

Moose smirked. "Hell, no. I just put it under his name 'cause he's an asshole."

"Uh-huh." I was starting to understand why the police always seemed like they didn't know what they were doing. It was mind-boggling trying to put all the pieces of this stuff together. "So the Miloseviches live near the Clearys, right?"

Moose looked over his shoulder, turning away again. "Yeah." He hefted his bucket onto table one.

I leaned against the next booth and took a shot in the dark, "I've heard they were really pissed at Mr. Cleary."

"Wouldn't you be?" Moose said, not looking up.

"But you still went there. To him. After."

He turned to face me then, taking a step closer. His jaw was clenched. "Listen. I don't know where you get off playing Mr. Righteous or the Hardy Boys here, but what I do or don't do is none of your business. If you're dancing around whether I had anything to do with your friend's shithead dad getting killed, the answer is no. Neither did Jessica's parents. The Miloseviches," he added, glaring at me. "So Fuck. Off."

Moose whirled back to his silverware, knocking the rolls he'd already done onto the floor. He cursed and kicked the leg of the table.

I decided to take his suggestion, making myself scarce for the rest of the shift. But it wasn't Jessica Milosevich's parents I was thinking about. It was Richie.

After work I swung by the track to get Tannis so we could meet everyone over at Trip's to talk about Nat's dad. Our Saturday night command performance. She was still racing laps, so I stood by the chain-link fence, watching the blue Thunderbird fly around the loop.

"Well, well," a deep voice said from behind me. "Riley Larkin."

I turned to see Tannis's brother striding across the gravel lot. "Hey, Jed." I shook the hand he offered, forcing myself not to wince. "I never got to tell you how much we enjoyed kicking your butt at the Dash." He squeezed harder, smiling when I yelped. I rubbed my hand gingerly when he finally let go. "What are you still doing here? I didn't know the marines gave so much vacation."

Jed nodded, the blond hair he'd always worn shaggy when he lived here now buzz-cut, military style. "They usually don't," he said shortly.

I nodded toward Tannis, who'd pulled over by the pole and was out of the car, talking to her dad. "She ready for the race tomorrow?"

"I guess." He shrugged. "My dad says her times have been off. And she's been acting weird. Weirder than usual, I mean."

"How so?"

"I dunno." Jed leaned over and spit something onto the dirt. "Crying and shit. Freaking out if I move her bag from one place to another. Just . . . weird."

"Well, it's been a weird few weeks here."

"You can say that again. Crazy shit about Randall Cleary, huh?"

Tannis's dad climbed behind the wheel and drove slowly toward the garages. Tannis pulled off her helmet, shaking her blonde hair and seeing me and Jed for the first time. She waved. "Be there in a few, Ri," she yelled. "I'm just gonna change up quick."

"'Kay!" I yelled back.

As she disappeared down the grandstand tunnel, I could feel Jed eyeing me.

"What?"

"Dude. Are you dating my sister?"

"No!" I squawked. "I mean, not that there's anything wrong with her or whatever. I'm just giving her a ride."

I cringed, but Jed ignored the obvious joke. "Okay,

man." He smirked. "But if you're the reason she's acting like a freak, I'm gonna kick your ass, 'cause it's making life hell."

"Seriously, Jed."

"Hey." He held up his hands, grinning. "None of my business, you know?" He smirked again. "Gonna go help out the old man."

Jed hoisted himself over the fence easily, tall and athletic, like Tannis and the rest of their family.

He'd reached the track's infield when Tannis reappeared, looking . . . well, shinier than usual. Jed saw her and turned back to me, still close enough that I could see his self-satisfied expression. "Yep," he called. "Have fun tonight, *friend*."

Tannis paused when she reached him, talked for a few seconds, then gave him a playful shove before continuing my way. She was wearing her usual ripped and faded Levi's, but some kind of silky shirt instead of the sweatshirts and fleeces I was used to seeing her in. And makeup.

"You finally do the wash?" I asked when she got to the dirt lot where I was waiting by my car.

"What?" She looked down at herself, plucking the shirt. "You mean this?"

"It's rather, uh, feminine for you," I said.

"I *am* a girl, Riley." She thrust out her chest, adding archly, "In case you haven't noticed."

"Thanks for the reminder," I said, feeling heat on my cheeks. I opened my door so I wouldn't have to look at her.

Tannis grinned at my embarrassment, yanking open the passenger side and sliding in. "Anyway, you don't wash silk, dumbass."

"Wow. And a domestic goddess, too. What a wife you'll make someday," I said as I started driving, and then realized immediately that if Jed were right and Tannis liked me, that'd be a really uncomfortable thing to say. I changed the subject. "You ready for tomorrow?"

Tannis frowned. "I guess." She seemed like she was going to say more, but rolled down the window instead.

"D'you mind?" I said, glancing over. "It's, like, twenty degrees out."

"Sorry," she said, not rolling it up. "I'm feeling a little queasy."

"You need me to pull over?"

She didn't answer. I slowed down. But then she shook her head. "No, I'm good." She rolled up the window.

"You sure?"

She nodded, and I hit the gas. Jed was right. She was acting weird.

"Jed's been back for a while, huh?"

"Yeah."

I pulled onto the bypass road toward Trip's. "Doesn't he have a wife and, like, a job down in Virginia?"

"I guess his job's flexible. And his wife's a bitch. *She's* probably why he's here so much."

"Oh."

"I wonder about that, you know?" Tannis said, obviously feeling better. "How people wind up with other people who seem like, just, the wrong match for them."

"Uh . . ." Where was this going? Her and Matty? I'd seen them talking in the halls a few times, and I'd always felt like I was having an out-of-body experience, seeing two separate worlds colliding.

But instead she said, "Like Trip and Sarah." That caught me off guard, but then Tannis added what I prayed she didn't know and would never say. "I know you want her, Riley."

My breath caught, and I felt hot, my palms and armpits sweaty. I pretended I hadn't heard, frowning at the radio, changing the station.

"You get all awkward when she's around."

I scowled at Tannis. "I do not."

"You do," she said. "Don't worry, She probably doesn't notice because you're *always* that way with her."

I flicked on my turn signal, nearing Trip's house. I was itching to tell her Sarah probably noticed everything, and, oh, by the way, she hadn't seemed to think I was awkward when we'd kissed. Though it was plenty awkward after that. "She's Trip's girlfriend," I said instead.

"Yup," Tannis said softly. "That she is."

We drove silently for a minute through the dark fields, the grass flat and barren in the sweep of the headlights. This was my least favorite time of year, everything dying and dull, not the bright greens of summer or the clean white of the snow. Just dead broken stalks of corn and browning brush.

Once when I was fourteen, my mom surprised me with tickets to a Red Sox game. Play-offs, no less. We escaped the house like that a lot then. It was this same time of year, but riding the train, it seemed like the closer we sped toward the city, the more alive things were, till we sat staring at the vibrant green infield of Fenway Park. We lingered after the game, getting food in a diner nearby, even trading our train tickets for a later ride home. "It'd be fun to live somewhere like that, wouldn't it?" she asked when we finally boarded our train after eleven.

I nodded, feeling a flutter of excitement through my sleepiness.

"Maybe someday we will," she said thoughtfully.

We never went back, though. Never talked about it again. Not after her visits to Dr. Williams became routine.

"Do you really think Trip's all that into her?" Tannis asked as we turned onto his street.

Trip and Sarah had been going out for over a year now. At first he'd told me everything. More than I wanted to know, really. How far he'd gotten with her. What she'd done to him the first night they'd hooked up. I don't know why I was his confidant. Maybe because I was so much less experienced than his football pals and it was safe to tell me stuff. Or because I'd been there when he'd decided to ask her out. After a while he stopped talking about that stuff. Then other things followed. College. Plans for next year. It was funny, because there'd been plenty of days in our lifetime of friendship when I'd wished Trip would just *shut up.* But once he did, I realized I missed it. Just like I'd missed him those first years of high school when he'd cut me loose. Not that I'd ever tell him any of that.

I parked, looking up the path at Trip's lit house and wondering if Tannis was into Trip or just sticking her nose into my business. I decided I didn't really care. I had enough other things to worry about. "Yeah," I finally answered, opening the door. "I do."

Tannis nodded. "Sucks to be you, huh?" She climbed out of the car and jogged to the door without waiting for me.

"I think we should list out what we know," Trip said when we were all in the basement with the door shut. Trip's mom was puttering around upstairs; his dad was "out." I tried not to think about where. "Sarah's going to whiteboard it," Trip said, motioning to an easel he'd set up.

"You're so professional," Tannis commented.

Trip ignored her and looked at Natalie, sitting on the couch, John Peters beside her. "Are you okay with that, Nat?"

She nodded, looking decidedly not okay.

"So," he said. "Suspects." Trip watched while Sarah wrote the heading on the board. "Galen Riddock," he said. "We know he was a customer, but he says he wasn't there that night."

"Even though he stole and pawned my mom's vase," Natalie said.

"But the handwriting didn't match," John reminded her.

"I can explain that," I said. Everyone turned to me.

"You can?" Nat said. "How?"

I hesitated, looking at John. "I know who took it and pawned it, but if I say, it has to stay between us. For now at least." Moose had been so honestly freaked-out by my accusations, I really felt like he'd been telling the truth. Not that I could know for sure. But I didn't want to be the one to turn his probation into something much worse over his vindictive act of stealing the vase.

"I don't know that we can promise that," Trip said finally, reading John's and Natalie's reactions. "Not without knowing what you're going to say."

"Someone admitted to me that he was there that night and took it. He pawned it under Galen's name because Galen's an ass. It was a prank."

Trip frowned. "Why'd he take it? And why was he—your mystery man—there that night at all?"

"I—" I hesitated, realizing Moose hadn't explained

why he'd gone there. Had it been to buy drugs? Or something else? *I figured he owed me*, he'd said. For what? Jessica Milosevich's death? "I don't know, actually," I admitted, wondering whether I was wrong to trust the things Moose had said.

"Can you just tell us, Riley?" Natalie asked. "Maybe if we know who it is, we can help figure out if it means anything."

And coming from her, it made up my mind, because, honestly, who did I owe more to . . . Moose or Natalie? So I told.

"Do you want to tell about the lighter, too?" Sarah prompted as she wrote his name on the whiteboard. I sighed, explaining what we'd found, but Natalie stopped me a sentence in.

"When was this?"

I looked at her, realizing suddenly that we'd never told her we'd gone back. Thankfully, Sarah took over, addressing Nat directly.

"We went to your house, Natalie. Riley and I. And mapped the . . ." She hesitated, obviously choosing words carefully. "The living room, the scene."

John raised his eyebrows. "Like forensics?"

Sarah nodded. "We've been studying it in physics. We thought it might help. I'm sorry, Nat." She winced. "I hope you're not mad."

Nat shrugged noncommittally, but was obviously not happy. "So, what about the lighter?"

I finished, explaining how I'd found it and why it mattered. John spoke up immediately. "There's no way the police would have missed that," he said.

None of us spoke, uncomfortable telling a cop's son the things we'd been saying among ourselves, but he got it.

"Listen, I know the police here don't process scenes like this often, and maybe you think they bungled it, and maybe in some ways they did. But think about it," he said, addressing me and Sarah particularly. "You were there, you did the forensics work too, so you know how painstaking it is and how carefully the whole area is looked at. Do you honestly think they'd have overlooked a lighter lying on top of the blood they were examining?"

No. I didn't. "Maybe someone planted it there afterward," I suggested.

"Who?" Tannis said.

"What about Richie Milosevich?" I could see all of their eyes widen. I went through all the connections—Moose's visits to the Miloseviches' house, how Richie had been the first to point the finger at Galen, the stuff about his sister and how his family had felt after. I had myself convinced by the end, until John said,

"That all makes sense except for one thing."

"What?"

"He and his parents have a rock-solid alibi for Dash weekend. They weren't even in town."

Sarah crossed the freshly written name off her white-board, leaving just Moose and Galen.

"And Moose swears he didn't do it. I think he's telling the truth. Plus, he's too short," I reminded her.

She nodded and crossed him off too.

"Wait," John said frowning. "What was that?"

Sarah told him what we'd come up with at the trailer.

John shook his head. "Something's not making sense here," he said. "I'm pretty sure my dad said it was just the opposite. They were *looking* for someone short."

"Well, that would *really* narrow the suspects," Tannis said. "Maybe you guys did it wrong."

"Sarah got it dead-on in class," I said defensively.

"No pun intended," Trip said.

Nat looked like she'd had just about enough.

"It's possible," I said. "I think we were careful . . ." I glanced at Sarah, who nodded. "But we're obviously far from experts."

"So where does that leave us?" Tannis asked, exasperated.

"Pretty much where the police are," John suggested wryly. "Without a clue."

CHAPTER 26

"HOW MUCH LONGER?" NATALIE ASKED. SHE WAS SITTING beside John Peters, huddled under a wool blanket. We'd come out to see Tannis's race, the last one of the season. The cars were all lined up, Tannis's father and brothers standing in the pits. I saw Jed hopping around, trying to stay warm.

"They should have gone by now," Trip said, glancing at the big clock. "If I'd known we'd be sitting out here for an hour, I'd have brought some beers and a cooler."

"You mean a heater," I said.

"Yeah, that, too."

The forecast had said it was supposed to hit forty, but sitting on the metal bleachers at the racetrack, it felt about twenty degrees colder. I could see my breath, and kicked myself for forgetting gloves.

I had a blanket all to myself, though. The fifth wheel. Nat and John. Trip and Sarah. Me.

"Look!" Natalie said, pointing to the track lights that finally turned on, signaling red to the drivers at starting positions. At the same time the loudspeaker announced the start of the race.

"Finally," Sarah said. She was sitting at the other end of the bleachers. I'd let them settle in first before choosing the farthest seat away. I wondered if she'd noticed.

The track lights changed to yellow, then green. The cars took off in clouds of dust and a roar of engines.

We could see right away it wasn't going to go well for Tannis.

I'd been to a handful of her races before, plus seen her practicing at the track, but I'd never seen her driving like she was here. She completely miscalculated the first curve, turning late, then swerving hard left and almost skidding out.

"Jeez," Trip said. "What is she doing?"

She made it around the next lap okay, but you could see that her timing was off, her accelerations erratic. Twice she almost bumped into other cars, and edged away at the last second, seemingly more by luck than intent.

"She's usually better than this, isn't she?" John asked, turning to me. He'd never been to a race, but it was pretty obvious this wasn't how you won them, and everyone knew

Tannis had plenty of trophies to show for her time at the track.

"Yeah," I said. Out of the corner of my eye I saw Sarah biting her lip. Nat's hands were clenched tight. I think we all felt that way, hanging on to the hope that Tannis would somehow pull it together in the remaining seven laps.

She came in dead last. We all looked at each other. I'd been dying to get out of the cold before, but now, not so much.

"This is going to suck," Trip said. Reluctantly we stood and walked toward the pits.

We waited to the side while Tannis talked with her dad and brothers. I wondered if maybe there'd been something wrong with her car. I caught a glimpse of her face, pale with dark circles under her eyes. She was sick, I realized.

Finally her family moved away, and Tannis came over.

"Hey." Natalie put her arm around Tannis, coming up to about her shoulder. "It's okay." Nat's nose wrinkled, and I realized Tannis was *really* sick. There was puke on her uniform and the car. She stank and was crying.

"It's okay, Tannis." Trip clapped her on the back, careful not to get too close. "What're you doing even trying to race with a stomach bug? You think you're some kind of iron man? Of course it was a tough day."

She didn't even smile, just swiped at her eyes. "It's not a stomach bug, Trip," she said dully, barely looking at him. "I'm pregnant."

* * *

"So . . . holy shit," Trip said. We were driving aimlessly through town the way Trip did sometimes when there was stuff on his mind that needed to come out. Nat and John had driven separately, and we'd already dropped Sarah off. Tannis, of course, had stayed at the track.

"Yeah," I agreed. "I can't . . . I mean, the whole thing . . ." I'd been shocked by her announcement but completely floored when she'd told us who the father was. Matty Gretowniak.

"Does he know?" I'd asked.

She'd glared at me. "Of course. You think I'd tell you dorks first?"

I'd wanted to ask what he'd said about it. What they were going to do. But those questions seemed way too personal. The kind of thing Tannis wouldn't hesitate to ask. Except she was the person in trouble.

"Sarah's been acting weird lately," Trip said.

My gut felt hollow. Oh God. Is *that* why we were driving and talking? Did he know?

"I wonder if Tannis told her?" he mused. "Got her freaked out."

"Maybe," I croaked.

He glanced over. "You okay?"

I nodded, clearing my throat. "Yeah, fine." I knew I shouldn't ask. Should change the subject to something less dangerous. But I wanted to know. "Weird how?"

Trip turned the corner, cruising toward the rec fields where he used to practice football drills while I read. "I don't know. Distant. Doesn't call me back as fast. Doesn't come over."

"Doesn't send you flowers," I said, feeling unbelievably guilty.

Trip snorted. "Exactly." He was looking out the window, and I thought back to that summer and how things might have been different now if I'd practiced too, made the football team. Or whether they'd have been just the same. Trip still drifting away to other friends, finding his way back to me when it suited him.

"I'm sure we've all been acting weird lately," I said. "It's been a weird couple of weeks."

"Understatement of the year," he said, pulling to the curb and abruptly changing the subject. "Want to go throw a ball for a while?"

I didn't but agreed anyway.

He pulled an old football from his trunk, and I went long, my half-frozen hands fumbling the ball.

"C'mon, Ri," he said, grinning. "No butterfingers."

"They're more like Popsicles, thank you very much." I threw him a bullet, which he caught against his chest.

"No excuses."

We passed back and forth a few more times before he said, "You get that this is another thing from that night coming true, right?"

I paused midthrow. Then nodded. I had, subconsciously if nothing else. Nat's dad. Tannis with kids. And of course, the one Trip didn't know about. Me and Sarah.

"It's only a matter of time before she realizes it and freaks," he said. "You still have those binoculars?"

"Yeah."

"Where?"

"At my house." Not 100 percent true. I'd moved them somewhere farther away, the sense of them in my underwear drawer too unsettling.

Trip nodded but didn't say more. I dropped a couple more passes before he said, "You had enough?"

"I'm fucking frozen," I told him.

"Maybe not the best day for football," he agreed.

"Don't be a wimp," I said, walking back to the car. He drove to my house, idled the car while I detangled myself from his seat belt when we got there.

"Hey, Ri," he said as I opened the door.

"What?"

"Good luck tomorrow."

"With what?"

"You know," he said. "Your dad."

My chest tightened. My mom and I always visited his grave on the anniversary of his death. Trip was the only one who knew about it. That he remembered meant something. "Thanks, man," I said, struggling to keep my voice even.

CHAPTER 27

THERE ARE THREE CEMETERIES IN BUFORD. MY DAD WAS BURIED in the one farthest from our house. I wouldn't have minded if it were across the country. The idea of his body in a box felt so wrong.

I preferred to think of him as perpetually sitting on a rock by the banks of Stipler's Creek like he had every summer he'd been alive. Dangling a line into the clear water, watching for the fish that you'd see long before they reached you.

But visiting his grave with my mom made it hard to hold on to that. She talked to him, and I couldn't help thinking really weird stuff, like how she was talking to a pile of dust. Or how he'd never be able to hear her through all that dirt.

"You ready?" she asked as I clomped down the stairs.

I nodded. My mom was wearing a skirt like she did every

year. *Like a fifties housewife*, he'd have teased her. They'd always been more the blue jeans and flip-flops types.

We'd both taken the day off, skipping school and work for the occasion. It was overcast and cold but not raining. Late October was a shitty time to visit a cemetery. Probably a shittier time to lie dying in the woods. He'd been shot clean through the gut. The other hunter hadn't even known it'd happened until he'd read about it in the paper. He came forward as a witness, having been up on Neversink that day, only to find out it was his shot that had killed my dad.

My memory of it is crystal clear: I was working on a ham radio with pieces my dad had left me and some barely legible instructions his dad had written about a hundred years before. I stopped when the phone rang, listening. Maybe I always did that, or maybe I had a sixth sense about that call.

And then a crash in the kitchen.

I walked out there, my heart thumping. My mom's teacup was broken, and there were brown splatters all across the floor. She wasn't even looking at it.

"Oh my God, oh my God."

She kept saying it over and over, crumpled on the floor, her jeans soaking up the tea she was sitting in.

I always thought of that moment as when my dad died, but it was actually the day before. He'd been dead for hours, lying in the woods alone while my mom and I had eaten dinner, said good night, gone about whatever our routine had been when I was thirteen and she was thirty-five. He'd broken one of his cardinal rules and hunted alone. *Not like him*, she always said. Not like *any* experienced, responsible hunter. Years later it struck me odd that he'd been gone overnight and we hadn't worried. But I'd pieced together enough of what had been going on with my parents around then that I hadn't asked. It probably hadn't been the first time my dad had disappeared like that.

I guess visiting his grave on a dreary day like this was only fitting. Then again, maybe I'd think of him differently if it were a blue-sky summer morning, remember the happy times rather than the depressing memories this trip always stirred up. I wish we could just pack it in, but my mom thought it was important to remember and respect. Every year there was less and less I remembered, grainy and nonsequential, like screen shots of an old and kind of sad movie.

My dad tinkering with wires and tools at his workbench, letting me watch by the side as long as I was quiet and didn't fidget.

Him bringing home the retriever puppy we had to give up for adoption six months later when he lost his job.

The time we drove to Maine with Trip's family and I got a hole in one at mini-golf. My dad boosted me onto his shoulders, paraded me around the course. We got ice cream later, and mine fell out of the cone onto the parking lot, but

I didn't care, still flying high from my golf triumph.

I mentioned that to my mom once. "You did so care," she countered. "You cried and whined for ten minutes for a new one."

"No, I didn't."

"You most certainly did. And your dad got it for you too," she said, ruffling my hair.

I spent most of the ride today thinking not about my dad but about Trip. Feeling both better about how I'd been handling the thing with Sarah and terrible that there was anything to handle in the first place. And what of the things yet to come? Me and her in bed. It wouldn't happen, I vowed. Couldn't.

My mom passed through the iron gates and wove down the roughly paved lanes, the worn and tilted grave markers turning gradually to newer, tidier ones until we got to my dad's section near the back. She pulled to the side, not that anyone else would need to pass. In our years of visiting, I don't think I'd seen another soul there.

"Ready?" I asked after a minute.

She took a breath and nodded. But didn't move.

"Mom?" I asked. "You okay?"

"I was just realizing how long it's really been, Riley," she said. "You were thirteen. Eighth grade, right?"

I nodded. I'd been mortified when old Miss Bussey had hugged me right in front of the whole class when I'd gone back to school, pressing me against her scratchy, mothbally sweater. I'd had to hold my breath and count to five so I wouldn't scream or wiggle away. I'd had practice by then. Lots of people had wanted to pat or hug or touch me at the funeral and after. I'd just wanted them all to go away.

"You've grown up without a dad," she said softly.

"I remember the things he taught me," I said. "About circuits and baseball and . . . other stuff. And you've filled in the rest just fine."

She looked over, smiling through teary eyes, and I knew it had been the right thing to say, even if it wasn't all true.

We got out then, tramped through the muddy grass, our boots squishing in the muck, leaving soft tracks to his marker.

"Hey, Wes," she said softly. My mom stood stiffly by the gray stone. It was too hard for her to squat down anymore, and wet besides. "It's been a busy year," she said, talking like she always did, as if he were just down there waiting all this time for his annual update. She covered work: fine (a lie). The house: still standing, needs some work we hope to get to this year (if we win the lottery). Me.

"He's so tall now, Wes," she said, glancing back at me with a smile. "A full head above me. What was he when you saw him last? Up to your chest? You wouldn't even recognize him. Except he's got your blue eyes." She paused. "He's taking the SATs this year, maybe heading off to college . . ." I heard my mom take a breath, her voice catching for a second. "I wish you could see what a great kid he's become. So smart and caring and hardworking." Her voice cracked gently. "You'd be so proud."

I wanted to run. Right then. Take off as fast as I could through row after row of stones. Out of here, away from the way this hurt, fast enough to turn today to yesterday and back to the night when we didn't think to call and find out where he was and why he wasn't home. Sarah had been right. I'd do anything to have him back. My chest burned with it, hot and tight, and I had to bite my lip, hard enough to draw blood, so I could stay there, steady for my mom, and not leave or cry or scream the way everything in me needed to just then.

"Riley?" I looked over at my mom, who'd stepped back and was beside me now. "Your turn." She gestured toward the gravestone.

I took a few hesitant steps forward. "Hi, Dad," I said, wishing my mom weren't standing there listening to every word I said. "Mom already filled you in on pretty much everything. So I . . . uh . . ." I fidgeted, then stopped, remembering how he'd look at me, his rough face softening, in the light and shadow by his basement workbench. "I miss you," I said, adding quietly, "a lot."

I stepped back, my left boot making a disgusting squelchy noise. My mom patted my back, leaning forward to put a wrapped cigar onto the headstone. "Smoke 'em if you got 'em," she said softly like she did every year. Then we walked silently back to the car.

The other thing we always did on his anniversary was make tacos. His favorite meal.

As much as I dreaded the day, this part felt warm and safe. I had run the gauntlet, completed another year's worth of rituals and trials. Now I could relax.

"When's the test?" she asked, handing me the grater and cheese.

"What test?"

She gave me a funny smile. "The SAT?"

Oh. That one. "Two weeks." I was still uncomfortable talking about it, but it was easier now that the house was warm again.

She started slicing tomatoes, saying, "I'm glad you did it, Riley."

I shook my head. "I shouldn't have. It was stupid—"

"No." She cut me off. "It wasn't. It's what you're supposed to be doing. You probably should have done it months ago, right?"

"Maybe." I shrugged uncomfortably. "It just seemed like there was never a good time."

"Sometimes you have to make it a good time." She smiled. "I guess you figured that out." My mom shook her head. "I can't believe you'll be graduating high school this year."

"Me either."

It struck me that these were the times—more than when bills came due or we had to shovel out the car—that I wished my dad were still alive. Wished that it weren't just me and her. Because even if we got the financial stuff figured out, the idea of leaving her here in this lonely house hurt.

"Maybe you should, you know, start dating, Mom."

Her eyebrows shot up. *"What?"*

"You know." I blushed. "Go out. With guys."

She stared at me, a different kind of smile stuck on her mouth. Half-amused, half-uncomfortable. "What brought this up?"

"I just think . . . I don't know," I fumbled, embarrassed. "Aren't you lonely?" I blurted finally, giving her a glance before studying my ragged fingernails.

"Lonely?" she said slowly. "No. Not really."

"But won't you be?" I asked. "When—" I quickly corrected myself, "*If* I go to college? Someday?"

She nodded thoughtfully. "Maybe," she said. "But I have friends here . . ."

I let the silence hang a minute, hoping she'd continue so I wouldn't have to. But she didn't.

"I know, Mom." Her friends were mostly people from church or work—with their own families and husbands—

who weren't going to spend their evenings cooking dinner with her. "But maybe it'd be nice to have a . . ." I couldn't quite bring myself to say it.

"Partner?" she said teasingly. "Companion?" She grinned. "It's very sweet that you worry about me, Riley, but you don't have to. Really. I'm fine and I'm happy."

I gave her a skeptical look.

"There are people who look out for me," she said comfortingly.

"But, Mom," I blurted, "he's married."

She gaped at me, speechless. I was a little shocked I'd actually said it too.

"Yes," she said after a minute, "but I can't change that."

"But you don't have to be . . . involved in it."

"What brought this up, Riley?"

Good question, one I wasn't sure I could answer. Something to do with Sarah and me and Trip. And the binoculars. "It's just . . . well, it doesn't seem right, Mom."

Her lips tightened, but she stayed calm. "It's probably hard for you to understand, Riley. But we have a history, he and I. It means something. I care about him. He cares about me."

Not enough to leave his wife, I wanted to say. That was the part that got me angriest, the way he used her. And she let him.

"It's not ideal," she was saying. "And I've agonized about

it a lot for a long time, but I can't be responsible for everyone's happiness. I'm happy, he's happy, and she's . . . well, no less happy than she would be any other way, I think."

I left it there. What else could I do? But I was disappointed, which is stupid, because parents are just people too, and most of the ones I knew—Trip's, Natalie's, mine—had proved time and again that they were far from perfect. I wanted my mom to be better, nobler. I didn't love her any less, but I think I respected her less. It might have been unfair, given my own conduct, but somehow that made it even clearer for me. If I could feel how wrong it was, having only done it once or twice, how could she have let it go on for years?

Not that my heart didn't skip a beat when my phone rang later, Sarah's name on the caller ID.

"I had a thought," she said when I picked up.

"Again?"

Sarah took a deep breath. "You know how John was saying something isn't adding up?"

"Yeah."

"Think about the things we know: what Galen said about that night, what we learned when we went back to the trailer, the lighter you found."

"So?"

"How do we know all that stuff?"

"Well, Trip talked to Galen—"

"How did we even start to suspect him in the first place?" she interrupted.

"Richie Milosevich said he was up there."

"Said it to who?" Sarah prodded.

I hesitated, thinking, and she continued.

"Who encouraged us to go back to the trailer to map? Where we just happened to find Moose's lighter?" she continued. "And who was the first one to tell us Nat's dad had been killed? Who heard it on the scanner?"

The answer to all of it was the same.

"Trip." His name dropped from my lips like a lead ball, her point chillingly clear. "You think he's been lying?" I said. "Why?"

"Why do you think?" she asked.

I thought about that a second, the answer obvious. "To protect someone," I said. "Like Natalie. Or Galen."

"Or himself."

CHAPTER 28

WE DECIDED TO TALK TO TRIP TOGETHER. HE WAS SUPPOSED TO go to Sarah's after football practice. He'd just find me waiting there also.

I'd tossed the situation around after talking to Sarah, and the next day too, looking for explanations and alternatives, but Sarah was right. Every angle could be drawn back to him. "But he was the one pressing us to investigate," I'd argued. "Why would he do that if he were involved?"

"Was he really, Ri?" she'd asked. "Think about it. Were we investigating, or just following up on things he was feeding us?"

"It was just you and me mapping the crime scene. He didn't even want to go."

"Maybe he'd already been up there," she'd said. "Left the lighter, moved things around. Who knows?"

"Why would he kill Natalie's dad?"

"I don't know." Sarah had paused and I'd listened to her soft breathing through the phone, pictured her in her living room, frowning, trying to figure it out. "Self-defense? To protect Natalie? Anger?"

None of those reasons really added up. Like lots of things in this puzzle. So we decided to ask Trip point-blank. Just the three of us.

I was there at seven on the dot, like we'd agreed. Plenty of time for Trip to finish practice and get there. Sarah opened the door and ushered me into the living room, warm and brightly lit. There was a tray of drinks on the coffee table.

"Did Martha Stewart move in?" I asked.

Sarah attempted a smile. "I was trying to keep busy." She took a shaky breath. "God, Riley, I'm nervous."

I nodded. "Me too." I checked my watch. 7:05. "What time was he coming?"

"Seven," she said.

We perched uneasily on the sofas. I looked around the room, realizing the bookshelves were bare. The walls too. "Where did everything go?"

"My dad." She shook her head. "He's 'decorating.'"

Silence fell again. "So . . . ," I said after a minute. "I guess I'll start when he comes in?"

"Okay." Her voice was strained, and when she looked

at me, I saw her eyes were filled with tears.

"Hey," I said, moving closer, catching her hands in mine. "Listen, whatever it is, it'll be okay."

She nodded, drawing a deep breath. "I know. I'm just so worried. And confused."

"I'm sure if Trip had anything to do with it, there was a very good reason."

"Then why wouldn't he just have come forward?"

That was the part I couldn't figure out either. "I don't know," I admitted. "But the three of us will talk it out. And help each other." *Whatever that means*, I thought.

She smiled tenderly. "Thank you, Riley," she said. "You always know how to say the right things."

I smiled back, still holding her hand, and impulsively gave her a quick kiss on the forehead.

Just as the front door opened.

Trip, late as usual, stared at us, whatever greeting he'd started, strangled in his throat.

I jumped up. "Hey, Trip."

He looked from me to Sarah, then back at me, glaring. "What the fuck?"

"What?" I asked innocently, my throat so tight I could barely speak.

Trip sneered. "What?" he mimicked. "I know you think I'm stupid, but do you think I'm blind, too?" He turned to Sarah. "What's he even doing here?"

"Trip," Sarah said, soothing. "We just wanted to talk to you. Relax. It's nothing."

"Really? It didn't look like nothing. It looked like you and Riley snuggled up on the couch and him kissing you." He looked from her to me. "Which part of that do I have wrong?"

"It's my fault, Trip," I said. "Sarah was upset, and I was trying to help." I took a breath. Time to man up. "I shouldn't have done that." God, what had I been thinking? "I'm sorry. I way overstepped."

"You can say that again." Trip was staring at me with such intensity I felt like I was shriveling up, especially because I could see he knew. How I felt about Sarah. And that I'd acted on it. I didn't know how—maybe just because he could read me so well—but he knew. He shook his head, his voice low. "That's just so *wrong*, man."

I was too ashamed to answer.

Sarah stepped hesitantly closer to him. "Trip," she said softly. "We need to talk about Nat's dad."

"Yeah," he said gruffly. "But I think we better talk about *this* first." He waved his hands at me and Sarah. "I thought I was imagining things, being paranoid. I figured there was *no way* my best friend and girlfriend could be hooking up." I'd never seen him so mad. And he had every right to be.

"Trip—" I started, but he cut me off.

"I mean, what kind of people would do that?" he shouted.

"Huh?" Sarah stood there silently, tears running down her face. Trip's jaw was clenched, his eyes blazing as he looked from her to me. I felt awful, like the smallest, most worthless piece of crap. "I guess I know the answer."

He turned around, yanked open the door, and slammed it behind him, without looking back.

We stood there, stunned.

"Oh my God, Riley. Should we go after him?" Sarah's face was pale, and I could see her hands shaking. "Riley?"

I had no idea. "No," I finally answered. I mean, what could we say to make it better? He was so angry, he wouldn't hear us anyway.

But there was a nagging worry about whether letting him stew was really the best idea.

I wish I'd had the sense to listen to it. To call him back in, tell him why we'd asked him there. Even own up to things, if that was what it took. I wish I'd told Trip whatever he needed to hear to stay.

Because after he left Sarah's, tires squealing as he zoomed away, I never saw him again.

CHAPTER 29

MY MOM WAS STANDING IN MY ROOM WHEN I WOKE UP. IT WAS dark, her thin shoulders silhouetted against the light from the hall.

"Mom?" I mumbled.

I heard a sniff, saw the shadow of her chest heave slightly. She was crying.

"Mom?" I sat up, all sleepiness gone. "What's wrong?" I thought she was sick again, needed to go to the hospital. But then she wouldn't have been standing here, wouldn't have been able to get out of bed.

"It's Trip."

We drove to the hospital together, my mom still crying, me numb as if my body had turned to stone or ice. Dr. Williams had called her, knowing our families were close, or had been. A car accident. Single vehicle. On old Ohoyo Road, not too far from Natalie's trailer.

My head was empty. Or maybe too full. But none of the stuff in there made sense. Sarah. That was all I could pick out, and then I immediately pushed it back, into the dark, deafening roar. Had she called him? Tried to explain? Had he gone back and gotten her? It wasn't until we were there, robotically stepping off the elevator, that I knew she was safe. She stood in the garish light with Natalie, and Tannis and her brothers, their parents, a cluster of pale faces and puffy, red, unseeing eyes. Trip's mom was huddled in a corner, his dad beside her.

I went to the girls. "What happened?"

Sarah looked at me, looked through me, her eyes unreadable, but not like they usually were. There was just nothing there. Hollow. Then she turned away.

"No one's sure yet," Tannis said. "It looks like he ran off the road, into a tree."

"God," I whispered. I didn't want to ask the next question. I could read the answer in the people in that cold, hard, bright hallway. "How bad?"

A doctor pushed through the door then, tugged at his mask. I remember every bit of detail from that moment—the clipboard in his hand, the streaks of blood on his shirt, his unshaven face like he slept there night after night. His eyes swept the room tiredly, then fixed on that corner and he walked slowly toward Trip's parents.

"Mr. and Mrs. Jones?"

Trip's mom looked up at him, and I saw her eyes meet his. Saw his head shake slightly. She screamed. And screamed and screamed. The sound of it piercing, shattering the brittle frame of me, over and over. They wheeled her away soon, but that sound lingered in the hallway like it would never, ever leave.

CHAPTER 30

THEY BURIED TRIP IN THE SAME CEMETERY AS MY DAD. IF I squinted, I could see my dad's marker across the field from where I stood, feeling wooden among other wooden figures. I wondered if the cigar was still there and whether we'd add Trip to our annual visits, dropping off a Bud Light or a new football when we came.

Lots of people were there. I knew almost everyone in the first row and second and third. The four of stood near the front, side-by-side—me, Nat, Tannis, and Sarah. I held Natalie's hand during the prayer, with Lu standing protectively behind her. I wanted to talk to Sarah, just her and me. I wanted her to look at me so I could find some spark of life in those deep, dark eyes. But her gaze skated vacantly past.

When the priest finished talking, my mom and I offered

condolences to Trip's parents. His mom was unresponsive, his dad mechanical, but affable as always.

Afterward, classmates whispered about what'd happened, the same as they'd whispered about Nat and her dad. I didn't ask for any of it but let their gossip seep in, piling into the empty, ugly hollow of my gut.

I should have told him, I thought. Over and over and over. I couldn't follow the train of thought long enough to figure out what I should have told him or when I could have made a difference. I knew only that I'd done something horribly, unspeakably wrong.

CHAPTER 31

TRIP'S DAD CAME BY THE HOUSE A COUPLE OF DAYS LATER. Maybe it was a couple of weeks. Time did a funny thing after, some days slipping away without notice while others stretched on endlessly. He stood on the front step, twisting his gloves in his hands like he was trying to wring the life out of them. It looked like someone had done the same to him. His face was so pale and sad that I couldn't muster even a trace of the anger I usually felt when I saw him.

He looked around the living room after I'd ushered him in, like he'd never been there. I waited, but he just kept sweeping his eyes around the room.

"My mom's out," I told him finally. "She's at work."

He started like I'd woken him, then shook his head. "I came to see you," he said.

I waited, wondering after the silence continued if I'd have

to restart him again, but finally he said slowly, "I knew your dad way back." He looked past me, toward the back door and yard, where he used to laugh and drink with my dad about a million years ago. "Of course, you already know that."

I didn't answer. I didn't want to hear him reminisce about how it had been before it had all split apart.

Mr. Jones took a deep breath. Then his shoulders fell heavily as he exhaled. "He was a good guy. A better friend to me than I ever was to him."

I shifted my weight subtly. "Mr. Jones, maybe we should—"

He held up a hand. "Hear me out, Riley. Please. I feel like I have to tell you. I owe it to him." He paused. "I feel like there's karma at work here. Payback. And I have to stop it now."

I wanted to tell him that whatever it was, it was okay. If there was a debt, it was paid back. With interest. I wanted to plug my ears, the way you do when you're four and your daddy is telling you he expects you to clean up the mess you made in the kitchen before he paddles your butt. But I wasn't four anymore, and I knew that if there were something karmic at work, my part of the bargain was to listen. So I did.

"I was supposed to be hunting with him the day he died." He saw the shock on my face and passed a hand over his forehead, trying to wipe away whatever he was feeling. "We had a fight. Had a bunch of them back then . . ."

His voice caught. After a minute he continued, "Instead of being a man and hashing it out or calling him up to say I couldn't go, I stood him up. Just didn't show up at the lot when I was supposed to. I figured that'd show him . . ." He trailed off like he'd lost his train of thought.

"It's okay," I said mechanically.

That woke him up. "No! No, it's not, Riley." He was fighting for composure. "It's not okay. Never okay. When Trip was doing that same thing to you, I made him fix it. You don't just throw away your friends."

Made Trip fix it? What did that mean? Had he sent Trip over to my house that June day before junior year? Forced him to be friends with me again? I didn't know what to say, but he didn't notice.

"Your dad thought there was something between me and your mom."

I cringed, and he kept going.

"There wasn't," Mr. Jones said quickly. "I always thought she was gorgeous. Your mom was so . . . alive. Back then," he added as an afterthought. "I told him that, but your dad was suspicious, always watching me—"

I had to interrupt. "Please." I held up my hand. "These are my *parents* you're talking about." I couldn't stand another minute of it—him and her and my dad. Trip and Sarah and me.

Mr. Jones rubbed at his forehead. "Right. I'm sorry." I saw him glance around the room, focus on the spot by the stairs where the carpet was worn down to the flecked padding underneath. It made me want to push a chair or box or lay a sheet on top to cover it up. He looked down, realizing he was holding something. The reason he was here.

"Your dad isn't here to provide for you," he said, fingering the thing in his hand, a wrinkled envelope. "At least part of that is my fault. I owe him," he continued. "And I don't have a son to provide for anymore." He said it dully, the words wooden, without real meaning, because if they'd had more form and life, both of us would have crumbled. He stuck the envelope out toward me. "Take it. Please."

He had to shake it once, insisting, before I finally, reluctantly took it.

"Open it," he said when it was obvious I didn't plan to.

I turned it over, saw that the back was unsealed, and glanced inside, feeling my throat constrict as I read the numbers on the cashier's check.

"I can't take this—" I shoved it back at him. I couldn't imagine what crazy idea made him think I'd let him hand me that kind of money.

"You have to," he interrupted. "It's earmarked for school. For—" His voice broke, edged to desperation when he continued. "What am I going to do with it? Pay bills? Remodel my house? For what? What does any of that mean? Take it. You're a smart kid. Use it to get yourself out of here. Do something good, something that'll mean something—"

"Stop." It was rude, but I couldn't listen anymore, couldn't hear the things I knew were coming. *For Trip. So he'll be remembered, valued. In his memory.* I kept the envelope. It felt like a deal with the devil.

I laid it on the table by the door, the envelope suddenly feeling too heavy to hold, laden with the responsibility of memorializing Trip. It wasn't the kind of thing I could say no to, even though everything in me told me I should. I was taking Trip's life. His college savings. His girlfriend. None of it had been my fault or on purpose, but it still felt very, very wrong. I had wanted Sarah and I'd wanted to leave here, but ohmygod, I didn't want either of them this way.

CHAPTER 32

OF COURSE, I REALIZED IT WAS THE FINAL PIECES.

Why Trip had never seen anything in the binoculars. No future.

How I'd pay for college.

It took Tannis a few days longer, but one day at lunch she said it. "We have to get rid of them. It's all coming true."

I looked at Natalie and Sarah, their eyes deeply vacant, something I'd come to accept as our general state of being. We were in a vacuum of meaning. We were statues, sitting together but none of us really there. Nothing mattered. Nothing seemed possible.

I would take the SATs the following weekend. I was leaving Buford. I'd go to college next year.

I didn't give a damn about any of it.

"You guys do it," Natalie said. "I'm not touching them.

I don't even want to see them again. Ever." Her voice was high, hysterical. Not that Tannis was much better.

I nodded. Thinking was so hard. Just do it. Go with it. "Okay. They're at my house. We'll go after school."

"I can't," Sarah said. "I have an appointment." She smiled mirthlessly. "My dad's making me see a shrink."

It would have been funny. But it wasn't. Sarah was the worst of all of us. I wanted to talk to her, tell her the things I wished I could believe about how it wasn't our fault and there was nothing we could have done. But she wouldn't even get near me alone. I hated it, and I was worried about her—it was the only real feeling I had these days—but I understood.

"So, just you and me," I said to Tannis. "You okay to go?"

"Well, my back hurts all the fucking time, I have to puke every morning, and I'm exhausted," she said, "but I don't think I'll ever sleep again until I know they've been mashed, bashed, burned, or destroyed. So, yeah, I'm good to go."

I nodded. "It's a date."

We walked to my house, her and me. Neither of us had a car that day. We could have asked her brother or someone else, maybe Matty, but it was too much effort.

"How are things with him?" I asked her on the walk. "And . . . stuff?" I couldn't bring myself to say "baby" or "pregnant." I didn't even like thinking it.

"Okay. I guess. We're talking about what to do." Tannis

smiled vaguely. "He really digs me," she said, looking over. "Isn't that funny?"

"Why? You're hot," I said. "At least that's what you've always told me."

Tannis nudged my arm playfully. "I just never thought . . . I don't know. He's not my usual type." She finished quietly, the sense of who her type was—had been—hanging there.

We walked in silence for a few minutes until Tannis asked, "Do you think they'll ever find out who killed Nat's dad?"

"Does it matter?" It slipped out before I realized how it'd sound.

"What do you mean?" Tannis looked at me like I was crazy. "Of course it matters."

"Yeah, I know. Sorry," I said, not meaning any of it. I couldn't tell Tannis the things Sarah and I had talked about. What we'd been planning to ask Trip. And how the whole thing was wrapped up in his death for me now. And because of that, wrapped up in my role in it, something I couldn't bear to think about too much. "No," I told her honestly. "I don't." Whether that was because the murderer was dead himself or because what Trip had known had been a key to the puzzle, I didn't know or care.

Tannis nodded. "Yeah, I've kind of been thinking that too," she said. "I read somewhere that most murders are solved in the first forty-eight hours."

"You can read?"

"Shove it, Ri," she said, before continuing. "I guess if the police haven't figured it out yet, they're probably not going to."

Tannis and I turned onto my walk. The power had been back on for almost two weeks, but I still had a second of apprehension when we pushed into the living room. I flicked on the light switch, and everything worked.

But something was still wrong.

It was that same prickly not-right feeling I'd had the day I'd caught my mom with Trip's dad.

"What?" Tannis asked, seeing me motionless just inside the door.

I listened, and a soft sound confirmed what I'd been thinking. "Someone's here," I told her quietly. Her eyes went wide. "Mom?" I called, already knowing from the missing car that it wasn't her.

No one answered. There was a creak and another, moving faster. The squeal of rusty hinges. My thoughts flew to my room. Moose's lighter in my drawer, traces of Mr. Cleary's blood on it. I should have given it to the cops.

"Stay here," I told Tannis. I strode through the hallway to the kitchen and yanked the back door open. I stepped out into the yard just in time to see a shadowy figure disappear into the woods.

"Stop!" I yelled. Like they were going to listen. I sprinted after them, dodging the branch that hung low at the start of the trail. It had been years since I'd hiked it, but I still remembered every twist of the path. I jogged up the steep section, careful to keep my eyes on the ground. It was easy to hit a stone or hole and sprain your ankle. I could hear the person ahead of me crashing through the brush, stepping on twigs as they went. What could they possibly want? The money Trip's dad had given me was tucked securely in a bank account. We had nothing else of value. Except the lighter, of value to only one person.

The trail's incline evened out as the path zigzagged around trees and brush. I kept up a jog. The person sounded farther ahead, but I knew I'd catch up. Another forty feet, and the trail seemed to disappear. To find it you had to climb through two fallen trees, their branches forming a knotted obstacle not unlike the maze of strings Sarah and I had created in the physics closet and at Natalie's trailer. I doubted the person ahead of me knew that.

I rounded the last bend, stepping into the small clearing before the trees.

It was empty.

And then I saw the slightest movement. Someone crouched behind a bush to the side of the trail. I might not have noticed if it had been a little darker. Or if her coat hadn't been bright red.

"Sarah?"

Nothing.

"I see you." I took a step closer. "You can come out."

She stood slowly, her long hair tangled, pieces of twigs and dead leaves clinging to it. There was a scratch across her cheek. She looked wild, her eyes jittery and desperate. It struck me that this was the first time since Trip had died that I'd actually seen her eyes, that she'd looked at me straight on.

"Sarah," I said gently, stepping toward her. "Are you okay? I've been really worried—" I stopped, seeing her shrink from my reach. I let my hand drop back. She didn't want me to touch her. I understood, but it stung. I'd only wanted to comfort her. She looked like she needed it.

"You were in my house," I said softly, afraid to scare her away. "Do you need something?"

She nodded, her eyes filling with tears. I could see them glittering.

"What, Sarah? Did you need to see me?"

She shook her head. Then said something, her voice too quiet.

"What?"

"The binoculars," she said louder. "I need the binoculars."

"What?" I noticed the deep hollows of her face and circles around her eyes and wondered if she'd gone over the edge. "Why?"

"Please, Riley," she said, the tears now running down

her cheeks. "Please don't make me explain. Just . . . just let me have them."

I felt a tickle of something, the same kind of warning I'd felt when we'd first found them that night at the cave. *Just give them to her,* my inner voice said. *Don't ask questions.* But I hadn't listened to it before, so why start now? I'm a slow learner like that.

"Sarah," I started. "I don't think that's a good idea," I said. "Why do you want them?"

She wiped at her face, leaving streaks of mud from the tears and dirt. "Riley . . . I . . ." She took a shaky breath. "I'm so sorry."

"For what, Sarah? The stuff that's happened . . ." I didn't want to say his name. "It's not your fault."

"No." She shook her head miserably. "You're wrong, Riley. It *is* my fault. All of it."

"Sarah—" I stepped toward her, meaning to soothe, but again she shrank away.

"They're mine," she said starkly. "The binoculars."

I froze. "What?"

"I'm the one who put them in the cave," she said. "Before that night when we found them. I've known what they were—or what they were supposed to be—all along. I just . . . I never thought . . ." She stopped, crying too hard to continue.

I didn't move, struggling to work through the words. I

wanted to believe she was crazy, as horrible as that would be. She *looked* crazy. But something told me she wasn't.

"What do you mean?" I heard myself ask.

Sarah pinched the bridge of her nose, her eyes squeezed shut. Then she wiped her hands harshly across both cheeks and took a deep unsteady breath. "My mom gave them to me. Before she left." Sarah barked an angry laugh. "I guess that's the thing. When you abandon your family, you leave something behind. Nat got a vase. I got these effed-up binoculars.

"She called them her déjà vu glasses," Sarah said hoarsely. She cleared her throat before continuing. "The first time I saw them, I must have been seven or eight. She was all excited about them, a new project she was tinkering with. I'd hear her and my dad talking about them from time to time, tossing around ideas of hypnosis and brain function. That was the kind of background chatter that went on in our house."

"Yeah, mine, too," I said, but Sarah didn't crack a smile.

"It's not a joke, Riley." She sucked her lip in, biting at it. I knew it wasn't. I didn't feel like laughing either. I felt like screaming or running away, the way I'd felt at my dad's grave on our anniversary visit. Wishing I could rewind time.

"I didn't think anything of it," Sarah continued. "I mean, why would I? I was a kid and there were always things my mom was making, new machines, new projects. This was just another of them, right?

"One day when I was ten, she sat me down in the kitchen. My dad was out, and I knew it was serious, because my mom didn't have sit-down conversations. That meant she'd have to stay still. And focus." Sarah smiled bitterly. "She brought them out.

"'Do you remember these?' she asked me.

"'Yes,' I told her. 'Your dish-a-view glasses.'

"She laughed. 'Déjà vu,' she corrected me. 'Do you know what that is?'

"I didn't, and she explained it. 'These glasses *make* that happen,' she said—"

"What does that mean?" I interrupted. My mouth was dry, and every nerve thrummed with energy. And fear.

She had known, I realized. That's what she was telling me. This whole time Sarah had known what they were. And now I was about to know too. Had I really seen my future?

"There are big parts of our brain that we never use," Sarah said. "That's what my dad's dissertation was about. The one my mom got so interested in. Dormant centers. There are a lot of theories about what goes on in there and whether people have untapped powers, ESP, telekinesis—"

"Crazy shit," I interrupted, feeling my heart pounding.

"A lot of it, yeah," Sarah said. "But there's *something* there. And my mom—and dad—thought there were ways to tap into it through a sort of hypnosis."

"The binoculars—her déjà vu glasses—hypnotize you?"

"They put you into a state where you can access things you normally can't."

"What kind of things?"

"Memories," Sarah said. "From the future."

I stared at her, her tangled hair and torn, dirty face. My mind was spinning through the possibilities and impossibilities of what she was saying. "Sarah—" But I couldn't finish the thought. I didn't know where it led.

"Do you remember what Mr. Ruskovich told you?" she asked. "About things traveling the through space-time continuum?"

I nodded. "Matter can't," I croaked.

"But energy can," Sarah finished quietly. "And brain waves create energy."

She let that hang, and I tried to process it. But my brain felt swollen, pounding against my skull.

"So the things we saw," I said slowly, "are thoughts and memories we have *in the future*?" I was trying to find sense in the words as I said them, but mostly it felt like I was just repeating what she'd said.

"Yes," she said, sounding relieved. "That's right, Riley. That's why she called them déjà vu glasses, because that's what gave her the idea to start with."

I just stared, and Sarah explained, "My mom thought that feeling of having done something before is so intense because we have the memory of it, the way it feels and looks and smells, it's all"—Sarah tapped her head—"stored up here."

It was so impossible, so crazy. There were so many ways I should have been able to shoot holes in this ridiculous story. If only I could think. "Why didn't you tell us before?" I asked mechanically, not even really aware that the words had come out, until I saw tears pooling in Sarah's eyes.

"She told me I couldn't," Sarah said.

"Who? Your mom?"

Sarah nodded. "She left about a week after the day she explained them to me. I heard her and my dad fighting downstairs. They didn't throw things or yell, but there was a certain way their voices were." Tears spilled over, running through the mud on Sarah's cheeks. "I was on my bed when she came in and sat beside me.

"'I have to go,' she told me. 'I wanted you to come, but . . . well, it's not that simple.'" Sarah was openly sobbing, her words coming in bursts between broken breaths. "I remember her winking at me," Sarah said bitterly. "Handing me that case with the binoculars and saying, 'It's just as well, sweets. I've got a job for you here. An important one.' Like my life wasn't falling apart. Like I gave a shit about her stupid glasses." Sarah spat the words out, swiping at her nose, her cheeks, with the sleeve of her jacket. She was a mess, her eyes wild, and I wondered again about her sanity.

"What was it, Sarah?" I asked gently, thinking maybe if I coaxed out the rest, we could go home. Back to my house or hers. To the hospital or the shrink her dad wanted her to see.

"She wanted me to get them where they needed to be," Sarah said dully.

"And where was that?"

She didn't answer, just kept staring at me, tears running down her face, glistening in the sun.

I felt a strange stillness, a dread-filled certainty—like that first night at the cave when I didn't want to open the box because I almost knew already what was inside and where it might lead—that I shouldn't ask. But I did.

"What, Sarah?" I demanded, fear making the words harsher than I meant them to be. "Where did they need to be?"

"With you," she whispered.

CHAPTER 33

HER WORDS WERE PERFECTLY DISTINCT, BUT INCOMPREHENSIBLE. "With me?"

"That's the thing I remember most about the night she left," Sarah said. "'You'll know, honey.'" Sarah's voice was higher, mimicking her memory. "'You'll look in them, and one day you'll see the boy I'm talking about. He's here. And when he looks like he does in these, you'll know its time. And you'll know how.'" Sarah closed her eyes, squeezing them tight like she could hold in the tears. I could barely think through the black, ugly buzzing in my head. The boy. Me.

"No," I heard myself say. "That can't be. If your mom invented something like that, she'd be famous. She'd have sold it for millions—"

"Sold it to who, Riley?" Sarah asked quietly. "So they could do *what*?"

She was right. It was the invention of the century, the millennium maybe. But who could you give it to? Who could you trust with something like that?

Certainly not a seventeen-year-old boy you didn't know.

Except maybe she did know me. In the future.

"Why?" I asked, still trying to pick through the mind-bending possibilities. "Why me?"

"You do something with them," Sarah said simply. "Something important. That's all she said. If I got them to you, they'd be safe and she'd come back for me."

I stared, aghast. "She told you that? If you gave me the binoculars, she'd come back?" It was a ridiculous, awful condition to put on someone, especially your kid.

Sarah's face crumpled, her voice strangled by sobs. "Yes."

"And?" I asked roughly. I knew it was mean, but I couldn't stop myself. "Has she?"

She shook her head, still sobbing. "No."

I went to her then, put my arms around her and she let me. I didn't feel like I usually did, close to Sarah. I felt cold. *I do something with them.* My mind rushed through all the things she'd said. Trying to figure out what, if any of it, could be true. Maybe she felt my hesitation, because she pulled away after a minute.

"Why did you come looking for them?" I asked. "If I'm supposed to have them, why are we here?"

"I never meant it to be like this, Riley," she said, her eyes desperate again. “All the things that happened . . . I didn’t know—”

The full truth and horror of it hit me then. All the things we’d seen. Sarah had known they’d happen.

“You didn’t know that Nat’s dad would be killed? After she saw that, you didn’t know?”

“I . . . I’d . . . I didn’t really think—”

“What about Tannis?” I pressed on. “And Trip?”

“I had no idea, Riley,” she said. Her voice was low and urgent. “You have to believe me. I didn’t know that would happen to Trip. I would never, ever have let it go—”

“Why didn’t you just tell us, Sarah?” I said loudly. “For God’s sake, it’s all we’ve talked about for weeks. This whole time, this whole charade about what they were—why didn’t you just confess?”

“And say what?” she asked miserably. “That I’d let Natalie’s dad die? What would you have thought of me? You can’t even imagine what I felt like. I didn’t want to believe it. I just meant to do what I’d been waiting so long to do.” Sarah squeezed her eyes shut again, hand pressing against her forehead. “It all went wrong. I tried to help. I thought if we could figure out what happened to Nat’s dad—who did it—maybe that’d somehow make it better.” She shook her head. “But it just got worse and worse—”

“How is it any worse—” The look on her face stopped me. “You know who did it?”

She didn't answer.

"Sarah?"

She hitched her breath and said, "Ask Nat."

"What?" I was incredulous. "She knows?"

Sarah nodded slowly, wiping at her eyes.

"So I should ask, and then what? She'll just tell me? God, what does Tannis know, the cure to cancer?" I was really angry. All this time, all the things that had happened, and one after another, the people around me, my "friends," had known the answers all along.

"Unlikely," Sarah said, a flash of a smile, sad and tired, at the corners of her lips. "Nat wasn't asleep," she said. "And she wasn't wearing her headphones that night."

"So?" Then I got it. "She heard everything."

Sarah nodded. "Tell her I told you that. I think she'll tell you the rest."

"Why don't you?"

"It's not my secret to tell, Riley," Sarah said. None of them were, it seemed. She'd rather just let me flounder around like an idiot with half the story.

We stood there for a minute, me trying to calm down and Sarah watching me, her tears subsiding.

"They weren't in your drawer," she said finally.

"No," I agreed. "I moved them."

She nodded, not surprised. "Can I have them back?"

I wondered what she'd do if I gave them to her. Wondered what the right answer was. Finally I shook my head. "I don't think so."

"Riley?" Tannis's voice was faint, calling from somewhere in my backyard. "You okay?"

Sarah and I looked at each other.

"Yeah," I yelled back to Tannis, my eyes on Sarah the whole time. "I'm okay. I'll be down in a minute." I waited, wondering how we would go on from here. What would happen next.

"Don't tell her, Riley," she said. "Please."

"Sarah—"

"Think about it," she pressed. "What did you say way back about Tannis? About how she'd feel if she knew it really was her future? Tell her they're gone, disappeared. Tell her you destroyed them. But don't tell her the truth."

"What about Nat?"

She shook her head.

"So . . . we're just going to keep this all a secret?"

"We've had a lot of practice, haven't we?" Sarah said sadly. She leaned forward then and kissed me softly. I could smell the faint flowery scent of her perfume, the shampoo she used, could feel the warmth of her cheek as she pressed it against mine. "Be careful with them," Sarah said. She turned away then, climbing deftly over the bramble of branches and moving along the trail, until even the red of her jacket faded away into the dark woods.

CHAPTER 34

I FIGURED WE'D TALK ABOUT IT AFTER I HAD TIME TO THINK through everything she'd said, that I'd be able to ask all the questions that ran through my brain even as I walked through the woods back toward my house. I told Tannis I'd fallen and the person had outrun me. We searched my room—her and I—and I made like they'd stolen some money I'd had lying on the desk, a watch, and the binoculars.

"You need to file a report," she insisted.

"Don't you think the cops have enough going on?"

Tannis considered it. "Maybe," she said. "Whoever stole them will get what's coming to them with those binoculars anyway."

I was relieved when Sarah wasn't at school the next day. I still didn't know what to say to her. Or how I felt. I was furious at first. And confused. Denying, then believing. Resentful.

I knew that if it was true, I should blame her mom, and intellectually I did. But it was hard to feel much for someone I'd never met, so my anger was mostly directed at Sarah.

After two days I started to worry.

I never expected she would be gone.

Tannis and I went to Sarah's house the third day she was absent, after her cell phone just rang and rang. We pounded on the door, peeked in the windows. It looked like it always had, boxes stacked everywhere. But all the plants were missing. Maybe she'd taken them with her or given them away. But that's how I knew she'd gone, because she wouldn't have left the plants in there to die without her to tend them.

Her note came a day later. I recognized her handwriting, spiky and cramped, on the envelope, and my heart sped up. It was postmarked somewhere in Delaware. I tore it open and pulled out the single page.

Riley,

I'm sorry to leave without saying good-bye in person. I wasn't sure what was best. I never, ever meant for things to happen like they did. I didn't know what we were getting into—what I was getting us into. I am so, so sorry. Please believe that.

I'm sure you're angry. I am too, though I have no right to be.

I told my dad everything, and we're going to find her. I deserve answers. We all do. I'll see you in Cambridge, if not before. I hope by then we can both forgive me.

Love,
Sarah

I read it twice, then a third time, forcing myself to stop after that. I felt like I had when my dad died, a sudden hole ripped in my world. I couldn't believe she'd just left like that.

"What the fuck?" Tannis said when I told her Sarah had written. "Where'd she go?"

"Some kind of family emergency," I said vaguely. I was watching Nat, the way her eyes looked shaded. More than just sad. Secretive.

"Is she coming back?" Nat asked.

"I don't know."

"And then there were three," Tannis said.

But there really weren't.

I noticed it over the next week when I tried to find a time to talk to Nat. She was with the skiers now. And John Peters, always John Peters. And when she saw me, she sometimes looked away.

So finally one day I biked to Lu's, my tires slipping now and then in the slush from our first snowfall, which had been quickly plowed into dirty gray heaps. The mountain was covered, mostly man-made with a topping of the "real deal," as the owners called it. It looked a lot different from how it had at the Dash, the hopeful start to our season. So different now and yet so the same as it always was, always would be.

I couldn't wait to leave Buford.

Lu's walk was neatly cleared, the sheer edges of the snow marked with a blower's lines. I rang the bell, hoping I'd timed it right, that Nat hadn't gone for some runs, just for fun.

She opened the door, surprised and not happy to see me. It took her a minute to recover.

"Hi, Nat."

"Riley," she said. "Hi. Sorry." She smiled a little. "I didn't expect you. Is everything okay?"

I nodded. "Can I come in?"

Nat hesitated, then stepped aside.

"Is Lu here?" I asked as she led me to the living room.

Nat paled. I didn't mean to freak her out, but she'd never tell me anything unless she was alone. "No." She turned to face me. "What's going on, Riley?"

I didn't want to just come out with it, but I could see Nat wasn't going to budge until I did. "Sarah told me some things before she left," I said. "I know you were awake that night."

She blanched and swallowed once. "So?" Natalie folded her arms defensively.

"So," I said. "That means you know who was there. And what happened."

She stayed rigid for a second, and I thought she was going to tell me to leave. Then her whole body sagged. Natalie sighed tiredly. "Yeah," she said. "I know."

Suddenly I didn't want to hear it. I had a flashback to Sarah and me standing in the woods behind my house. I'd hardly slept these past nights, all the things she'd said bouncing around. Once you heard things like that, things you weren't meant to or didn't want to, you couldn't take it back. But Nat was already talking.

"You know who was there that night too. The whole town does," she said. "Just like they always do. Do you have any idea what it's like to listen to your dad whooping it up with your classmates? Snorting coke with Galen Riddock? Selling dope and lighting up with your lab partner or the girl who sits behind you in chem? Do you know what it feels like when they look at you after that?" Her voice rose. "After they see how you live?"

"No." But I could imagine. And it was mortifying.

"No," she agreed. "You don't. I wasn't wearing my headphones and I wasn't sleeping, because I was worried about him. It was like living with a little kid that you have to constantly watch to be sure he doesn't hurt himself. Except with my dad, it wasn't just himself he'd hurt." Nat paused and took a breath. "I wanted to keep an ear out, make sure he was okay."

"And?" I prompted gently.

"And I heard Galen come and go, and then your buddy."

"Moose?"

She nodded. "He bought, and my dad badgered him to stay, even though Moose never does. But this time he did. They sat out there for a while doing whatever, and then he left."

I was relieved. It wasn't Moose, after all.

"I was about to go out to talk to my dad, see if I could get him to go to bed. I could hear him stumbling around out there, he was so wasted." Nat paused, struggling not to cry. "I'd had a bad feeling all night. Nervous, but I couldn't figure out why."

Suddenly I was nervous too.

Nat took a deep breath. "And then I heard the door open again."

"Moose came back?"

She shook her head. "I thought it was him too, but then I heard my dad say, 'Who the fuck 'er you?'

"And the person said, 'You killed my sister.'"

It felt like my heart stopped. "Richie?"

She nodded. "He started going off about how Jessica was always careful, would never have taken too much, that my dad must have cut the drugs with something else." Natalie looked sick. "I just sat there in my room, listening to all of it. All this horrible, horrible stuff. And my dad shouting back at him. I mean, who has to deal with this, right?" Her voice was rising again. I would have told her no one did and no one should, but I was afraid to interrupt.

"My dad went after him. Things were banging around, drawers or doors slamming. I heard someone get hit." Nat winced. "And then my dad said, 'Oh, you got a gun? Well, me too.'" Nat look a sharp breath. "The last thing he said was, 'Hey, that's *mine*.'" Natalie buried her face in her hands, her shoulders shaking.

"Nat . . ." I reached over to touch her, already piecing together the rest and feeling awful about making her go through this. "It's okay—"

"It's not okay," she exploded, her head whipping up. "Don't say that! I knew what was coming, Riley." Tears were dripping from her eyes, down her cheeks, but she didn't seem to notice. "I knew from the second I heard Richie's voice. It was like being at the eye doctor and they're showing you all the letters and flipping through the different lenses, and then, suddenly, everything is totally clear." Words were spilling frantically from Natalie's mouth, like they had to come fast or not at all. "It's what I saw that night," she said. "All of it. I knew they were going to fight and Richie would have my dad's gun and . . . and that he'd shoot him." The tears were wetting her shirt, and Natalie wiped at her nose, saying quietly, "I knew it was coming, and I didn't stop it."

"Nat," I said slowly, "how could you? Richie had a gun and—"

"I could have gone out there and interrupted before they got to that point. Or called the cops. I could have done lots of stuff, Riley," she said, her voice dropping low. "You know the worst thing about what I saw in the binoculars?"

I shook my head, transfixed by the loathing on her face. "The way I felt," she said hoarsely. "Yeah, I was scared and horrified. But there was another part of me that felt free. Like someone had taken this huge responsibility I could never escape, and *poof!* it was gone. I felt so relieved." She drew in a ragged breath, her voice shaky. "That's what I remembered when I stood there, listening. When I let my dad die and did nothing."

It was silent in the town house. Nat's face was wet with tears, and I thought about the way I felt about the money Mr. Jones had given me. Freedom at an unthinkable price.

"Why didn't you tell?" I asked finally.

"Who?" she said. "The cops? And explain that I'd stood in my room and let it happen?"

"There was a gun out there, Nat. They'd have understood."

She continued like I hadn't spoken, "And fry Richie

Milosevich? Ruin his life? Have his parents lose another kid because of my dad and the awful things he'd already done to them? To other people in town? To me?" She whispered the last part.

"But . . ." I hesitated, but I had to ask it. "Aren't you worried, Nat? I mean, the cops might figure it out someday . . . " I trailed off, seeing the look on her face. "What?"

"They're not as stupid as you think, Ri," she said. "Richie's alibi was that he was out of town with his parents. So either they're covering for him or the cops are covering for all of them." Nat shrugged. "Even if the police don't know, I imagine they're not looking real hard for answers. That's the thing about having a dad no one likes. I'm the only one that'll miss him." She wiped her eyes finally. "He was a mess. But he was still my dad."

"What about justice?" I asked.

"This is Vermont justice," Nat said. "Live and let live. Or whatever."

If I hadn't lived there my whole life, I might not have believed it.

"How did Sarah figure it out?" I asked. And when?

"She didn't," Nat said. "I told her. After Trip. She was so wrecked. I could tell she was blaming herself. She said she and Trip had a fight . . ." Nat looked at me searchingly, but I wasn't going to talk about it. Not with her or anyone else. Ever. "I thought it would help her," Natalie said.

"She really seemed like she was losing it." She shook her head. "If I'd known she was going to go blabbing it around, I wouldn't have."

"I'm not going to tell anyone."

"Yeah," she said. "That's what Sarah said too."

"Really, Nat. I promise."

She nodded dismissively. "Nothing I can do about it," she said. "Once I leave this place next year, I'm never coming back."

I nodded. It was what we were all feeling, all planning, I guessed.

Except for Tannis, who, if the binoculars were right, was never leaving.

CHAPTER 35

I GAVE THE LIGHTER BACK TO MOOSE THE NEXT WEEK. JUST LAID it on the counter where he was rolling silverware. He and I didn't talk much anymore. Not that we'd ever been buddies.

He ignored me at first, barely flicking his eyes to what I'd put there. Then he realized what it was. Moose put down the utensils and turned to me, his eyes wary and defiant.

"You left it at the Miloseviches', didn't you?" I asked.

He didn't say anything, but the answer was in his eyes. I pushed it toward him.

"Take it," I said. "I'm not going to tell."

He eyed me, unsure, like it might be a trick, then quickly took it. The lighter disappeared into his pocket. "I didn't do it," Moose said quietly.

"I know."

"He . . . I didn't even—"

I held up a hand. "Don't tell me." I didn't want the details about whether Moose and Richie had plotted the whole thing, watching outside the trailer as Galen had gone in and come out, or whether Moose had stolen Mr. Cleary's gun, maybe as a prank like the vase, or had just told Richie where to find it. I already knew more things than I should, and none of it seemed to be doing me any good.

"But—" I could see him dying to spill the whole story.

"Moose," I warned. "Don't."

He shut his mouth, eyeing me suspiciously. "You're not going to say anything?" he said. "To the cops? Or anyone?"

"No. Live and let live," I told him. "Or whatever."

It was weird being around him afterward. And around Nat. And Tannis. I knew all their secrets and more. I knew Tannis and Matt would wind up keeping the baby. And that she'd have two more and that even if there were moments of regret, there'd be happy ones too.

None of them knew my secrets, of course. The only person who did was gone.

A month has passed now, and Sarah still hasn't come back. I thought she might write again or call. She hasn't done either.

Rather than going to the cafeteria, where I'd have to avoid my friends and the table where the five of us used to sit, I started leaving school at lunch. They let us do that—open lunch. Sometimes I'd just walk and walk until I couldn't really feel my toes anymore. Most days I'd go to the town library, do my homework long before I needed to or noodle around on the Internet, looking up theories about the brain and hypnosis and energy. Hoping for something that'd prove Sarah wrong, show that the things she'd told me were impossible. I didn't find it.

One day, early on, I looked up Cambridge, too. Sarah had mentioned it in her letter, and I couldn't put my finger on whether it was something we'd talked about or a joke I couldn't remember.

A cityscape popped up on the computer—red brick buildings, a river spanned by arching bridges. And a building that was eerily familiar. I looked at it for a long, long time. Vast and oddly shaped, like it had been built with kids' blocks, chunks left out by accident. And row after row of little square windows stacked on top of one another. I'd never seen anything like it.

Except in my vision that very first night at the cave. The building out the window of my dorm room, against the cloudless blue sky.

Simmons Hall, it was called. A dorm at MIT.

I'd always hoped I'd leave Buford, but I'd never allowed myself to dream that big. MIT. Would I really wind up there someday? I'd taken the SATs and sent in my applications, but not there. Still, I'd seen it.

And so, it seemed, had Sarah.

What did it mean?

I didn't want to believe her story. It seemed impossible that the binoculars did what she'd said, or that her mom made them or left them with Sarah or asked her to give them to me. But I only had to look at Trip and Tannis and Nat's dad to believe the first, and Nat, and even myself were proof of the impossible situations parents give their kids sometimes.

So, was that my future—me and Sarah at MIT? Or had I misinterpreted or misremembered something, the way we can with memories? Was it a future I'd create, now that the idea had been planted, the way the binoculars had pushed me toward the SATs and Sarah and all the things that had come after? If they had. The chicken or the egg, decision or destiny?

I keep going round and round, trying to put the pieces together. About Sarah. About the binoculars. It took me a while to even realize how she knew where to leave them—the only way she could have guessed that I'd find them in the back of a cave. She must have seen that moment in them before.

How many other times had she looked, and what did she know?

And what had her mother known that made her think the binoculars belonged with me?

I've read and reread Sarah's letter, poring over the words for meaning. Especially the end. *Love, Sarah*, she'd written. Had she meant that? Or was that just how she signed her letters?

Would we really be together someday? And did I still want that?

That was the one question I could answer: Yes. I did. I knew how I'd sign a letter, if I knew where to send her one.

I saw an old movie once about this guy who thought he was living a regular boring life—family, job, house, all that—but it turned out he was the star of a reality TV show. He was the only one who didn't know. Everyone else was in on the joke.

That was kind of how I felt. Like none of the things or people in my life—Natalie, my mom, Trip's dad, Sarah, the cops—were quite who I thought they were.

I don't remember how that movie ended, whether it was happy or sad or what happened to that guy. So it's kind of like my life that way too.

Except now I have a way to see how it ends.

I feel the temptation sometimes. It burns. Wanting to

know if I'll see her, what we'll say. I have the binoculars. I could look.

But I won't.

And neither will anyone else.

I'm the only one who knows where they are. I'm not telling, and regardless of what Sarah or her crazy mom thought my future was, I'm not using them again.

At least, I think I'm not.

About the Author

JEN NADOL grew up in Reading, Pennsylvania, and graduated from American University with a BA in literature. She's lived in Washington, DC, Boston, New York City, and now, an old farmhouse north of the city with her husband and three sons. When she's not writing, she's probably tending to the farmhouse or the sons, reading, cooking, skiing, or sleeping. She is also the author of *The Mark* and *The Vision*. Find her online at jennadolbooks.com, on Twitter, and on Facebook.